THE CLASSIC TREASURY
OF ANIMAL STORIES

THE CLASSIC TREASURY
OF ANIMAL STORIES

KEY PORTER BOOKS

Canadian Cataloguing in Publication Data

Main entry under title:

The classic treasury of animal stories

ISBN 1-55013-867-7

1. Animals — Literary collections.   2. Children's stories.

PZ5.C55 1997   j808.8'0362   C97-930353-2

The publisher gratefully acknowledges the assistance of the Canada Council and the Ontario Arts Council.

Key Porter Books Limited
70 The Esplanade
Toronto, Ontario
Canada M5E 1R2

Electronic Formatting: Heidi Palfrey

Printed and bound in Spain

97 98 99 00 6 5 4 3 2 1

TABLE OF CONTENTS

CUNNING BRER RABBIT

ONE DAY BRER Bear decided to set out and dig himself a store of peanuts for the winter. Brer Rabbit, hiding in the bushes, saw Brer Bear with his donkey and his cart and heard him calling out to his missus that he would be back at the end of the day with a cartload of the best peanuts around.

Brer Rabbit thought to himself that he and his missus needed a pile of peanuts for the winter, too. And Brer Rabbit wasn't one to do a lot of work if he thought he could get someone else to do it for him.

So he rooted around his burrow and found a red kerchief that he wrapped around his neck. He tied it tightly, ran out to where Brer Bear would be passing by, and lay down in the middle of the road.

Brer Bear spent a very busy day gathering nuts and was coming home with a full cart when he saw Brer Rabbit lying in the road.

"Why, that looks like Brer Rabbit dead in the road with his throat cut wide open," said Brer Bear. "Mm-mh. The missus sure will be happy when I tell her I've got peanuts and a rabbit for rabbit stew."

Brer Bear got down from his cart, picked up Brer Rabbit, and threw him in the back with the load of peanuts. No sooner was Brer Bear's back turned than Brer Rabbit sprang up and jumped out of the cart with Brer Bear's entire load of peanuts.

Brer Bear didn't notice a thing.

Brer Bear pulled up to the tree where he and Missus Bear had set up house and called out, "Come on out, Missus. It was a great day. Peanuts here; rabbit there."

Missus Bear shuffled out and looked in the cart where she could see only a few peanuts rolling around. She scratched her head, looked grumpily around and said, "Peanuts gone; rabbit, too."

The following day, Brer Bear started out again. "Don't lose those peanuts today. It's getting late in the year," Missus Bear called out.

Meanwhile, Brer Fox, who had been lurking in the bushes and had seen Brer Rabbit's trick, decided that a good trick was worth repeating.

"I'll do the same thing," he said to himself and went looking for a red kerchief he could tie around his neck.

Brer Fox wasn't nearly as smart as everyone thought, though. He went right to the very same place in the road where Brer Bear had found Brer Rabbit. He lay down just like Brer Rabbit had and waited.

A little while later, Brer Bear came around that corner in the road and saw Brer Fox lying there.

"Why, there's that thief from yesterday. Looks like somebody done run him over but good this time. Missus Bear will have meat stew for sure today."

Saying this, he climbed down and lifted up Brer Fox. "Oh boy," thought Brer Fox to himself. "Here come my peanuts."

But instead of throwing Brer Fox into the back of the cart, Brer Bear swung him around and bashed him against the cart's wheel.

"You look mighty dead to me," Brer Bear muttered to himself, "but today I'm just going to make sure."

Poor Brer Fox just barely managed to escape Brer Bear's licking.

It just goes to show that you can't get away with the same trick twice.

THE MOCK TURTLE'S STORY

In Alice's Adventures in Wonderland, *Alice follows a
white rabbit into a hole and lands in a magical
world where everything is topsy-turvy. After many adventures,
she finds herself playing in a curious croquet game led
by the Queen of Hearts.*

"YOU CAN'T THINK how glad I am to see you again, you dear old thing!" said the Duchess, as she tucked her arm affectionately into Alice's, and they walked off together.

Alice was very glad to find her in such a pleasant temper, and thought to herself that perhaps it was only the pepper that had made her so savage when they met in the kitchen. "When *I'm* a Duchess," she said to herself (not in a very hopeful tone though), "I won't have any pepper in my kitchen *at all*. Soup does very well without—Maybe it's always pepper that makes people hot-tempered," she went on, very much pleased at having found out a new kind of rule, "and vinegar that makes them sour—and camomile that makes them bitter—and—and barley-sugar and such things that make children sweet-tempered. I only wish people knew *that*: then they wouldn't be so stingy about it, you know—"

She had quite forgotten the Duchess by this time, and was a little startled when she heard her voice close to her ear. "You're thinking about something, my dear, and that makes you forget to talk. I can't tell you just now what the moral of that is, but I shall remember it in a bit."

"Perhaps it hasn't one," Alice ventured to remark.

"Tut, tut, child!" said the Duchess. "Everything's got a moral, if only you can find it." And she squeezed herself up closer to Alice's side as she spoke.

Alice did not much like her keeping so close to her: first, because the Duchess was *very* ugly, and secondly, because she was exactly the right height to rest her chin on Alice's shoulder, and it was an uncomfortably sharp chin. However, she did not like to be rude, so she bore it as well as she could.

"The game's going on rather better now," she said by way of keeping up the conversation a little.

"'Tis so," said the Duchess: "and the moral of that is—'Oh, 'tis love, 'tis love, that makes the world go round!'"

"Somebody said," Alice whispered, "that it's done by everybody minding their own business!"

"Ah, well! It means much the same thing," said the Duchess, digging her sharp little chin into Alice's shoulder as she added, "and the moral of *that* is—'Take care of the sense, and the sounds will take care of themselves.'"

"How fond she is of finding morals in things!" Alice thought to herself.

"I daresay you're wondering why I don't put my arm round your waist," said the Duchess after a pause: "the reason is, that I'm doubtful about the temper of your flamingo. Shall I try the experiment?"

"He might bite," Alice cautiously replied, not feeling at all anxious to have the experiment tried.

"Very true," said the Duchess: "flamingos and mustard both bite.

And the moral of that is—'Birds of a feather flock together.'"

"Only mustard isn't a bird," Alice remarked.

"Right, as usual," said the Duchess: "what a clear way you have of putting things!"

"It's a mineral, I *think*," said Alice.

"Of course it is," said the Duchess, who seemed ready to agree to everything that Alice said; "there's a large mustard-mine near here. And the moral of that is—'The more there is of mine, the less there is of yours.'"

"Oh, I know!" exclaimed Alice, who had not attended to this last remark, "it's a vegetable. It doesn't look like one, but it is."

"I quite agree with you," said the Duchess, "and the moral of that is— 'Be what you would seem to be'—or, if you'd like it put more simply— 'Never imagine yourself not to be otherwise than what it might appear to others that what you were or might have been was not otherwise than what you had been would have appeared to them to be otherwise.'"

"I think I should understand that better," Alice said very politely, "if I had it written down: but I can't quite follow it as you say it."

"That's nothing to what I could say if I chose," the Duchess replied in a pleased tone.

"Pray don't trouble yourself to say it any longer than that," said Alice.

"Oh, don't talk about trouble!" said the Duchess. "I make you a present of everything I've said as yet."

"A cheap sort of present!" thought Alice. "I'm glad they don't give birthday presents like that!" But she did not venture to say it out loud.

"Thinking again?" the Duchess asked, with another dig of her sharp little chin.

"I've a right to think," said Alice sharply, for she was beginning to feel a little worried.

"Just about as much right," said the Duchess, "as pigs have to fly: and the m—"

But here, to Alice's great surprise, the Duchess's voice died away, even in the middle of her favorite word "moral," and the arm that was linked into hers began to tremble. Alice looked up, and there stood the Queen in front of them, with her arms folded, frowning like a thunderstorm.

"A fine day, your Majesty!" the Duchess began in a low, weak voice.

"Now, I give you fair warning," shouted the Queen, stamping on the ground as she spoke; "either you or your head must be off, and that in about half no time! Take your choice!"

The Duchess took her choice, and was gone in a moment.

"Let's go on with the game," the Queen said to Alice, and Alice was too much frightened to say a word, but slowly followed her back to the croquet-ground.

The other guests had taken advantage of the Queen's absence, and were resting in the shade: however, the moment they saw her, they hurried back to the game, the Queen merely remarking that a moment's delay would cost them their lives.

All the time they were playing the Queen never left off quarreling with the other players, and shouting "Off with his head!" or "Off with her head!" Those whom she sentenced were taken into custody by the soldiers, who of course had to leave off being arches to do this, so that by the end of half an hour or so there were no arches left, and all the players, except the King, the Queen, and Alice, were in custody, and under sentence of execution.

Then the Queen left off, quite out of breath, and said to Alice, "Have you seen the Mock Turtle yet?"

"No," said Alice. "I don't even know what a Mock Turtle is."

"It's the thing Mock Turtle Soup is made from," said the Queen.

"I never saw one, or heard of one," said Alice.

"Come on, then," said the Queen, "and he shall tell you his history."

As they walked off together, Alice heard the King say in a low voice, to the company generally, "You are all pardoned." "Come, *that's* a good thing!" she said to herself, for she had felt quite unhappy at the number of executions the Queen had ordered.

They very soon came upon a Gryphon, lying fast asleep in the sun. "Up, lazy thing!" said the Queen, "and take this young lady to see the Mock Turtle, and to hear his history. I must go back and see after some executions I have ordered;" and she walked off, leaving Alice alone with the Gryphon. Alice did not quite like the look of the creature, but on the whole she thought it would be quite as safe to stay with it as to go after that savage Queen: so she waited.

The Gryphon sat up and rubbed its eyes: then it watched the Queen till she was out of sight: then it chuckled. "What fun!" said the Gryphon, half to itself, half to Alice.

"What *is* the fun?" said Alice.

"Why, *she*," said the Gryphon. "It's all her fancy, that: they never executes nobody, you know. Come on!"

"Everybody says 'come on!' here," thought Alice, as she went slowly after it: "I never was so ordered about before in all my life, never!"

They had not gone far before they saw the Mock Turtle in the distance, sitting sad and lonely on a little ledge of rock, and, as they came nearer, Alice could hear him sighing as if his heart would break. She pitied him deeply. "What is his sorrow?" she asked the Gryphon, and the Gryphon answered, very nearly in the same words as before, "It's all his fancy, that: he hasn't got no sorrow, you know. Come on!"

So they went up to the Mock Turtle, who looked at them with large eyes full of tears, but said nothing.

"This here young lady," said the Gryphon, "she wants for to know your history, she do."

"I'll tell it her," said the Mock Turtle in a deep, hollow tone: "sit down, both of you, and don't speak a word till I've finished."

So they sat down, and nobody spoke for some minutes. Alice

thought to herself, "I don't see how he can *ever* finish, if he doesn't begin." But she waited patiently.

"Once," said the Mock Turtle at last, with a deep sigh, "I was a real Turtle."

These words were followed by a very long silence, broken only by an occasional exclamation of "Hjckrrh!" from the Gryphon, and the constant heavy sobbing of the Mock Turtle. Alice was very nearly getting up and saying, "Thank you, sir, for your interesting story," but she could not help thinking there *must* be more to come, so she sat still and said nothing.

"When we were little," the Mock Turtle went on at last, more calmly, though still sobbing a little now and then, "we went to school in the sea. The master was an old Turtle—we used to call him Tortoise—"

"Why did you call him Tortoise, if he wasn't one?" Alice asked.

"We called him Tortoise because he taught us," said the Mock Turtle angrily; "really you are very dull!"

"You ought to be ashamed of yourself for asking such a simple question," added the Gryphon; and then they both sat silent and looked at poor Alice, who felt ready to sink into the earth. At last the Gryphon said to the Mock Turtle, "Drive on, old fellow! Don't be all day about it!" and he went on in these words:—

"Yes, we went to school in the sea, though you mayn't believe it—"

"I never said I didn't!" interrupted Alice.

"You did," said the Mock Turtle.

"Hold your tongue!" added the Gryphon, before Alice could speak again. The Mock Turtle went on.

"We had the best of educations—in fact, we went to school every day—"

"*I've* been to a day-school too," said Alice; "you needn't be so proud as all that."

"With extras?" asked the Mock Turtle a little anxiously.

"Yes," said Alice, "we learned French and music."

"And washing?" said the Mock Turtle.

"Certainly not!" said Alice indignantly.

"Ah! Then yours wasn't a really good school," said the Mock Turtle in a tone of great relief. "Now at *ours* they had at the end of the bill, 'French, music, *and washing*—extra.'"

"You couldn't have wanted it much," said Alice; "living at the bottom of the sea."

"I couldn't afford to learn it," said the Mock Turtle with a sigh. "I only took the regular course."

"What was that?" enquired Alice.

"Reeling and Writhing, of course, to begin with," the Mock Turtle replied: "and then the different branches of Arithmetic—Ambition, Distraction, Uglification, and Derision."

"I never heard of 'Uglification,'" Alice ventured to say. "What is it?"

The Gryphon lifted up both its paws in surprise. "Never heard of uglifying!" it exclaimed. "You know what to beautify is, I suppose?"

"Yes," said Alice, doubtfully: "it means—to—make—anything—prettier."

"Well then," the Gryphon went on, "if you don't know what to uglify is, you *are* a simpleton."

Alice did not feel encouraged to ask any more questions about it, so she turned to the Mock Turtle, and said, "What else had you to learn?"

"Well, there was Mystery," the Mock Turtle replied, counting off the subjects on his flappers—"Mystery, ancient and modern, with Seaography: then Drawling—the Drawling-master was an old conger-eel, that used to come once a week: *he* taught us Drawling, Stretching, and Fainting in Coils."

"What was *that* like?" said Alice.

"Well, I can't show it you, myself," the Mock Turtle said: "I'm too stiff. And the Gryphon never learnt it."

"Hadn't time," said the Gryphon: "I went to the Classical master, though. He was an old crab, *he* was."

"I never went to him," the Mock Turtle said with a sigh: "he taught Laughing and Grief, they used to say."

"So he did, so he did," said the Gryphon, sighing in his turn, and both creatures hid their faces in their paws.

"And how many hours a day did you do lessons?" said Alice, in a hurry to change the subject.

"Ten hours the first day," said the Mock Turtle: "nine the next, and so on."

"What a curious plan!" exclaimed Alice.

"That's the reason they're called lessons," the Gryphon remarked: "because they lessen from day to day."

This was quite a new idea to Alice, and she thought it over a little before she made her next remark. "Then the eleventh day must have been a holiday?"

"Of course it was," said the Mock Turtle.

"And how did you manage on the twelfth?" Alice went on eagerly.

"That's enough about lessons," the Gryphon interrupted in a very decided tone: "tell her something about the games now."

THE BREMEN TOWN MUSICIANS

A CERTAIN MAN HAD an ass which for many years carried sacks to the mill without tiring. At last, however, its strength was worn out and it was no longer of any use for work. Accordingly, its master began to ponder as to how best to cut down its keep. But the ass, seeing there was mischief in the air, ran away and started on the road to Bremen. There he thought he could become a town musician.

When he had been traveling a short time, he fell in with a hound, who was lying panting on the road as though he had run himself off his legs.

"Well, what are you panting so for, Growler?" said the ass.

"Ah," said the hound, "just because I am old, and every day I get weaker. And also, because I can no longer keep up with the pack, my master wanted to kill me, so I took my departure. But now how am I to earn my bread?"

"Do you know what?" said the ass. "I am going to Bremen and shall there become a town musician. Come with me and take your part in the music. I shall play the lute, and you shall beat the kettledrum."

The hound agreed and they went on.

A short time afterwards they came upon a cat sitting in the road, with a face as long as a wet week.

"Well, why are you so cross, Whiskers?" asked the ass.

"Who can be cheerful when he is out at elbows?" said the cat. "I am getting on in years and my teeth are blunted, and I prefer to sit by the stove and purr instead of hunting round after mice. Just because of this my mistress wanted to drown me. I made myself scarce, but now I don't know where to turn."

"Come with us to Bremen," said the ass. "You are a great hand at serenading, so you can become a town musician." The cat consented and joined them.

Next the fugitives passed by a yard where a barnyard fowl was sitting on the door, crowing with all its might.

"You crow so loud you pierce one through and through," said the ass. "What is the matter?"

"Why? Because Sunday visitors are coming tomorrow, the mistress has no pity, and she has ordered the cook to make me into soup. So I shall have my neck wrung tonight. Now I am crowing with all my might while I can."

"Come along, Red-comb," said the ass. "You had much better come with us. We are going to Bremen and you will find a much better fate there. You have a good voice, and when we make music together there will be quality in it."

The cock allowed himself to be persuaded and they all four went off together. They could not, however, reach the town in one day, and by evening they arrived at a wood, where they determined to spend the night. The ass and the hound lay down under a big tree. The cat and the cock settled themselves in the branches, the cock flying right up to the top, which was the safest place for him. Before going to sleep he looked round once more in every direction. Suddenly it seemed that he saw a light burning in the distance. He called out to his comrades that there must be a house not far off, for he saw a light.

"Very well," said the ass. "Let us set out and make our way to it, for the entertainment here is very bad."

The hound thought some bones or meat would suit him too, so they set out in the direction of the light. They soon saw it shining

more clearly and getting bigger and bigger, till they reached a brightly lighted robbers' den. The ass, being the tallest, approached the window and looked in.

"What do you see, old Jackass?" asked the cock.

"What do I see?" answered the ass. "Why, a table spread with delicious food and drink, and robbers seated at it enjoying themselves."

"That would just suit us," said the cock.

"Yes, if we were only there," answered the ass.

Then the animals took counsel as to how to set about driving the robbers out. At last they hit upon a plan.

The ass was to take up his position with his forefeet on the window sill, the hound was to jump on his back, the cat to climb up onto the hound, and last of all the cock was to up and perch on the cat's head. When they were thus arranged, at a given signal they all began to perform their music. The ass brayed, the hound barked, the cat mewed, and the cock crowed. Then they dashed through the window, shivering the panes. The robbers jumped up at the terrible noise. They thought nothing less than that the devil was coming in upon them and fled into the wood in the greatest alarm. Then the four animals sat down to table and helped themselves according to taste, and they ate as though they had been starving for weeks. When they had finished, they extinguished the light and looked for sleeping places, each one to suit his taste.

The ass lay down on a pile of straw, the hound behind the door, the cat on the hearth near the warm ashes, and the cock flew up to the rafters. As they were tired from the long journey, they soon went to sleep.

When midnight was past, and the robbers saw from a distance that the light was no longer burning and that all seemed quiet, the chief said, "We ought not to have been scared by a false alarm." And he ordered one of the robbers to go and examine the house.

Finding all quiet, the messenger went into the kitchen to kindle a light. And taking the cat's glowing, fiery eyes for live coals, he held a match close to them so as to light it. But the cat would stand no non-sense—it flew at his face, spat, and scratched. He was terribly frightened and ran away.

He tried to get out the back door, but the hound, who was lying there, jumped up and bit his leg. As he ran across the pile of straw in front of the house, the ass gave him a good sound kick with his hind legs; while the cock, who had awakened at the uproar quite fresh and gay, cried out from his perch, "Cock-a-doodle-doo."

Thereupon the robber ran back as fast as he could to his chief and said, "There is a gruesome witch in the house who breathed on me and scratched me with her long fingers. Behind the door there stands a man with a knife, who stabbed me, while in the yard lies a black monster who hit me with a club. And upon the roof the judge is seated, and he called out, 'Bring the rogue here!' So I hurried away as fast as I could."

Thenceforward the robbers did not venture again to the house, which pleased the four Bremen musicians so much that they never wished to leave it again.

THE BEGINNING OF THE ARMADILLOS

T HIS, O BEST Beloved, is another story of the High and Far-Off Times. In the very middle of those times was a Stickly-Prickly Hedgehog, and he lived on the banks of the turbid Amazon, eating shelly snails and things. And he had a friend, a Slow-and-Solid Tortoise, who lived on the banks of the turbid Amazon, eating green lettuces and things. And so *that* was all right, Best Beloved. Do you see?

But also, and at the same time, in those High and Far-Off Times, there was a Painted Jaguar, and he lived on the banks of the turbid Amazon too; and he ate everything that he could catch. When he could not catch deer or monkeys he would eat frogs and beetles; and when he could not catch frogs and beetles he went to his Mother Jaguar, and she told him how to eat Hedgehogs and Tortoises.

She said to him ever so many times, graciously waving her tail, "My son, when you find a Hedgehog you must drop him into the water and then he will uncoil, and when you catch a Tortoise you must scoop him out of his shell with your paw." And so that was all right, Best Beloved.

One beautiful night on the banks of the turbid Amazon, Painted Jaguar found Stickly-Prickly Hedgehog and Slow-and-Solid Tortoise sitting under the trunk of a fallen tree. They could not run away, and so Stickly-Prickly curled himself up into a ball, because he was a Hedgehog, and Slow-and-Solid Tortoise drew in his head and feet into his shell as far as they would go, because he was a Tortoise; and so *that* was all right, Best Beloved. Do you see?

"Now attend to me," said Painted Jaguar, "Because this is very important. My mother said that when I meet a Hedgehog I am to drop him into the water and then he'll uncoil, and when I meet a Tortoise I am to scoop him out of his shell with my paw. Now which of you is Hedgehog and which is Tortoise because, to save my spots, I can't tell."

"Are you sure of what your Mummy told you?" said Stickly-Prickly Hedgehog. "Are you quite sure? Perhaps she said that when you uncoil a Tortoise you must shell him out of the water with a scoop, and when you paw a Hedgehog you must drop him on the shell."

"Are you sure of what your Mummy told you?" said Slow-and-Solid Tortoise. "Are you quite sure? Perhaps she said that when you water a Hedgehog you must drop him into your paw, and when you meet a Tortoise you must shell him till he uncoils."

"I don't think it was at all like that," said Painted Jaguar, but he felt a little puzzled; "but, please, say it again more distinctly."

"When you scoop water with your paw you uncoil it with a Hedgehog," said Stickly-Prickly. "Remember that, because it's important."

"*But*," said the Tortoise, "when you paw your meat you drop it into a Tortoise with a scoop. Why can't you understand?"

"You are making my spots ache," said Painted Jaguar; "and besides, I didn't want your advice at all. I only wanted to know which of you is Hedgehog and which is Tortoise."

"I shan't tell you," said Stickly-Prickly. "But you can scoop me out of my shell if you like."

"Aha!" said Painted Jaguar. "Now I know you're Tortoise. You thought I wouldn't! Now I will." Painted Jaguar darted out his paddy-paw just as Stickly-Prickly curled himself up, and of course Jaguar's paddy-paw was just filled with prickles. Worse than that, he knocked Stickly-Prickly away and away into the woods and the bushes, where it was too dark to find him. Then he put his paddy-paw into his mouth, and of course the prickles hurt him worse than ever. As soon as he could speak he said, "Now I know he isn't Tortoise at all. But"—and then he scratched his head with his un-prickly paw—"how do I know that this other is Tortoise?"

"But I *am* Tortoise," said Slow-and-Solid. "Your mother was quite right. She said that you were to scoop me out of my shell with your paw. Begin."

"You didn't say she said that a minute ago," said Painted Jaguar, sucking the prickles out of his paddy-paw. "You said she said something quite different."

"Well, suppose you say that I said that she said something quite different, I don't see that it makes any difference; because if she said what you said I said she said, it's just the same as if I said what she said she said. On the other hand, if you think she said that you were to uncoil me with a scoop, instead of pawing me into drops with a shell, I can't help that, can I?"

"But you said you wanted to be scooped out of your shell with my paw," said Painted Jaguar.

"If you'll think again you'll find that I didn't say anything of the kind. I said that your mother said that you were to scoop me out of my shell," said Slow-and-Solid.

"What will happen if I do?" said the Jaguar most sniffily and most cautious.

"I don't know, because I've never been scooped out of my shell before; but I tell you truly, if you want to see me swim away you've only got to drop me into the water."

"I don't believe it," said Painted Jaguar. "You've mixed up all the things my mother told me to do with the things that you asked me whether I was sure that she didn't say, till I don't know whether I'm on my head or my painted tail; and now you come and tell me something I *can* understand, and it makes me more mixy than before. My mother told me that I was to drop one of you two into the water, and as you seem so anxious to be dropped I think you don't want to be dropped. So jump into the turbid Amazon and be quick about it."

"I warn you that your Mummy won't be pleased. Don't tell her I didn't tell you," said Slow-and-Solid.

"If you say another word about what my mother said—" the Jaguar answered, but he had not finished the sentence before Slow-and-Solid quietly dived into the turbid Amazon, swam under water for a long way, and came out on the bank where Stickly-Prickly was waiting for him.

"That was a very narrow escape," said Stickly-Prickly. "I don't like Painted Jaguar. What did you tell him that you were?"

"I told him truthfully that I was a truthful Tortoise, but he wouldn't believe it, and he made me jump into the river to see if I was, and I was, and he is surprised. Now he's gone to tell his Mummy. Listen to him!"

They could hear Painted Jaguar roaring up and down among the trees and the bushes by the side of the turbid Amazon, till his Mummy came.

"Son, son!" said his mother ever so many times, graciously waving her tail, "what have you been doing that you shouldn't have done?"

"I tried to scoop something that said it wanted to be scooped out of its shell with my paw, and my paw is full of per-ickles," said

Painted Jaguar.

"Son, son!" said his mother ever so many times, graciously waving her tail, "by the prickles in your paddy-paw I see that that must have been a Hedgehog. You should have dropped him into the water."

"I did that to the other thing; and he said he was a Tortoise, and I didn't believe him, and it was quite true, and he has dived under the turbid Amazon, and he won't come up again, and I haven't anything at all to eat, and I think we had better find lodgings somewhere else. They are too clever on the turbid Amazon for poor me!"

"Son, son!" said his mother ever so many times, graciously waving her tail, "now attend to me and remember what I say. A Hedgehog curls himself up into a ball and his prickles stick out every which way at once. By this you may know the Hedgehog."

"I don't like this old lady one little bit," said Stickly-Prickly, under the shadow of a large leaf. "I wonder what else she knows?"

"A Tortoise can't curl himself up," Mother Jaguar went on, ever so many times, graciously waving her tail. "He only draws his head and legs into his shell. By this you may know the Tortoise."

"I don't like this old lady at all—at all," said Slow-and-Solid Tortoise. "Even Painted Jaguar can't forget those directions. It's a great pity that you can't swim, Stickly-Prickly."

"Don't talk to me," said Stickly-Prickly. "Just think how much better it would be if you could curl up. This *is* a mess! Listen to Painted Jaguar."

Painted Jaguar was sitting on the banks of the turbid Amazon sucking prickles out of his paw and saying to himself—

> "Can't curl, but can swim—
> Slow-and-Solid, that's him!
> Curls up, but can't swim—
> Stickly-Prickly, that's him!"

"He'll never forget that this month of Sundays," said Stickly-Prickly. "Hold up my chin, Slow-and-Solid. I'm going to try to learn to swim. It may be useful."

"Excellent!" said Slow-and-Solid; and he held up Stickly-Prickly's chin, while Stickly-Prickly kicked in the waters of the turbid Amazon.

"You'll make a fine swimmer yet," said Slow-and-Solid. "Now, if you can unlace my backplates a little, I'll see what I can do towards curling up. It may be useful."

Stickly-Prickly helped to unlace Tortoise's backplates, so that by twisting and straining Slow-and-Solid actually managed to curl up a tiddy wee bit.

"Excellent!" said Stickly-Prickly; "but I shouldn't do any more just now. It's making you black in the face. Kindly lead me into the water once again and I'll practice that side-stroke which you say is so easy." And so Stickly-Prickly practiced, and Slow-and-Solid swam alongside.

"Excellent!" said Slow-and-Solid. "A little more practice will make you a regular whale. Now, if I may trouble you to unlace my back and front plates two holes more, I'll try that fascinating bend that you say is so easy. Won't Painted Jaguar be surprised!"

"Excellent!" said Stickly-Prickly, all wet from the turbid Amazon. "I declare, I shouldn't know you from one of my own family. Two holes, I think, you said? A little more expression, please, and don't grunt quite so much, or Painted Jaguar may hear us. When you've finished, I want to try that long dive which you say is so easy. Won't Painted Jaguar be surprised!"

And so Stickly-Prickly dived, and Slow-and-Solid dived alongside.

"Excellent!" said Slow-and-Solid. "A leetle more attention

to holding your breath and you will be able to keep house at the bottom of the turbid Amazon. Now I'll try that exercise of wrapping my hind legs round my ears which you say is so peculiarly comfortable. Won't Painted Jaguar be surprised!"

"Excellent!" said Stickly-Prickly. "But it's straining your backplates a little. They are all overlapping now, instead of lying side by side."

"Oh, that's the result of exercise," said Slow-and-Solid. "I've noticed that your prickles seem to be melting into one another, and that you're growing to look rather more like a pine-cone, and less like a chestnut-burr, than you used to."

"Am I?" said Stickly-Prickly. "That comes from my soaking in the water. Oh, won't Painted Jaguar be surprised!"

They went on with their exercises, each helping the other, till morning came; and when the sun was high they rested and dried themselves. Then they saw that they were both of them quite different from what they had been.

"Stickly-Prickly," said Tortoise after breakfast, "I am not what I was yesterday; but I think that I may yet amuse Painted Jaguar."

"That was the very thing I was thinking just now," said Stickly-Prickly. "I think scales are a tremendous improvement on prickles—to say nothing of being able to swim. Oh, *won't* Painted Jaguar be surprised! Let's go and find him."

By and by they found Painted Jaguar, still nursing his paddy-paw that had been hurt the night before. He was so astonished that he fell three times backward over his own painted tail without stopping.

"Good morning!" said Stickly-Prickly. "And how is your dear gracious Mummy this morning?"

"She is quite well, thank you," said Painted Jaguar, "but you must forgive me if I do not at this precise moment recall your name."

"That's unkind of you," said Stickly-Prickly, "seeing that this time yesterday you tried to scoop me out of my shell with your paw."

"But you hadn't any shell. It was all prickles," said Painted Jaguar. "I know it was. Just look at my paw!"

"You told me to drop into the turbid Amazon and be drowned," said Slow-and-Solid. "Why are you so rude and forgetful today?"

"Don't you remember what your mother told you?" said Stickly-Prickly—

"Can't curl, but can swim—
Stickly-Prickly, that's him!
Curls up, but can't swim—
Slow-and-Solid, that's him!"

Then they both curled themselves up and rolled round and round Painted Jaguar till his eyes turned truly cart-wheels in his head.

Then he went to fetch his mother.

"Mother," he said, "there are two new animals in the woods today, and the one that you said couldn't swim, swims, and the one that you said couldn't curl up, curls; and they've gone shares in their prickles, I think, because both of them are scaly all over, instead of one being smooth and the other very prickly; and, besides that, they are rolling round and round in circles, and I don't feel comfy."

"Son, son!" said Mother Jaguar ever so many times, graciously waving her tail, "a Hedgehog is a Hedgehog, and can't be anything but a Hedgehog; and a Tortoise is a Tortoise, and can never be anything else."

"But it isn't a Hedgehog, and it isn't a Tortoise. It's a little bit of both, and I don't know its proper name."

"Nonsense!" said Mother Jaguar. "Everything

has its proper name. I should call it Armadillo till I found out the real one. And I should leave it alone."

So Painted Jaguar did as he was told, especially about leaving them alone; but the curious thing is that from that day to this, O Best Beloved, no one on the banks of the turbid Amazon has ever called Stickly-Prickly and Slow-and-Solid anything except Armadillo. There are Hedgehogs and Tortoises in other places, of course (there are some in my garden); but the real old and clever kind, with their scales lying lippety-lappety one over the other, like pine-cone scales, that lived on the banks of the turbid Amazon in the High and Far-Off Days, are always called Armadillos, because they were so clever.

So *that's* all right, Best Beloved. Do you see?

> I've never sailed the Amazon,
>   I've never reached Brazil;
> But the *Don* and the *Magdalena*,
>   They can go there when they will!
>
>   Yes, weekly from Southampton,
>   Great Steamers, white and gold,
>   Go rolling down to Rio
>   (Roll down—roll down to Rio!)
>
>   And I'd like to roll to Rio
>   Some day before I'm old!
>
> I've never seen a Jaguar,
>   Nor yet an Armadill—
> O dilloing in his armor,
>   And I s'pose I never will,

Unless I go to Rio
These wonders to behold—
Roll down—roll down to Rio—
Roll really down to Rio!
Oh, I'd love to roll to Rio
Some day before I'm old!

THEN THERE WERE THREE

Cry Wild is the story of a Canadian timber wolf. Although the story is imaginary, it is based on the author's close observation of wolves and his long experience in the north country. In this excerpt the pup, Silverfeet, and his brother and sisters, have their first, brutal encounter with another inhabitant of the wilderness—a black bear.

SILVERFEET WAS NINE days old when his eyes began to open. The cubs were alone in the den that afternoon, for the bitch wolf had gone on a hunt with her mate. She had been forced by hunger to abandon the young ones. Had she been with a pack, she would not have gone and there would have been no hunger in the den; but although her mate was a good hunter he had been unable, alone, to bring down enough game for their needs. The dog had brought hares and groundhogs, and now and then a grouse, but such fare is meager for two full-grown timber wolves, inadequate for a she-wolf nursing young. In the middle of plenty, these two efficient, powerful hunters were suffering want. Yet there was nothing really unusual about this. Wolves were created to hunt in packs; they are sociable animals that band together for survival. The dog and his mate, before the coming of the pups, had made an efficient, if small, hunting pack, but the dog alone could not hope to provide enough of the big game needed for the survival of the cubs. So the two had paired again and they had gone to hunt, perforce leaving the cubs unguarded.

Silverfeet and his brother and sisters were unaware of these things. They had nursed from their mother before she left the den, and now they made small dog-noises as they huddled together. Silverfeet had one of his black sister's ears clamped firmly in his mouth, and he was sucking it, comforting himself as a human baby might do with his thumb. At first, when the gummy lids of his right eye separated just a crack, exposing the eye to the sunlight that slanted into the cave, panic seized him and he let go of his sister's ear and tried to bury his head beneath the squirming bodies of the others. For some moments he continued to try to escape the light and then his second eyelid parted a little, chasing away more darkness. Fear was overcome by curiosity. Silverfeet withdrew his head from the bundle of living fur into which he had thrust it, and blinked owlishly towards the cave mouth. The strong light hurt his eyes and he turned away, but there was a fascination in that light. He had to stare at it. Slowly the pain of the light became less and less, until at last it left him altogether and for the first time he could see, though dimly.

That afternoon all the wolf pups gained their vision. Until then they had been guided by their ears and by their nostrils. They had crawled around and over one another, and had wandered aimlessly around the den chamber. Now they had eyes to guide them. They discerned each other for the first time and they recognized the smells and sounds of the den with their eyes. It was a wonderful experience. And if it frightened them at first, it held new promise.

The four rose to unsteady legs and peered at one another, smelling each other and sniffing about the chamber. They were small and feeble and their muscles would not co-ordinate properly, but the light drew them. Silverfeet was the first to make for it—slowly, wobbling, as often crawling as walking, but determined to reach the daylight that beckoned so persuasively. And the others followed. The four inched their way towards the outside on their short, rubbery legs, ignorant of the dangers that lurked there. Now and then one would sit down and rest a moment before setting off again.

Their progress was uneven but it took them closer and closer to their objective. Finally they were at the den entrance. Silverfeet stopped abruptly, dazzled by the sun. The others huddled around him, small, scared, and excited; four precocious animal children reaching too soon the great, green world. Silverfeet's chubby little body was toppled forward by the combined weight of the others. He rolled a little way outside, stopped, recovered, and scrambled slowly to his feet. He moved two steps forward, paused undecided, and peered back to see what the others were doing. The small gray bitch was just then moving, intent on following Silverfeet; the black bitch was sprawled flat on her belly at the cave mouth; the brindled little dog was still framed by the opaqueness of the cave, but he, too, was beginning to follow.

At last the four cubs were outside. They again huddled together, fear beginning to crowd their senses. They were so small and so unsure, and this new world was so big, even to their myopic sight. Silverfeet, not really knowing why, felt the urge to return to the safe darkness of the den and he began to walk again, but his senses were too weak and he did not know which way to go. Instead of retracing his steps, he moved farther away from the cave. His brother and sisters followed, a ragged little group that traveled but inches at a time. Some instinct warned Silverfeet that he was going in the wrong direction; perhaps the smell of the den became weaker in his nostrils, perhaps fear sharpened his senses. He stopped and the others stopped with him. They sat undecided.

The squirrel that lived near the den had been watching the young wolves. Squatting lazily on his nesting branch he had followed their ungainly progress from the cave mouth with the intent curiosity that all wild things display towards newness in their territory. Suddenly he sat upright and riveted his gaze upon an area of tangled scrubland a bare quarter of a mile from the den. The cubs continued with their antics, still trying to return to the security of their nursery.

The squirrel had lost all interest in them; his entire attention was devoted to the place he was watching. From his high vantage point he could see the brush moving. His keen ears caught a heavy sound coming from the area. Suddenly the squirrel chittered his alarm cry. He kept up the churring for perhaps half a minute, then he bolted up the tree and disappeared into his nesting hole. The cubs were oblivious of this. They heard the noise that the squirrel made, but they did not know that this was an alarm, alerting the forest to the presence of a dangerous prowler.

Silverfeet had succeeded in pointing himself in the right direction at last. Wobbling, he was slowly making his way towards the cave mouth. His sisters were following, but his brother had lost his bearings and was wandering farther away.

From the direction of the scrub patch a pig-like grunt disturbed the stillness of the afternoon. On its heels came the crackling of brush. Presently, the shaggy bulk of a black bear emerged into view. The bear's shambling course was erratic. He paused now and then to snuffle at something on the ground. Once he stopped at a dead log; with two slow smashes of his powerful forepaws, he tore it to pieces and stooped to lick up the ants from within the rotting wood, enjoying the pungent taste of the acidy bodies. When he had lapped up the last scurrying ant, he ambled up the hill towards the wolf den. Suddenly he stopped. Wolf scent had penetrated his nostrils. He was interested and cautious. He knew the smell of the wolf den, and he knew that in that den he could expect to find some young; these would be delicate mouthfuls for the still winter-hungry bear. But he knew also the savagery of timber wolves protecting their young, and so he paused, advanced a couple of steps, and paused once more, working his nostrils and flicking his ears, trying to locate the adult wolves. A few yards farther on he detected the smell of the cubs. He squinted, trying with his poor vision to locate their whereabouts, at the same time deciding that the parent wolves were not present. He quickened his steps, and the scent of the pups guided him unerringly towards the feebly-moving shape of the brindled male.

Returning home from a successful deer hunt, the parent wolves had picked up the scent of the bear. Now they were rushing towards the den, pausing occasionally to track the bear's progress, aware that he was heading directly for their den. The wolves were half a mile from home, but their progress was swift. They raced in their fastest gallop, jumping dead-falls, smashing their way through brush in an effort to get to their pups ahead of the marauding bear.

They burst out of the forest in view of their den just as the black bear seized the body of the brindled cub. The big bear stood on all fours, facing the cave entrance and eyeing the remaining pups. The little male was entirely hidden within his great jaws. He bit down, and the life was crushed from the little brindled body. At this moment two furious, savage things unleashed themselves upon the bear.

With flashing fangs and upcurled lips the wolves bore into the attack, smashing into the bear from either side. The bitch seized the bear's left hind leg, the dog sank his teeth into the hairy right flank. The bear whirled, shaking off both wolves with ease. He dropped the body of the pup. The wolves attacked again, their throaty growls of rage mingled with the bear's roar of surprise. The bear rushed the dog, trying to clasp him in his strong arms and crush him to death. While he was doing this the bitch struck him hard in the shoulder, knocking him off his feet. In a trice the dog wolf hit again and slashed a furrow in one of the bear's ears.

The bear was nimble. Quickly he regained his feet and charged the she-wolf; the tactic was repeated. While the she retreated out of reach, the dog bore in from the other side. Slowly the two wolves were easing the bear away from the cubs. The fight was fierce, and the noise of it filled the forest with fear. The three remaining pups, meanwhile, lay as though frozen, their instincts telling them to stay that way while the life and death struggle raged on; not even a whimper escaped them.

The bear was trying to run from the wolves now. Repeatedly he sought to gallop away, but each time he was met by one of the charging wolves. Again and again they bit at him. Time after time the bear tried to crush them. If he was slow with his biting jabs, he was fast with his forepaws. The

fight seemed to have come to an impasse. But if the bear wanted to escape, the wolves wanted even more to get him away from the den.

Step by step, yard by yard, they drew him away, until at last they were down the slope and close to the brush out of which the bear had come. The dog had a wound on his right shoulder, where one of the bear's claws had raked him. Blood came, but the wound was not serious. The bear was bleeding from several bites, but these, too, were only superficial. His shaggy coat of matted hair made him almost impervious to the fangs of the wolves.

The wolves paused for a fraction of time, and the bear took advantage of the moment to wheel and charge into the heavy brush. The dog pursued him. The bitch hesitated, the mother instinct conquering her desire for vengeance. She climbed the slope to her pups.

She went first to the three, and smelled them and licked them, noting that they were unharmed. She turned to the dead cub then, licked it all over, and nuzzled it as though urging it to move. The bitch whined and licked her baby again. Carefully she opened her mouth and picked it up. It looked at first as though she were going to eat it, for the small body hardly protruded from either side of her jaws, but this is the way in which wolves carry their young. She turned and entered the den and deposited the dead pup in the nesting chamber. In a moment she was back outside, and one by one she carried her other pups to safety. She lay down with them, and Silverfeet and his sisters suckled from her. The dead pup lay on his back near her front paws; she nuzzled him and pushed him towards her dugs. She looked to the cave mouth and listened to the progress of the chase.

The dog wolf had no desire now to attack the bear, but he kept chasing him, pushing him out of his country, always near but never actually closing with him. They ran in this fashion for about two miles. At last the dog stopped. The bear kept traveling, grotesquely agile, looking like a moving black ball as he raced at top speed to disappear over a hilltop. The dog waited a few moments and listened, and when he could hear the bear no more he turned and raced for home.

THE GRASSHOPPER
AND THE ANTS

ON A BEAUTIFUL sunny winter day some ants had their winter store of food out to dry. A grasshopper came by and gazed hungrily at the food. As the ants paid no attention to him, he finally said, "Won't you please give me something to eat? I'm starving." "Did you not store away food last summer for use now?" asked the ants. "No," replied the grasshopper, "I was too busy enjoying myself in dancing and singing." "Well, then," said the ants, "live this winter on your dancing and singing, as we live on what we did."

No one has a right to play all the time,
or he will have to suffer for it.

44

ANDREW LANG

HOW SOME WILD ANIMALS BECAME TAME ONES

A Lapp Fairytale

ONCE UPON A time there lived a miller who was so rich that, when he was going to be married, he asked to the feast not only his own friends but also the wild animals who dwelt in the hills and woods round about. The chief of the bears, the wolves, the foxes, the horses, the cows, the goats, the sheep, and the reindeer, all received invitations; and as they were not accustomed to weddings they were greatly pleased and flattered, and sent back messages in the politest language that they would certainly be there.

The first to start on the morning of the wedding-day was the bear, who always liked to be punctual; and, besides, he had a long way to go, and his hair, being so thick and rough, needed a good brushing before it was fit to be seen at a party. However, he took care to awaken very early, and set off down the road with a light heart. Before he had walked very far he met a boy who came whistling along, hitting at the tops of the flowers with a stick.

"Where are you going?" said he, looking at the bear in surprise, for he was an old acquaintance, and not generally so smart.

"Oh, just to the miller's marriage," answered the bear carelessly. "Of course, I would much rather stay at home, but the miller was so anxious I should be there that I really could not refuse."

45

"Don't go, don't go!" cried the boy. "If you do you will never come back! You have got the most beautiful skin in the world—just the kind that everyone is wanting, and they will be sure to kill you and strip you of it."

"I had not thought of that," said the bear, whose face turned white, only nobody could see it. "If you are certain that they would be so wicked—but perhaps you are jealous because nobody has invited *you*?"

"Oh, nonsense!" replied the boy angrily, "do as you see fit. It is your skin, and not mine; I don't care what becomes of it!" And he walked quickly on with his head in the air.

The bear waited until he was out of sight, and then followed him slowly, for he felt in his heart that the boy's advice was good, though he was too proud to say so.

The boy soon grew tired of walking along the road, and turned off into the woods, where there were bushes he could jump and streams he could wade; but he had not gone far before he met the wolf.

"Where are you going?" asked he, for it was not the first time he had seen him.

"Oh, just to the miller's marriage," answered the wolf, as the bear had done before him. "It is rather tiresome, of course—weddings are always so stupid; but still one must be good-natured!"

"Don't go!" said the boy again. "Your skin is so thick and warm, and winter is not far off now. They will kill you, and strip it from you."

The wolf's jaw dropped in astonishment and terror. "Do you *really* think that would happen?" he gasped.

"Yes, to be sure, I do," answered the boy. "But it is your affair, not mine. So good morning," and on he went. The wolf stood still for a few minutes, for he was trembling all over, and then crept quietly back to his cave.

Next the boy met the fox whose lovely coat of silvery gray was shining in the sun.

"You look very fine!" said the boy, stopping to admire him, "are you going to the miller's wedding too?"

"Yes," answered the fox; "it is a long journey to take for such a thing as that, but you know what the miller's friends are like—so dull and heavy! It is only kind to go and amuse them a little."

"You poor fellow," said the boy pityingly. "Take my advice and stay at home. If you once enter the miller's gate his dogs will tear you in pieces."

"Ah, well, such things *have* occurred, I know," replied the fox gravely. And without saying any more he trotted off the way he had come.

His tail had scarcely disappeared, when a great noise of crashing branches was heard, and up bounded the horse, his black skin glistening like satin.

"Good morning," he called to the boy as he galloped past, "I can't wait to talk to you. I have promised the miller to be present at his wedding-feast, and they won't sit down till I come."

"Stop! stop!" cried the boy after him, and there was something in his voice that made the horse pull up. "What is the matter?" asked he.

"You don't know what you are doing," said the boy. "If once you go there you will never gallop through these woods any more. You are stronger than many men, but they will catch you and put ropes around you, and you will have to work and to serve them all the days of your life."

The horse threw back his head at these words, and laughed scornfully.

"Yes, I am stronger than many men," answered he, "and all the ropes in the world would not hold me. Let them bind me as fast as they will, I can always break loose, and return to the forest and freedom."

And with this proud speech he gave a whisk of his long tail, and galloped away faster than before.

But when he reached the miller's house everything happened as the boy had said. While he was looking at the guests and thinking how much handsomer and stronger he was than any of them, a rope was suddenly flung over his head, and he was thrown down and a bit thrust between his teeth. Then, in spite of his struggles, he was dragged to a stable, and shut up for several days without any food, till his spirit was broken and his coat had lost its gloss. After that he was harnessed to a plow, and had plenty of time to remember all he had lost through not listening to the counsel of the boy.

When the horse had turned a deaf ear to his words the boy wandered idly along, sometimes gathering wild strawberries from a bank, and sometimes plucking wild cherries from a tree, till he reached a clearing in the middle of the forest. Crossing this open space was a beautiful milk-white cow with a wreath of flowers round her neck.

"Good morning," she said pleasantly, as she came up to the place where the boy was standing.

"Good morning," he returned. "Where are you going in such a hurry?"

"To the miller's wedding; I am rather late already, for the wreath took such a long time to make, so I can't stop."

"Don't go," said the boy earnestly; "when once they have tasted your milk they will never let you leave them, and you will have to serve them all the days of your life."

"Oh, nonsense; what do *you* know about it?" answered the cow, who always thought she was wiser than other people. "Why, I can run twice as fast as any of them! I should like to see anybody try to keep me against my will." And, without even a polite bow, she went on her way, feeling very much offended.

But everything turned out just as the boy had said. The company had all heard of the fame of the cow's milk, and persuaded her to give them some, and then her doom was sealed. A crowd gathered round her, and held her horns so that she could not use them, and, like the horse, she was shut in the stable, and only let out in the mornings, when a long rope was tied round her head, and she was fastened to a stake in a grassy meadow.

And so it happened to the goat and to the sheep.

Last of all came the reindeer, looking as he always did, as if some serious business was on hand.

"Where are you going?" asked the boy, who by this time was tired of wild cherries, and was thinking of his dinner.

"I am invited to the wedding," answered the reindeer, "and the miller has begged me on no account to fail him."

"O fool!" cried the boy, "have you no sense at all? Don't you know that when you get there they will hold you fast, for neither beast nor bird is as strong or as swift as you?"

"That is exactly why I am quite safe," replied the reindeer. "I am so strong that no one can bind me, and so swift that not even an arrow can catch me. So, goodbye for the present, you will soon see me back."

But none of the animals that went to the miller's wedding ever came back. And because they were self-willed and conceited, and would not listen to good advice, they and their children have been the servants of men to this very day.

THE OWL AND THE PUSSY-CAT

THE OWL AND the Pussy-cat went to sea
In a beautiful pea-green boat:
They took some honey, and plenty of money
Wrapped up in a five-pound note.
The Owl looked up to the stars above,
And sang to a small guitar,
"O lovely Pussy, O Pussy, my love,
What a beautiful Pussy you are,
        You are,
        You are!
What a beautiful Pussy you are!"

Pussy said to the Owl, "You elegant fowl,
How charmingly sweet you sing!
Oh! let us be married; too long we have tarried:
But what shall we do for a ring?"
They sailed away, for a year and a day,
To the land where the bong-tree grows;
And there in a wood a Piggy-wig stood,
With a ring at the end of his nose,
        His nose,
        His nose,
With a ring at the end of his nose.

50

"Dear Pig, are you willing to sell for one shilling
Your ring?" Said the Piggy, "I will."
So they took it away, and were married next day
By the Turkey who lives on the hill.
They dined on mince and slices of quince,
Which they ate with a runcible spoon;
And hand in hand, on the edge of the sand,
They danced by the light of the moon,
   The moon,
   The moon,
They danced by the light of the moon.

THE GREAT SEA SERPENT

THERE ONCE WAS a little fish. He was of good family; his name I have forgotten—if you want to know it, you must ask someone learned in these matters. He had one thousand and eight hundred brothers and sisters, all born at the same time. They did not know their parents and had to take care of themselves. They swam around happily in the sea. They had enough water to drink—all the great oceans of the world. They did not speculate upon where their food would come from, that would come by itself. Each wanted to follow his own inclinations and live his own life; not that they gave much thought to that either.

The sun shone down into the sea and illuminated the water. It was a strange world, filled with the most fantastic creatures; some of them were so big and had such huge jaws that they could have swallowed all eighteen hundred of the little fish at once. But this, too, they did not worry about, for none of them had been eaten yet.

The little fishes swam close together, as herring or mackerel do. They were thinking about nothing except swimming. Suddenly they heard a terrible noise, and from the surface of the sea a great thing was cast among them. There was more and more of it; it was endless and had neither head nor tail. It was heavy and every one of the small fishes that it hit was either stunned and thrown aside or had its back broken.

The fishes—big and small, the ones who lived up near the waves and those who dwelled in the depths—all fled, while this monstrous serpent grew longer and longer as it sank deeper and deeper, until at last it was hundreds of miles long, and lay at the bottom of the sea, crossing the whole ocean.

All the fishes—yes, even the snails and all the other animals that live in the sea—saw or heard about the strange, gigantic, unknown eel that had descended into the sea from the air above.

What was it? We know that it was the telegraph cable, thousands of miles long, that human beings had laid to connect America and Europe.

All the inhabitants of the sea were frightened of this new huge animal that had come to live among them. The flying fishes leaped up from the sea and into the air; and the gurnard, since it knew how, shot up out of the water like a bullet. Others went down into the depths of the ocean so fast that they were there before the telegraph cable. They frightened both the cod and the flounder, who were swimming around peacefully, hunting and eating their fellow creatures.

A couple of sea cucumbers were so petrified that they spat out their own stomachs in fright; but they survived, for they knew how to swallow them again. Lots of lobsters and crabs left their shells in the confusion. During all this, the eighteen hundred little fishes were separated; most of them never saw one another again, nor would they have recognized one another if they had. Only a dozen of them stayed in the same spot, and after they had lain still a couple of hours their worst fright was over and curiosity became stronger than fear.

They looked about, both above and below themselves,

and there at the bottom of the sea they thought they saw the monster that had frightened them all. It looked thin, but who knew how big it could make itself or how strong it was. It lay very still, but it might be up to something.

The more timid of the small fish said, "Let it lie where it is, it is no concern of ours." But the tiniest of them were determined to find out what it was. Since the monster had come from above, it was better to seek information about it up there. They swam up to the surface of the ocean. The wind was still and the sea was like a mirror.

They met a dolphin. He is a fellow who likes to jump and to turn somersaults in the sea. The dolphin has eyes to see with and ought to have seen what happened, and therefore the little fishes approached it. But a dolphin only thinks about himself and his somersaults; he didn't know what to say, so he didn't say anything, but looked very proud.

A seal came swimming by just at that moment, and even though it eats small fishes, it was more polite than the dolphin. Luckily it happened to be full, and it knew more than the jumping fish. "Many a night have I lain on a wet stone—miles and miles away from here—and looked toward land, where live those treacherous creatures who call themselves, in their own language, men. They are always hunting me and my kind, though usually we manage to escape. That is exactly what happened to the great sea serpent that you are asking about—it got away from them. They had it in their power for ever so long, and kept it up on land. Now men wanted to transport it to another country, across the sea.—Why? you may ask, but I can't answer.—They had a lot of trouble getting it on board the ship. But they finally succeeded; after all, it was weakened from its stay on land. They rolled it up, round and round into a coil. It wiggled and writhed, and what a lot of noise it made! I heard it. When the ship got out to sea, the great eel slipped overboard. They tried to stop it. I saw them, there were dozens of hands holding onto its body. But they couldn't. Now it is lying down at the bottom of the sea, and I guess it will stay there for a while."

"It looks awfully thin," said the tiny fishes.

"They have starved it," explained the seal. "But it will soon get its old figure and strength back. I am sure it is the great sea serpent: the one men are so afraid of that they talk about it all the time. I had not believed it existed, but now I do. And that was it." With a flip of its tail, the seal dived and was gone.

"How much he knew and how well he talked," said one of the little fishes admiringly. "I have never known so much as I do now—I just hope it wasn't all lies."

"We could swim down and look," suggested the tiniest of the tiny fishes. "And on the way down we could hear what the other fishes think."

"We wouldn't move a fin to know anything more," said all the other tiny fishes, turned, and swam away.

"But I will," shouted the tiniest one, and swam down into the depths. But he was far away from where the great sea serpent had sunk. The little fish searched in every direction. Never had he realized that the world was so big. Great shoals of herring glided by like silver boats, and behind them came schools of mackerel that were even more splendid and brilliant. There were fishes of all shapes, with all kinds of markings and colors. Jellyfish, looking like transparent plants, floated by, carried by the currents. Down at the bottom of the sea the strangest things grew: tail grasses and palm-shaped trees whose every leaf was covered with crustaceans.

At last the tiny fish spied a long dark line far below it and swam down to it. It was not the giant serpent but the railing of a sunken ship, whose upper and lower decks had been torn in two by the pressure of the sea. The little fish entered the great cabin, where the terrified passengers had gathered as the ship went down; they had all drowned and the currents of the sea had carried their bodies away, except for two of them: a young woman who lay on a bench with her babe in her arms. The sea rocked them gently; they looked as though they were sleeping. The little fish grew frightened as he looked at them. What if they were to wake? The cabin was so quiet and so lonely that the tiny fish hurried away again, out into the light, where there were other fishes. It had not swum very far when it met a young whale; it was awfully big.

"Please don't swallow me," pleaded the little fish. "I am so little you could hardly taste me, and I find it such a great pleasure to live."

"What are you doing down here?" grunted the whale. "It is much too deep for your kind." Then the tiny fish told the whale about the great eel—or whatever it could be—that had come from the air and descended into the sea, frightening even the most courageous fishes.

"Ha, ha, ha!" laughed the whale, and swallowed so much water that it had to surface in order to breathe and spout the water out. "Ho-ho . . . ha-ha. That must have been the thing that tickled my back when I was turning over. I thought it was the mast of a ship and was just

about to use it as a back scratcher; but it must have been that. It lies farther out. I think I will go and have a look at it; I haven't anything else
to do."

The whale swam away and the tiny fish followed it, but not too
closely for the great animal left a turbulent wake behind it.

They met a shark and an old sawfish. They, too, had heard about
the strange great eel that was so thin and yet longer than any other fish.
They hadn't seen it but wanted to.

A catfish joined them. "If that sea serpent is not thicker than an
anchor cable, then I will cut it in two, in one bite," he said, and opened
his monstrous jaws to show his six rows of teeth. "If I can make a mark
in an anchor I guess I can bite a stem like that in two."

"There it is," cried the whale. "Look how it moves, twisting and
turning." The whale thought he had better eyesight than the others. As
a matter of fact he hadn't; what he had seen was merely an old conger-
eel, several yards long, that was swimming toward them.

"That fellow has never caused any commotion in the sea before, or
frightened any other big fish," said the catfish with disgust. "I have met
him often."

They told the conger about the new sea serpent and asked him if he
wanted to go with them to discover what it was.

"I wonder if it is longer than I am," said the conger eel, and
stretched himself. "If it is, then it will be sorry."

"It certainly will," said the rest of the company. "There are enough
of us so we don't have to tolerate it if we don't want to!" they
exclaimed, and hurried on.

They saw something that looked like a floating island that was having trouble keeping itself from sinking. It was an old whale. His head
was overgrown with seaweed, and on his back were so many mussels
and oysters that its black skin looked as if it had white spots.

"Come on, old man," the young whale said. "There is a new fish in the ocean and we won't tolerate it!"

"Oh, let me stay where I am!" grumbled the old whale. "Peace is all I ask, to be left in peace. Ow! Ow! . . . I am very sick, it will be the death of me. My only comfort is to let my back emerge above the water, then the sea gulls scratch it: the sweet birds. That helps a lot as long as they don't dig too deep with their bills and get into the blubber. There's the skeleton of one still sitting on my back. It got stuck and couldn't get loose when I had to submerge. The little fishes picked his bones clean. You can see it. . . . Look at him, and look at me. . . . Oh, I am very sick."

"You are just imagining all that," said the young whale. "I am not sick, no one that lives in the sea is ever sick."

"I am sorry!" said the old whale. "The eels have skin diseases, the carp have smallpox, and we all suffer from worms."

"Nonsense!" shouted the shark, who didn't like to listen to that kind of talk. Neither did the others, so they all swam on.

At last they came to the place where part of the telegraph cable lies, that stretches from Europe to America across sand shoals and high mountains, through endless forests of seaweed and coral. The currents move as the winds do in the heavens above, and through them swim schools of fishes, more numerous than the flocks of migratory birds that fly through the air. There was a noise, a sound, a humming, the ghost of which you hear in the great conch shell when you hold it up to your ear.

"There is the serpent!" shouted the bigger fish and the little fishes too. They had caught sight of some of the telegraph cable but neither the beginning nor the end of it, for they were both lost in the far distance. Sponges, polyps, and gorgonia swayed above it and leaned against it, sometimes hiding it from view. Sea urchins and snails climbed over it; and great crabs, like giant spiders, walked tightrope along it. Deep blue sea cucumbers—or whatever those creatures are called who eat with their whole body—lay next to it; one would think that they were trying to smell it. Flounders and cod kept turning from side to side, in order to be able to listen to what everyone was saying. The starfishes had dug themselves down in the mire; only two of their points were sticking up, but they had eyes on them and were staring at the black snake, hoping to see something come out of it.

The telegraph cable lay perfectly still, as if it were lifeless; but inside, it was filled with life: with thoughts, human thoughts.

"That thing is treacherous," said the whale. "It might hit me in the stomach, and that is my weak point."

"Let's feel our way forward," said one of the polyps. "I have long arms and flexible fingers. I've already touched it, but now I'll take a firmer grasp."

And it stuck out its arms and encircled the cable. "I have felt both its stomach and its back. It is not scaly. I don't think it has any skin either. I don't believe it lays eggs and I don't think it gives birth to live children."

The conger-eel lay down beside the cable and stretched itself as far as it could. "It is longer than I am," it admitted. "But length isn't everything. One has to have skin, a good stomach and, above all, suppleness."

The whale—the young strong whale!—bowed more deeply than it ever had before. "Are you a fish or a plant?" he asked. "Or are you a surface creation, one of those who can't live down here?"

The telegraph didn't answer, though it was filled with words. Thoughts traveled through it so fast that they took only seconds to move from one end to the other: hundreds of miles away.

"Will you answer or be bitten in two?" asked the ill-mannered shark.

All the other fishes repeated the question: "Answer or be bitten in two?"

The telegraph cable didn't move; it had its own ideas, which isn't surprising for someone so full of thoughts. "Let them bite me in two," it thought. "Then I will be pulled up and repaired. It has happened to lots of my relations, that are not half as long as I am." But it didn't speak, it telegraphed; besides, it found the question impertinent; after all, it was lying there on official business.

Dusk had come. The sun was setting, as men say. It was fiery red, and the clouds were as brilliant as fire—one more beautiful than the other.

"Now comes the red illumination," said the polyp. "Maybe the thing will be easier to see in that light, though I hardly think it worth looking at."

"Attack it! Attack it!" screamed the catfish, and showed all his teeth.

"Attack it! Attack it!" shouted the whale, the shark, the swordfish, and the conger-eel.

They pushed forward. The catfish was first; but just as it was going to bite the cable the swordfish, who was a little too eager, stuck its

sword into the behind of the catfish. It
was a mistake, but it kept the catfish from using the full
strength of its jaw muscles.

There was a great
muddle in the mud.
The sea cucumbers,
the big fishes, and the
small ones swam around in circles; they
pushed and shoved and squashed and ate each other up. The crabs and
the lobsters fought, and the snails pulled their heads into their houses.
The telegraph cable just minded its own business, which is the proper
thing for a telegraph cable to do.

Night came to the sky above, but down in the ocean millions and
millions of little animals illuminated the water. Crayfish no larger than
the head of a pin gave off light. It is incredible and wonderful; and
quite true.

All the animals of the sea looked at the telegraph cable. "If only we
knew what it was—or at least what it wasn't," said one of the fishes.
And that was a very important question.

An old sea cow—human beings call them mermen and mermaids—
came gliding by. This one was a mermaid. She had a tail and short arms
for splashing, hanging breasts, and seaweed and parasites on her
head—and of these she was very proud. "If you want learning and
knowledge," she said, "then I think I am the best equipped to give it to
you. But I want free passage on the bottom of the sea for myself and
my family. I am a fish like you, and a reptile by training. I am the most
intelligent citizen of the ocean. I know about everything under the
water and everything above it. The thing that you are worrying about
comes from up there; and everything from above is dead and power-

less, once it comes down here. So let it lie, it is only a human invention and of no importance."

"I think it may be more than that," said the tiny fish.

"Shut up, mackerel!" said the sea cow.

"Shrimp!" shouted the others, and they meant it as an insult.

The sea cow explained to them that the sea serpent who had frightened them—the cable itself, by the way, didn't make a sound—was not dangerous. It was only an invention of those animals up on dry land called human beings. When she finished talking about the sea serpent, she gave a little lesson in the craftiness and wickedness of men: "They are always trying to catch us. That is the only reason for their existence. They throw down nets, traps, and long fishing lines that have hooks, with bait attached to them, to try and fool us. This is probably another—bigger—fishing line. They are so stupid that they expect us to bite on it. But we aren't as dumb as that. Don't touch that piece of junk. It will unravel, fall apart, and become mud and mire—the whole thing. Let it lie there and rot. Anything that comes from above is worthless; it breaks or creaks; it is no good!"

"No good!" said all the creatures of the sea, accepting the mermaid's opinion in order to have one.

The little tiny fish didn't agree, but it had learned to keep its thoughts to itself. "That enormously long snake may be the most marvelous fish in the sea. I have a feeling that it is."

"Marvelous!" we human beings agree; and we can prove that it is true.

The great sea serpent of the fable has become a fact. It was constructed by human skill, conceived by human intelligence. It stretches from the Eastern Hemisphere to the Western, carrying messages from country to country faster than light travels from the sun down to the earth. Each year the great serpent grows. Soon it will stretch across all the great oceans, under the storm-whipped waves and the grasslike water, through which the skipper can look down as if he were sailing through the air and see the multitude of fish and the fireworks of color.

At the very depths is a *Midgards-worm*, biting its own tail as it circumscribes the world. Fish and reptiles hit their heads against it; it is impossible to understand what it is by looking at it. Human thoughts expressed in all the languages of the world, and yet silent: the snake of knowledge of good and evil. The most wonderful of the wonders of the sea: our time's great sea serpent!

THE RAVEN AND THE GOOSE

An Inuit Legend

DO YOU KNOW why the raven is so black, so dull and black in color? It is all because of its own obstinacy. Now listen.

It happened in the days when all the birds were getting their colors and the pattern in their coats. And the raven and the goose happened to meet, and they agreed to paint each other.

The raven began, and painted the other black, with a nice white pattern showing between.

The goose thought that very fine indeed, and began to do the same by the raven, painting it a coat exactly like its own.

But then the raven fell into a rage, and declared the pattern was frightfully ugly, and the goose, offended at all the fuss, simply splashed it black all over.

And now you know why the raven is black.

COYOTE AND WATER SERPENT

A LONG TIME AGO, when the earth was still young, Coyote and Water Serpent were the best of friends. They would drop by each other's house whenever it occurred to them to do so. Coyote and Water Serpent were young in those days and their story had not yet unfolded.

One morning after Water Serpent had finished his breakfast, he decided to visit his good friend Coyote. As he neared Coyote's house he could see smoke rising and knew his friend was at home.

"Hello," he shouted into Coyote's den. "Anyone home? May I come in to visit?"

"Of course," replied Coyote, being a friendly sort of fellow. "Come share the warmth of my fire and have a chat."

Water Serpent poked his head into Coyote's house and started to slide in. Now, although he had not yet reached his adult size, Water Serpent was a very big snake. He slid in one coil, which bumped up against each wall of the room, and it was not all of him. He slithered some more and another coil overlapped the first and it was not all of him. He slid and slithered and piled coil upon coil until Coyote was pushed to the very edge of his firepit. When Water Serpent was all the way in and comfortable, there was no room for Coyote. He was forced to sit, all scrunched up, close to the heat of the fire.

But Water Serpent was his friend and soon they began to gossip about what was happening in the village nearby and when the rains might start. All the while, Water Serpent seemed not to notice his

friend's discomfort, and Coyote, being the sort that he was, fell to scheming and planning how he would get back at his friend.

Finally, Water Serpent announced his departure, saying, "Come to visit me soon. Don't stay away too long." And he began to leave. Unlike most other creatures, it took quite some time for him to emerge completely from Coyote's home, and he was still slithering out when Coyote settled upon his plan.

Coyote was so anxious to put his scheme in action that he rushed through his supper and ran out into the evening. Soon he came to a spot full of juniper trees. It was just what he was looking for. He stripped the bark from some trees, picked up some yucca leaves, and arrived back home with his arms laden.

Once inside, Coyote started working. He worked all night. By the time the morning sun crept into his den, he had fashioned a tail from the juniper bark and yucca leaves. It looked just like Water Serpent's tail and it was almost as long.

Coyote was very pleased with himself and with his plan, but the tail needed one last finishing touch so that Water Serpent would believe it was really Coyote's tail. He started pulling tufts of fur from his body and sticking them onto the tail, and soon indeed it looked just like the rest of him.

"I can't wait till it's time to visit Water Serpent," he thought to himself. "Then he'll know what it's like to be squashed and squeezed and made uncomfortable in your own home."

The next day Coyote and his new tail made their way over to Water Serpent's house.

"Anyone home?" he called out. "May I come in?"

"Of course. Come on in," answered Water Serpent, and Coyote proudly began his entrance.

"I don't know what's happening to me," he said to Water Serpent, "but all of a sudden I seem to have grown this very long tail. It's almost as long as yours. I can't imagine where it came from. You'll have to excuse me if I take up more room than usual."

And, since Coyote thought he was going to teach Water Serpent a lesson, he, too, draped his tail around the whole room. Water Serpent had a big house, but soon he was crushed up against one side of the room, his coils in an uncomfortable knot. Coyote, appearing not to notice, began to talk. He talked all afternoon, enjoying his trick. But Water Serpent saw what Coyote was up to and knew that the tail wasn't a real one.

At suppertime Coyote took his leave, humming and thinking to himself that Water Serpent had fallen for his trick. He was very proud of himself. But Water Serpent was at home, thinking, "That Coyote, he's always up to something. He really thought I wouldn't notice that his tail was fake."

Soon it was Water Serpent's turn to visit. As he came near Coyote's house, Coyote quickly tied on his tail and went to the opening of his den to greet his friend.

Water Serpent said, "I think you should know that since we last met I've grown again. I'm not sure we'll both fit in your house any more."

"Oh, I'm sure we will. Here, I'll come out and you go in first."

Water Serpent went in and in and in and in and in. There wasn't any room for Coyote after all. To be polite, he was forced to sit outside and entertain his friend from there. It was very chilly that day and as Coyote grew colder and colder, he found himself wishing that his friend would go home.

But Water Serpent had no intention of leaving. He was quite happy to make his friend uncomfortable in retaliation for Coyote's last visit. So he stayed, and they chatted about this and that, and only when Coyote's teeth began to chatter did he say, "Well, I must be going now."

"If you insist," replied the shivering Coyote, who was already trying to push past Water Serpent's coils in his rush to get to the fire. By the time the last of Water Serpent's tail was finally out of his house, Coyote had already hatched another plan to get even.

That evening Coyote returned to the stand of junipers. He dragged even more bark and yucca back to his house than he had before. Once again he made the bark and yucca leaves ready for tail-making.

When he was finished, Coyote was sure he had the longest tail in the whole world. Certainly it was long enough to force Water Serpent to sit outside when he went to visit the next bitterly cold day.

So Coyote waited for a cold day. And waited. The weather turned unseasonably warm. Coyote was not very good at biding his time, but now he was patient. He knew the wait would be worth it.

The fourth day was bright and cold and just right for Coyote's visit. He got ready in a hurry and was soon at Water Serpent's house.

"Here I am at last," he called out. "It's been a long time since we visited. May I come in?"

"Of course. How nice to see you," replied Water Serpent.

"I should warn you," Coyote shouted into the house, "that since you last saw me, I, too, have grown quite a bit. There may not be room in your house for both of us."

And with that, Coyote began to drag his tail into Water Serpent's house. It was soon obvious that Coyote's tail would fill every nook and cranny in the house, and Water Serpent politely offered to take his turn sitting outside.

"Oh no, you mustn't on my account," said Coyote. "You'll catch your death of cold."

"It's not that chilly," responded Water Serpent. "I'll be fine."

And so they idled the day away talking of things near and far. Water Serpent grew colder and colder and he, too, began to wish that his friend would go home.

But Coyote was enjoying his revenge and he was not about to cut his visit short. Water Serpent was so cold he thought his eyes would turn to ice. He was so cold his nose began to run. He thought Coyote would never leave.

As the sun began to set, Coyote finally roused himself from his place next to Water Serpent's cozy fire and announced his departure. When he disappeared into the distance over a small hill and his tail was still leaving Water Serpent's house, Water Serpent thought, "This is

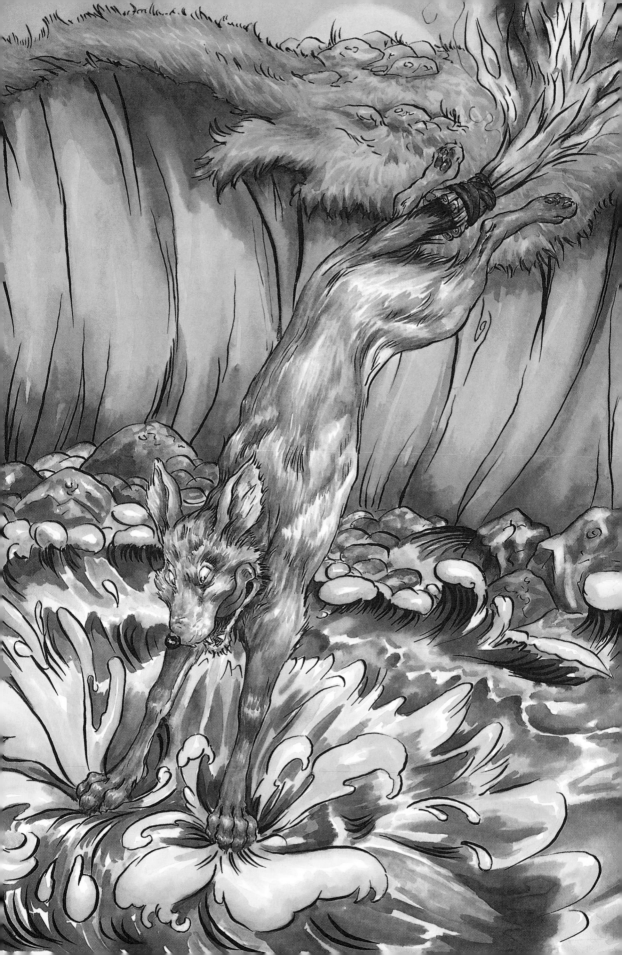

getting out of hand. I'm going to have to do something to end this silly competition. Coyote will never stop. He's a petty, vengeful wretch. He made me almost freeze to death!"

At just that moment, the last of Coyote's tail brushed past the fire and the angry Water Serpent knew what he was going to do. He grabbed the end of the tail and stuck it in the fire.

Meanwhile, Coyote had topped another rise. He was so in love with his tail that he felt he just had to turn around and admire it again. In doing so, he noticed a fire way off in the distance and thought that a brush fire had started near Water Serpent's house. But when Coyote looked again, the fire seemed to be following him. He thought men were perhaps having a coyote drive and that it would be unwise to return to his house just yet.

So Coyote veered off in a new direction. His walk became a trot; his trot a run. Everywhere he looked there seemed to be brush fires now. He was unaware that the swishing of his own tail had started the fires. He was only conscious that they seemed to be catching up to him. The faster he ran, the more the sparks flew from his burning tail and set ablaze the dry grasses.

Coyote, in a panic now, thought only of reaching the river. He had no idea that he was being chased by his own burning tail. He was certain that unknown enemies were hunting him down, beating him out of cover with the use of fire.

But as he approached the river, Coyote took one last look behind him. The fire had reached him, and he at last realized that he had been running away from his own tail. He jumped into the river and was never seen again.

When Coyote did not return, Water Serpent was not a bit upset. "Served him right," he muttered to himself. "Coyote could never leave well enough alone. Always making trouble and scheming. Now he'll not bother us again."

And so Water Serpent lost his best friend. Who knows, he may be alone still.

E. NESBIT

THE LAST OF THE DRAGONS

OF COURSE YOU know that dragons were once as common as motor-omnibuses are now, and almost as dangerous. But as every well-brought-up prince was expected to kill a dragon, and rescue a princess, the dragons grew fewer and fewer till it was often quite hard for a princess to find a dragon to be rescued from. And at last there were no more dragons in France and no more dragons in Germany, or Spain, or Italy, or Russia. There were some left in China, and are still, but they are cold and bronzy, and there were never any, of course, in America. But the last real live dragon left was in England, and of course that was a very long time ago, before what you call English History began. This dragon lived in Cornwall in the big caves amidst the rocks, and a very fine big dragon it was, quite seventy feet long from the tip of its fearful snout to the end of its terrible tail. It breathed fire and smoke, and rattled when it walked, because its scales were made of iron. Its wings were like half-umbrellas—or like bat's wings, only several thousand times bigger. Everyone was very frightened of it, and well they might be.

Now the King of Cornwall had one daughter, and when she was sixteen, of course she would have to go and face the dragon: such tales are always told in royal nurseries at twilight, so the Princess knew what she had to expect. The dragon would not eat her, of course—because the prince would come and rescue her. But the Princess could not help thinking it would be much pleasanter to have nothing to do with the dragon at all—not even to be rescued from him. "All the princes I know are such very silly little boys," she told her father. "Why must I be rescued by a prince?"

"It's always done, my dear," said the King, taking his crown off and putting it on the grass, for they were alone in the garden, and even kings must unbend sometimes.

"Father, darling," said the Princess presently, when she had made a daisy chain and put it on the King's head, where the crown ought to have been. "Father, darling, couldn't we tie up one of the silly little princes for the dragon to look at—and then *I* could go and kill the dragon and rescue the prince? I fence much better than any of the princes we know."

"What an unladylike idea!" said the King, and put his crown on again, for he saw the Prime Minister coming with a basket of new-laid Bills for him to sign. "Dismiss the thought, my child. I rescued your mother from a dragon, and you don't want to set yourself up above her, I should hope?"

"But this is the *last* dragon. It is different from all other dragons."

"How?" asked the King.

"Because he *is* the last," said the Princess, and went off to her fencing lessons, with which she took great pains. She took great pains with all her lessons—for she could not give up the idea of fighting the dragon. She took such pains that she became the strongest and boldest and most skillful and most sensible princess in Europe. She had always been the prettiest and nicest.

And the days and years went on, till at last the day came which was the day before the Princess was to be rescued from the dragon. The Prince who was to do this deed of valor was a pale prince, with large eyes and a head full of mathematics and philosophy, but he had unfortunately neglected his fencing lessons. He was to stay the night at the palace, and there was a banquet.

After supper the Princess sent her pet parrot to the Prince with a note. It said:

"Please, Prince, come onto the terrace. I want to talk to you without anybody else hearing.—The Princess."

So, of course, he went—and he saw her gown of silver a long way off shining among the shadows of the trees like water in starlight. And when he came quite close to her he said: "Princess, at your service," and bent his cloth-of-gold-covered knee and put his hand on his cloth-of-gold-covered heart.

"Do you think," said the Princess earnestly, "that you will be able to kill the dragon?"

"I will kill the dragon," said the Prince firmly, "or perish in the attempt."

"It's no use your perishing," said the Princess.

"It's the least I can do," said the Prince.

"What I'm afraid of is that it'll be the most you can do," said the Princess.

"It's the only thing I can do," said he, "unless I kill the dragon."

"Why you should do anything for me is what I can't see," said she.

"But I want to," he said. "You must know that I love you better than anything in the world."

When he said that he looked so kind that the Princess began to like him a little.

"Look here," she said, "no one else will go out tomorrow. You know they tie me to a rock and leave me—and then everybody scurries home and puts up the shutters and keeps them shut till you ride through the town in triumph shouting that you've killed the dragon, and I ride on the horse behind you weeping for joy."

"I've heard that that is how it is done," said he.

"Well, do you love me well enough to come very quickly and set me free—and we'll fight the dragon together?"

"It wouldn't be safe for you."

"Much safer for both of us for me to be free, with a sword in my hand, than tied up and helpless. *Do* agree."

He could refuse her nothing. So he agreed. And next day everything happened as she had said.

When he had cut the cords that tied her to the rock they stood on the lonely mountain-side looking at each other.

"It seems to me," said the Prince, "that this ceremony could have been arranged without the dragon."

"Yes," said the Princess, "but since it has been arranged with the dragon—"

"It seems such a pity to kill the dragon—the last in the world," said the Prince.

"Well then, don't let's," said the Princess; "let's tame it not to eat princesses but to eat out of their hands. They say everything can be tamed by kindness."

"Taming by kindness means giving them things to eat," said the Prince. "Have you got anything to eat?"

She hadn't, but the Prince owned that he had a few biscuits. "Breakfast was so very early," said he, "and I thought you might have felt faint after the fight."

"How clever," said the Princess, and they took a biscuit in each hand. And they looked here, and they looked there, but never a dragon could they see.

"But here's its trail," said the Prince, and pointed to where the rock was scarred and scratched so as to make a track leading to a dark cave. It was like cart-ruts in a Sussex road, mixed with the marks of sea gulls' feet on the sea-sand. "Look, that's where it's dragged its brass tail and planted its steel claws."

"Don't let's think how hard its tail and its claws are," said the Princess, "or I shall begin to be frightened—and I know you can't tame anything, even by kindness, if you're frightened of it. Come on. Now or never."

She caught the Prince's hand in hers and they ran along the path towards the dark mouth of the cave. But they did not run into it. It really was so very *dark*.

So they stood outside, and the Prince shouted: "What ho! Dragon there! What ho within!" And from the cave they heard an answering voice and great clattering and creaking. It sounded as though a rather large cotton-mill were stretching itself and waking up out of its sleep.

The Prince and the Princess trembled, but they stood firm.

"Dragon—I say, dragon!" said the Princess, "do come out and talk to us. We've brought you a present."

"Oh yes—I know your presents," growled the dragon in a huge rumbling voice. "One of those precious princesses, I suppose? And I've got to come out and fight for her. Well, I tell you straight, I'm not going to do it. A fair fight I wouldn't say no to—a fair fight and no favor—but one of these put-up fights where you've got to lose—no! So I tell you. If I wanted a princess I'd come and take her, in my own time—but I don't.

What do you suppose I'd do with her, if I'd got her?"

"Eat her, wouldn't you?" said the Princess, in a voice that trembled a little.

"Eat a fiddle-stick end," said the dragon very rudely. "I wouldn't touch the horrid thing."

The Princess's voice grew firmer. "Do you like biscuits?" she said.

"No," growled the dragon.

"Not the nice little expensive ones with sugar on the top?"

"*No*," growled the dragon.

"Then what *do* you like?" asked the Prince.

"You go away and don't bother me," growled the dragon, and they could hear it turn over, and the clang and clatter of its turning echoed in the cave like the sound of the steam-hammers in the Arsenal at Woolwich.

The Prince and Princess looked at each other. What *were* they to do? Of course it was no use going home and telling the King that the dragon didn't want princesses—because His Majesty was very old-fashioned and would never have believed that a new-fashioned dragon could ever be at all different from an old-fashioned dragon. They could not go into the cave and kill the dragon. Indeed, unless he attacked the Princess it did not seem fair to kill him at all.

"He must like something," whispered the Princess, and she called out in a voice as sweet as honey and sugar-cane:

"Dragon! Dragon dear!"

"WHAT?" shouted the dragon. "Say that again!" and they could hear the dragon coming towards them through the darkness of the cave. The Princess shivered, and said in a very small voice:

"Dragon! Dragon dear!"

And then the dragon came out. The Prince drew his sword, and the Princess drew hers—the beautiful silver-handled one that the Prince had brought in his motor-car. But they did not attack; they moved slowly back as the dragon came out, all the vast scaly length of him, and lay along the rock—his great wings half-spread and his silvery sheen gleaming like diamonds in the sun. At last they could retreat no further—the dark rock behind them stopped their way—and with their backs to the rock they stood swords in hand and waited.

The dragon drew nearer and nearer—and now they could see that he was not breathing fire and smoke as they had expected—he came crawling slowly towards them wriggling a little as a puppy does when it wants to play and isn't quite sure whether you're not cross with it.

And then they saw that great tears were coursing down its brazen cheek.

"Whatever's the matter?" said the Prince.

"Nobody," sobbed the dragon, "ever called me 'dear' before!"

"Don't cry, dragon dear," said the Princess. "We'll call you 'dear' as often as you like. We want to tame you."

"I *am* tame," said the dragon—"that's just it. That's what nobody but you has ever found out. I'm so tame that I'd eat out of your hands."

"Eat what, dragon dear?" said the Princess. "Not biscuits?" The dragon slowly shook his heavy head.

"Not biscuits?" said the Princess tenderly. "What, then, dragon dear?"

"Your kindness quite undragons me," it said. "No one has ever asked any of us what we like to eat—always offering us princesses, and then rescuing them—and never once, 'What'll you take to drink the King's health in?' Cruel hard I call it," and it wept again.

"But what would you like to drink our health in?" said the Prince. "We're going to be married today, aren't we, Princess?"

She said that she supposed so.

"What'll I take to drink your health in?" asked the dragon. "Ah, you're something like a gentleman, you are, sir. I don't mind if I do, sir. I'll be proud to drink your and your good lady's health in a tiny drop of"—its voice faltered—"to think of you asking me so friendly like," it said. "Yes, sir, just a tiny drop of puppuppuppuppu-petrol—tha-that's what does a dragon good, sir—"

"I've lots in the car," said the Prince, and was off down the mountain like a flash. He was a good judge of character and he knew that with this dragon the Princess would be safe.

"If I might make so bold," said the dragon, "while the gentleman's away—p'raps just to pass the time you'd be so kind as to call me Dear again, and if you'd shake claws with a poor old dragon that's never been anybody's enemy but his own—well, the last of the dragons'll be the proudest dragon that's ever been since the first of them."

It held out an enormous paw, and the great steel hooks that were its

claws closed over the Princess's hand as softly as the claws of the Himalayan bear will close over the bit of bun you hand it through the bars at the Zoo.

And so the Prince and Princess went back to the palace in triumph, the dragon following them like a pet dog. And all through the wedding festivities no one drank more earnestly to the happiness of the bride and bridegroom than the Princess's pet dragon—whom she had at once named Fido.

And when the happy pair were settled in their own kingdom, Fido came to them and begged to be allowed to make himself useful.

"There must be some little thing I can do," he said, rattling his wings and stretching his claws. "My wings and claws and so on ought to be turned to some account—to say nothing of my grateful heart."

So the Prince had a special saddle or howdah made for him—very long it was—like the tops of many tramcars fitted together. One hundred and fifty seats were fitted to this, and the dragon, whose greatest pleasure was now to give pleasure to others, delighted in taking parties of children to the seaside. It flew through the air quite easily with its hundred and fifty little passengers—and would lie on the sand patiently waiting till they were ready to return. The children were very fond of it, and used to call it Dear, a word which never failed to bring tears of affection and gratitude to its eyes. So it lived, useful and respected, till quite the other day when someone happened to say, in his hearing, that dragons were out-of-date, now so much new machinery had come in. This so distressed him that he asked the King to change him into something less old-fashioned, and the kindly monarch at once changed him into a mechanical contrivance. The dragon, indeed, became the first airplane.

THE HARE AND THE TORTOISE

A HARE WAS ONCE boasting about how fast he could run when a tortoise, overhearing him, said, "I'll run you a race." "Done," said the hare and laughed to himself; "but let's get the fox for a judge." The fox consented and the two started. The hare quickly outran the tortoise, and knowing he was far ahead, lay down to take a nap. "I can soon pass the tortoise whenever I awaken." But unfortunately, the hare overslept himself; therefore when he awoke, though he ran his best, he found the tortoise was already at the goal.

Slow and steady wins the race.

THE SPRINGFIELD FOX

THE HENS WERE disappearing. My uncle was wrathy. He determined to conduct the war himself, and sowed the woods with poison baits, trusting to luck that our own dogs would not get them. He indulged in contemptuous remarks on my bygone woodcraft, and went out evenings with a gun and the two dogs, to see what he could destroy.

Vix knew right well what a poisoned bait was; she passed them by or else treated them with active contempt, but one she dropped down the hole of an old enemy, a skunk, who was never afterward seen. Formerly old Scarface was always ready to take charge of the dogs, and keep them out of mischief. But now that Vix had the whole burden of the brood, she could no longer spend time in breaking every track to the den, and was not always at hand to meet and mislead the foes that might be coming too near.

The end is easily foreseen. Ranger followed a hot trail to the den, and Spot, the fox-terrier, announced that the family was at home, and then did his best to go in after them.

The whole secret was now out, and the whole family doomed. The hired man came around with pick and shovel to dig them out, while we and the dogs stood by. Old Vix soon showed herself in the near woods, and led the dogs away off down the river, where she shook them off when she thought proper, by the simple device of springing on a sheep's back. The frightened animal ran for several hundred yards, then Vix got off, knowing that there was now a hopeless gap in the scent, and returned to the den. But the dogs, baffled by the break in the trail, soon did the same, to find Vix hanging about in despair, vainly trying to decoy us away from her treasures.

Meanwhile Paddy plied both pick and shovel with vigor and effort. The yellow, gravelly sand was heaping on both sides, and the shoulders of the sturdy digger were sinking below the level. After an hour's digging, enlivened by frantic rushes of the dogs after the old fox, who hovered near in the woods, Pat called:

"Here they are, sor!"

It was the den at the end of the burrow, and cowering as far back as they could, were the four little woolly cubs.

Before I could interfere, a murderous blow from the shovel, and a sudden rush from the fierce little terrier, ended the lives of three. The fourth and smallest was barely saved by holding him by his tail high out of reach of the excited dogs.

He gave one short squeal, and his poor mother came at the cry, and circled so near that she would have been shot but for the accidental protection of the dogs, who somehow always seemed to get between, and whom she once more led away on a fruitless chase.

The little one saved alive was dropped into a bag, where he lay quite still. His unfortunate brothers were thrown back into their nursery bed, and buried under a few shovelfuls of earth.

We guilty ones then went back into the house, and the little fox was soon chained in the yard. No one knew just why he was kept alive, but in all a change of feeling had set in, and the idea of killing him was without a supporter.

He was a pretty little fellow, like a cross between a fox and a lamb. His woolly visage and form were strangely lamb-like and innocent, but one could find in his yellow eyes a gleam of cunning and savageness as unlamb-like as it possibly could be.

As long as anyone was near he crouched sullen and cowed in his shelter-box, and it was a full hour after being left alone before he ventured to look out.

My window now took the place of the hollow basswood. A number of hens of the breed he knew so well were about the cub in the yard. Late that afternoon as they strayed near the captive there was a sudden rattle of the chain, and the youngster dashed at the nearest one and would have caught him but for the chain which brought him up with a jerk. He got on his feet and slunk back to his box, and though he afterward made several rushes he so gauged his leap as to win or fail within the length of the chain and never again was brought up by its cruel jerk.

As night came down the little fellow became very uneasy, sneaking out of his box, but going back at each slight alarm, tugging at his chain, or at times biting it in fury while he held it down with his forepaws. Suddenly he paused as though listening, then raising his little black nose he poured out a short quavering cry.

Once or twice this was repeated, the time between being occupied in worrying the chain and running about. Then an answer came. The faraway *yap-yurrr* of the old fox. A few minutes later a shadowy form appeared on the wood-pile. The little one slunk into his box, but at once returned and ran to meet his mother with all the gladness that a fox could show. Quick as a flash she seized him and turned to bear him away by the road she came. But the moment the end of the chain was reached the cub was rudely jerked from the old one's mouth, and she, scared by the opening of a window, fled over the wood-pile.

An hour afterward the cub had ceased to run about or cry. I peeped out, and by the light of the moon saw the form of the mother at full length on the ground by the little one, gnawing at something—the clank of iron told what, it was the cruel chain. And Tip, the little one, meanwhile was helping himself to a warm drink.

On my going out she fled into the dark woods, but there by the shelter-box were two little mice, bloody and still warm, food for the cub brought by the devoted mother. And in the morning I found the chain was very bright for a foot or two next the little one's collar.

On walking across the woods to the ruined den, I again found signs of Vixen. The poor heart-broken mother had come and dug out the bedraggled bodies of her little ones.

There lay the three little baby foxes all licked smooth now, and by them were two of our hens fresh killed. The newly heaved earth was printed all over with tell-tale signs—signs that told me that here by the side of her dead she had watched like Rizpah. Here she had brought their usual meal, the spoil of her nightly hunt. Here she had stretched herself beside them and vainly offered them their natural drink and yearned to feed and warm them as of old; but only stiff little bodies under their soft wool she found, and little cold noses still and unresponsive.

A deep impress of elbows, breast, and hocks showed where she had lain in silent grief and watched them for long and mourned as a wild mother can mourn for its young. But from that time she came no more to the ruined den, for now she surely knew that her little ones were dead.

Tip the captive, the weakling of the brood, was now the heir to all her love. The dogs were loosed to guard the hens. The hired man had orders to shoot the old fox on sight—so had I, but was resolved never to see her. Chicken-heads, that a fox loves and a dog will not touch, had been poisoned and scattered through the woods; and the only way to the yard where Tip was tied, was by climbing the wood-pile after braving all other

dangers. And yet each night old Vix was there to nurse her baby and bring it fresh-killed hens and game. Again and again I saw her, although she came now without awaiting the querulous cry of the captive.

The second night of the captivity I heard the rattle of the chain, and then made out that the old fox was there, hard at work digging a hole by the little one's kennel. When it was deep enough to half bury her, she gathered into it all the stack of the chain, and filled it again with earth. Then in triumph thinking she had gotten rid of the chain, she seized little Tip by the neck and turned to dash off up the wood-pile, but alas! only to have him jerked roughly from her grasp.

Poor little fellow, he whimpered sadly as he crawled into his box. After half an hour there was a great outcry among the dogs, and by their straight-away tonguing through the far woods I knew they were chasing Vix. Away up north they went in the direction of the railway and their noise faded from hearing. Next morning the hounds had not come back. We soon knew why. Foxes long ago learned what a railroad is; they soon devised several ways of turning it to account. One way is when hunted to walk the rails for a long distance just before a train comes. The scent, always poor on iron, is destroyed by the train and there is always a chance of hounds being killed by the engine. But another way more sure, but harder to play, is to lead the hounds straight to a high trestle just ahead of the train, so that the engine overtakes them on it and they are surely dashed to destruction.

This trick was skillfully played, and down below we found the mangled remains of old Ranger and learned that Vix was already wreaking her revenge.

That same night she returned to the yard before Spot's weary limbs could bring him back and killed another hen and brought it to Tip, and stretched her panting length beside him that he might quench his thirst. For she seemed to think he had no food but what she brought.

It was that hen that betrayed to my uncle the nightly visits.

My own sympathies were all turning to Vix, and I would have no hand in planning further murders. Next night my uncle himself watched, gun in hand, for an hour. Then when it became cold and the moon clouded over he remembered other important business elsewhere, and left Paddy in his place.

But Paddy was "onaisy" as the stillness and anxiety of watching worked on his nerves. And the loud bang! bang! an hour later left us sure only that powder had been burned.

In the morning we found Vix had not failed her young one. Again next night found my uncle on guard, for another hen had been taken. Soon after dark a single shot was heard, but Vix dropped the game she was bringing and escaped. Another attempt made that night called forth another gun-shot. Yet next day it was seen by the brightness of the chain that she had come again and vainly tried for hours to cut that hateful bond.

Such courage and staunch fidelity were bound to win respect, if not toleration. At any rate, there was no gunner in wait next night, when all was still. Could it be of any use? Driven off thrice with gun-shots, would she make another try to feed or free her captive young one?

Would she? Hers was a mother's love. There was but one to watch them this time, the fourth night, when the quavering whine of the little one was followed by that shadowy form above the wood-pile.

But carrying no fowl or food that could be seen. Had the keen huntress failed at last? Had she no head of game for this her only charge, or had she learned to trust his captors for his food?

No, far from all this. The wild-wood mother's heart and hate were true. Her only thought had been to set him free. All means she knew she tried, and every danger braved to tend him well and help him to be free. But all had failed.

Like a shadow she came and in a moment was gone, and Tip seized on something dropped, and crunched and chewed with relish what she brought. But even as he ate, a knife-like pang shot through and a scream of pain escaped him. Then there was a momentary struggle and the little fox was dead.

The mother's love was strong in Vix, but a higher thought was stronger. She knew right well the poison's power; she knew the poison bait, and would have taught him had he lived to know and shun it too. But now at last when she must choose for him a wretched prisoner's life or sudden death, she quenched the mother in her breast and freed him by the one remaining door.

It is when the snow is on the ground that we take the census of the woods, and when the winter came it told me that Vix no longer roamed the woods of Erindale. Where she went it never told, but only this, that she was gone.

Gone, perhaps, to some other far-off haunt to leave behind the sad remembrance of her murdered little ones and mate. Or gone, maybe, deliberately, from the scene of a sorrowful life, as many a wild-wood mother has gone, by the means that she herself had used to free her young one, the last of all her brood.

ALL GONE

THERE WAS ONCE a cat called Slyboots, who, after having lived most of her life with a rich widow in a very comfortable house, suddenly found herself without a home. She had seen a good deal of the world, and knew how hard it might prove for a creature like herself no longer young and in this sad state of affairs to live easy. Besides, she was indolent by nature, had been brought up in luxury, and could only hope for the best. With this in mind, she struck up an acquaintance with a mouse. At first they merely exchanged the time of day; and if they met by chance in one of the rooms of the empty mansion, it was the mouse who was quickly gone. And when, later, it came to a little talk and gossiping between them, the mouse much preferred to be on the other side of her hole in the wainscot. But she was a simple and good-natured little creature, if vain and fond of flattery, and was so proud of her fine new acquaintance that she at length put aside all doubts, qualms, and misgivings, and agreed to keep house with the cat.

A very good bargain this was for Slyboots. The mouse had not only agreed to do all the housework—sweep, dust, tidy, and keep things neat and trim; but she it was who at night went scampering off in the dark from house to house, snuffing out wheresoever good food and dainties were to be found—meat and marrow, bones and scraps, cheese and butter. She knew every cranny and crevice and hole; and if any larder door had been left ajar, the cat soon heard of it. All Slyboots had to do was to steal out and fetch in what they needed (and the mouse needed very little), and to idle away the rest of the day in daydreaming and drowsing at home in ease and idleness. It was a hot and thundery summer when first they met, no weather for exercise; so this way of life suited her very well; and she never ceased whispering sly pleasant little speeches in the mouse's small round ear whenever she appeared in sight or they sat together at meals. And so the time went by until it drew on towards autumn.

"There is one little matter that is troubling me," said the cat one evening, after a private look round the house when the mouse had been out marketing. "A trifle as yet, my dear, but yet worth your pondering over. We have *no* provision for the winter. Not a morsel. And, since we are now living alone, we have none of these clumsy, selfish humans to help us. Winter will be our hungry time. I am strong and lusty and can, of course, fend for myself. It's little you I am thinking of. It troubles me. The cold will come—frost and snow and bitter winds. Doors and windows will be shut. You mustn't risk your precious life too often. There are traps, and I know what a temptation toasted cheese may be; there are—er—hungry enemies always in wait. Now what shall we do about the winter?"

At this, the simple mouse could scarcely contain herself for pride. "Ah, my dear friend, I long ago thought of that. When I was living alone. Before I had your precious, precious company. Come with me, and you shall share a little secret."

Without another word she went into the back parts of a dusty old closet and showed the cat where, by hook and by crook, she had stowed away a fine, large, earthenware gallipot brim-full of fat. "That jar, my dear, contains all my hard-won savings; and I would rather starve than waste it."

"Starve," said the cat, and stared, her tail-tip twitching softly from side to side. She sniffed. She purred. "Excellent," she cried again and again. "How clever! How ingenious! How thoughtful and how wise! There is but one little doubt in my mind, my dear. Is this cupboard safe? Surely the rats or—other creatures—might get in here *any* fine moonlight night."

At this the mouse was much alarmed. At length, after long and anxious discussion, the cat said, "Wainscots are good, cupboards are good, cellars are good; so are holes in the ground, hollows in trees, empty houses, caves, chasms and grottoes. But there is no place in the wide world, my dear, where a treasure like ours can be more safely stowed away than in a church. A church. Not even the wickedest thieves and robbers would dare to steal anything out of a church. St. Thomas's is the very place. It's cold. Most days it's empty, and there is a broken pane of glass under the belfry. I know the very place where we can hide the pot—behind a stone tomb, my dear—where no one would look for it. It shall be done tomorrow; and we will not so much as touch, taste, or even think of it until we are really and truly in *need* of it. No, my dear."

So towards evening next day they set out together to the church. The pot was hidden in its niche behind the tomb, not a soul being by to see them there. And as darkness came on, they stole out of the church and returned home. The days passed in peace and quiet; and they seemed to be closer friends than ever.

But it was not very long before the cat began to grow a little weary of the mouse's company, looks, and ways; and to pine on and on even for but just one secret sniff of the great gallipot of fat. As time went on she could think of little else; and, paws tucked in, would sit brooding all day in a corner, sulky and silent.

"I hope, dear friend," said the mouse at last, "you are not in any trouble, not indisposed, not ill?"

"Dear me, no!" the cat replied. "*Me*, ill! Never. Still, there is a little something on my mind. It is this. My favorite cousin who lives nine streets away has just brought a small, handsome son into the world. A beautiful little creature, creamy-white with cinnamon-brown patches, and I have been asked to be his godmother. They live in a fine house, and on the fat of the land; and it is, of course, a great honor. No need to tell *you* that, my dear! But I have been unable to decide whether or not to go to this christening only because I felt that, well, you *might* be a little hurt—a *little* hurt perhaps, at not having been asked to come too."

"Hurt!" said the mouse, stifling a gasp and a shiver at the very thought of being a guest in such a company. "Certainly not, my dear. I'll take every care of the house while you are gone, and shall be almost as happy alone thinking of you in the feasting and merrymaking as if I were with you. And if there *should* be any morsel very much to my taste at the christening, I am sure you will remember me. There's nothing like a sip and a suppet of sweet red christening wine! Please not to forget me!"

But the cat had no such cousin, not she. Nor had she been invited to be a godmother. By no means. Without another word, she slipped out of doors, and first this turning, then that, stole on and made her way straight to the church, looked, listened, then crawled in through the hole in the belfry window which was easily wide enough to admit her without brushing her whiskers. Once safe inside, in the cool great empty place, she had soon pushed off the lid of the pot. Crouched up in the niche behind the stone image, she at once set to at her feast.

Nor did she desist until she had licked off the complete upper layer of the rich ripe fat. After which, well fed, she replaced the pot in its hiding-place, stole out of the church, and took a walk upon the roofs of the town, on the lookout for other little opportunities. She then stretched herself out in the sun, sleeked herself with her long well-oiled tongue from chin to tail-tip, licking her chops whenever she thought of her feast; composed herself for a nap, and it was far on in the evening before she returned home.

"So here you are," said the mouse, "safe and sound. I've waited supper, my dear. But I was beginning to get anxious. I hope you've had a happy day."

"Happy enough," said the cat.

"And what name did they give the infant?"

"'Name?' 'Name?'" repeated the cat. "Why Top-off!"

"Topoff!" murmured the mouse. "*Topoff*! That is an odd, uncommon name—a very odd name."

"Usual or not, what does it signify?" said the cat. "It's no worse than *Crumbstealer* or *Cheesepicker*, I suppose, as so many of *your* godchildren seem or ought to be called." And at that the mouse fell silent.

Before long Mistress Slyboots was seized with yet another fit of longing for the fat. The savor and sweetness of the pot haunted her very dreams. And at last she said to the mouse, "You must do me yet another favor, my dear, and once more for an hour or two manage the house in my absence. I am again asked to be godmother, friends at a little distance too—and, as this time the infant is jet-black with a milk-white ring round its neck, a rare thing indeed if you knew anything about it, I simply cannot refuse."

The good kind mouse consented, and, waving Slyboots farewell from the porch, returned humbly into the house. And she—the cat—sly, gluttonous creature—she crept out once more by her short cuts and along the town walls to the church, and in at St. Thomas's window. And this time she half emptied the delicious pot of fat.

"It's a strange thing," she thought to herself licking her chops, now this side, now that, "but nothing in this world ever tastes so good as the dainties one keeps to oneself." And she was well satisfied with her day's work.

The stars were already shining bright by the time she came back home. And a glossy, comfortable creature she looked as she stepped delicately into the house.

"And what is the name of your god-child this time?" enquired the mouse.

"'Name?' 'This time?' What a nose, my dear, you have for trifles! Why Half-gone," answered the cat, with an inward grin.

"*Halfgone*! do you say? Well! Halfgone! I never heard so strange a name in the whole of my life! I'll wager *that* name's not in the Calendar!"

"The Calendar," cried the cat, "what's the Calendar to me? *Halfgone* was the name I said; and a plump, needle-clawed, silky-whiskered little creature it is." The mouse trembled a little at sight of her speaking these words, and presently crept off to bed.

For a time matters went much as usual; and all was friendly once more. But not so many days had gone by before the cat's mouth began to water again. She would actually wake up in the middle of the morning, licking her chops at rich flavors which although they were but memories seemed to be on her very tongue. She paced about, restless and yawning, stared at nothing, and became so contrary and morose that her house-mate the mouse would hide herself away in her room for hours together merely to be out of reach of her sullen stare.

And then one fine October afternoon, the cat delayed no longer, but cried out in a loud voice to the mouse, "All good things go in threes, my dear. You will scarcely credit it; but I am asked to stand godmother yet again. This time the child is rarest tortoiseshell—of a pattern and coloring never seen outside a Queen's palace. It has opened its eyes, and it mews, my dear, a complete octave—an infant seven days old! Think of it! Why, it can happen but once in a century—if that. But it's blood that tells. I hate, I grieve, I can't endure to leave you lonely, beds unmade, rooms unswept. But how can I help myself? How can I resist? And you so much amused at my family names! Ah, well; I bear no grudge. Jeer if it pleases you. I shall not be hurt."

"*Topoff! Halfgone!*" murmured the mouse. "They were certainly odd names. They made me a little thoughtful. Perhaps you are growing a little tired of me. And now another to come!"

"Ah, but you sit at home," said the cat, "in your demure dark-gray fur coat and that long dainty tail, and you are filled with fancies. That's because you so seldom venture out in the daytime. You are *too* dainty, you don't eat enough. No variety: nothing rich. You think too much. We must keep up with the times. We must turn over a new leaf." With that she pricked up her whiskers, and off she went.

During the cat's absence the mouse cleaned the house from top to bottom, putting everything in spotless trim. And while she scrubbed and polished, there was no time for sad, perplexing thoughts.

Meanwhile Slyboots was cowering greedily over the pot in the church; and this time she licked it as clean as a whistle. There wasn't a speck, not a vestige or flavor of fat left.

"When everything is finished, one may have a little peace," she said to herself. And thoroughly satisfied, she enjoyed a long dreamless sleep in the sunshine, took a jaunt through the town, gossiped with friends, saw the sights, and did not return home till well after midnight. At the first whisper of her at the door, the mouse looked out and at once enquired what name had been chosen for the third child.

"It will give you no more pleasure than the others," said the cat, with a surly glare. "We called him *All-gone*."

"'*Allgone!*'" cried the mouse. "'*Allgone!*' Oh, but how strange, how outlandish a name! Never in all my born days could I believe there was such a name. *Allgone!* Never. Nowhere."

"Well," said the cat, "you have heard it now. And that's the end of that." Whereupon she yawned as if her head would split in two, and went off to bed.

From that night on, Slyboots received no further invitation to stand godmother, and was so short with the mouse when she enquired after her three godchildren that little more was said about the matter. Summer gone, she grew more and more sulky and ill-natured as the days of autumn drew in, and hardly ceased complaining of the food, professing that she was an invalid, had a dainty stomach, and needed constant care and every nourishment.

At last, one cold frosty morning the mouse crept up to her bedside and said, "My dear, it is nearly winter now. There is scarcely anything but rinds of vegetables to be found outside. Do you not agree it would be a very pleasant thing if we started off together and enjoyed just a taste or two of our pot of fat?"

Her face twinkled all over at the thought of it; and indeed, poor thing, having been so long skimped even of her crumbs, she was by now little but a packet of bones.

The cat opened her mouth as she lay in bed: "By all means," said she, "by all means. And you will enjoy your taste as you call it exactly as much as you would enjoy putting out that dainty tongue of yours at the window to flout the full moon!"

"What can *that* mean?" thought the mouse to herself. But she was too much excited to put her question into words. Off she scampered to make ready for the journey.

They set out, and as soon as the sexton's back was turned among the gravestones, they crept in at the belfry window. So cold and stony and gloomy was it inside the great church that a shiver ran down the mouse's spine, while her mouth watered the more. And at last they came to the hiding-place. And there was the pot, its parchment top tied down, and as neat as a new pin.

And the cat said, grinning, "My dear, *you* shall open it; *you* shall have first nibble; *you* shall first enjoy what we have so long been look-ing forward to. But leave a morsel for me!"

Whereupon Mistress Mouse nibbled through the string, pushed off the cover, paused, and stared. The pot was empty. Bare.

"Oh! Ah! Alas! Alackaday!" broke out Slyboots in a wild shrill cater-wauling. "Robbers, robbers! Thieves, thieves!" Her voice echoed dreadful and hollow in the cold church, and died away. The mouse turned slowly, and out of her little round bright jet-black eyes gazed at her friend.

"Aha!" she cried bitterly, "I see; oh, I see. Now I begin to under-stand. Now I know. Friend that you professed yourself; true, faithful friend that you *are*! First it was '*Topoff.*' Next it was '*Halfgone.*' And last it was . . ."

"Hold your tongue this instant," yelled the cat, bristling all over. "Another syllable, and—"

"'*Allgone*,'" squeaked the mouse with her last breath.

For scarcely were the words out of her mouth, when Slyboots, claws extended, and with a yell of rage, had pounced upon her and swallowed her down.

"Truly," said she, as she turned away from the empty pot, and sallied out of the church, "that was a sad end to an old friendship. But such is the way of the world."

A LION AND A MOUSE

A MOUSE ONE day happened to run across the paws of a sleeping lion and wakened him. The lion, angry at being disturbed, grabbed the mouse, and was about to swallow him, when the mouse cried out, "Please, kind Sir, I didn't mean it; if you will let me go, I shall always be grateful; and, perhaps, I can help you someday." The idea that such a little thing as a mouse could help him so amused the lion that he let the mouse go. A week later the mouse heard a lion roaring loudly. He went closer to see what the trouble was and found his lion caught in a hunter's net. Remembering his promise, the mouse began to gnaw the ropes of the net and kept it up until the lion could get free. The lion then acknowledged:

Little friends might prove great friends.

A WOLF IN SHEEP'S CLOTHING

A CERTAIN WOLF, being very hungry, disguised himself in a sheep's skin and joined a flock of sheep. Thus, for many days he could kill and eat sheep whenever he was hungry, for even the shepherd did not find him out. One night after the shepherd had put all his sheep in the fold, he decided to kill one of his own flock for food; and without realizing what he was doing, he took out the wolf and killed him on the spot.

It really does not pay to pretend to be what you are not.

THE ELEPHANT'S CHILD

This story is from a book by Rudyard Kipling called the Just So *Stories. Like the other stories in the book, it offers a wonderfully clever and funny explanation of why animals are . . . just so.*

IN THE HIGH and Far-Off Times the Elephant, O Best Beloved, had no trunk. He had only a blackish, bulgy nose, as big as a boot, that he could wriggle about from side to side; but he couldn't pick up things with it. But there was one Elephant—a new Elephant— an Elephant's Child—who was full of 'satiable curtiosity, and that means he asked ever so many questions. *And* he lived in Africa, and he filled all Africa with his 'satiable curtiosities. He asked his tall aunt, the Ostrich, why her tail-feathers grew just so, and his tall aunt the Ostrich spanked him with her hard, hard claw. He asked his tall uncle, the Giraffe, what made his skin spotty, and his tall uncle, the Giraffe, spanked him with his hard, hard hoof. And still he was full of 'satiable curtiosity! He asked his broad aunt, the Hippopotamus, why her eyes were red, and his broad aunt, the Hippopotamus, spanked him with her broad, broad hoof; and he asked his hairy uncle, the Baboon, why melons tasted just so, and his hairy uncle, the Baboon, spanked him with his hairy, hairy paw. And *still* he was full of 'satiable curtiosity! He asked questions about everything that he saw, or heard, or felt, or smelt, or touched, and all his uncles and aunts spanked him. And still he was full of 'satiable curtiosity!

One fine morning in the middle of the Precession of the Equinoxes this 'satiable Elephant's Child asked a new fine question that he had never asked before. He asked, "What does the Crocodile have for dinner?" Then everybody said, "Hush!" in a loud and dretful tone, and they spanked him immediately and directly, without stopping, for a long time.

By and by, when that was finished, he came upon Kolokolo Bird sitting in the middle of a wait-a-bit thorn-bush, and he said, "My father has spanked me, and my mother has spanked me; all my aunts and uncles have spanked me for my 'satiable curtiosity; and *still* I want to know what the Crocodile has for dinner!"

Then Kolokolo Bird said, with a mournful cry, "Go to the banks of the great gray-green, greasy Limpopo River, all set about with fever-trees, and find out."

That very next morning, when there was nothing left of the Equinoxes, because the Precession had preceded according to precedent, this 'satiable Elephant's Child took a hundred pounds of bananas (the little short red kind), and a hundred pounds of sugar cane (the long purple kind), and seventeen melons (the greeny-crackly kind), and said to all his dear families, "Goodbye. I am going to the great gray-green, greasy Limpopo River, all set about with fever-trees, to find out what the Crocodile has for dinner." And they all spanked him once more for luck, though he asked them most politely to stop.

Then he went away, a little warm, but not at all astonished, eating melons, and throwing the rind about, because he could not pick it up.

He went from Graham's Town to Kimberley, and from Kimberley to Khama's Country, and from Khama's Country he went east by north, eating melons all the time, till at last he came to the banks of the great gray-green, greasy Limpopo River, all set about with fever-trees, precisely as Kolokolo Bird had said.

Now you must know and understand, O Best Beloved, that till that very week, and day, and hour, and minute, this 'satiable Elephant's Child had never seen a Crocodile, and did not know what one was like. It was all his 'satiable curtiosity.

The first thing that he found was a Bi-Colored-Python-Rock-Snake curled round a rock.

"'Scuse me," said the Elephant's Child most politely, "but have you seen such a thing as a Crocodile in these promiscuous parts?"

"*Have* I seen a Crocodile?" said the Bi-Colored-Python-Rock-Snake, in a voice of dretful scorn. "What will you ask me next?"

"'Scuse me," said the Elephant's Child, "but could you kindly tell me what he has for dinner?"

Then the Bi-Colored-Python-Rock-Snake uncoiled himself very quickly from the rock, and spanked the Elephant's Child with his scalesome, flailsome tail.

"That is odd," said the Elephant's Child, "because my father and my mother, and my uncle and my aunt, not to mention my other aunt, the Hippopotamus, and my other uncle, the Baboon, have all spanked me for my 'satiable curtiosity—and I suppose this is the same thing."

So he said goodbye very politely to the Bi-Colored-Python-Rock-Snake, and helped to coil him up on the rock again, and went on, a little warm, but not at all astonished, eating melons, and throwing the rind about, because he could not pick it up, till he trod on what he thought was a log of wood at the very edge of the great grey-green, greasy Limpopo River, all set about with fever-trees.

But it was really the Crocodile, O Best Beloved, and the Crocodile winked one eye—like this!

"'Scuse me," said the Elephant's Child most politely, "but do you happen to have seen a Crocodile in these promiscuous parts?"

Then the Crocodile winked the other eye, and lifted half his tail out of the mud; and the Elephant's Child stepped back most politely, because he did not wish to be spanked again.

"Come hither, Little One," said the Crocodile. "Why do you ask such things?"

"'Scuse me," said the Elephant's Child most politely, "but my father has spanked me, my mother has spanked me, not to mention my tall aunt, the Ostrich, and my tall uncle, the Giraffe, who can kick ever so hard, as well as my broad aunt, the Hippopotamus, and my hairy uncle, the Baboon, *and* including the Bi-Colored-Python-Rock-Snake, with the scalesome, flailsome tail, just up the bank, who spanks harder than any of them; and so, if it's quite all the same to you, I don't want to be spanked any more."

"Come hither, Little One," said the Crocodile, "for I am the Crocodile," and he wept crocodile-tears to show it was quite true.

Then the Elephant's Child grew all breathless, and panted, and kneeled down on the bank and said, "You are the very person I have been looking for all these long days. Will you please tell me what you have for dinner?"

"Come hither, Little One," said the Crocodile, "and I'll whisper."

Then the Elephant's Child put his head down close to the Crocodile's musky, tusky mouth, and the Crocodile caught him by his little nose, which up to that very week, day, hour, and minute, had been no bigger than a boot, though much more useful.

"I think," said the Crocodile—and he said it between his teeth, like this—"I think today I will begin with Elephant's Child!"

At this, O Best Beloved, the Elephant's Child was much annoyed, and he said, speaking through his nose, like this, "Led go! You are hurtig be!"

Then the Bi-Colored-Python-Rock-Snake scuffled down from the bank and said, "My young friend, if you do not now, immediately and instantly, pull as hard as ever you can, it is my opinion that your acquaintance in the large-pattern leather ulster" (and by this he meant the Crocodile) "will jerk you into yonder limpid stream before you can say Jack Robinson."

This is the way Bi-Colored-Python-Rock-Snakes always talk.

Then the Elephant's Child sat back on his little haunches, and pulled, and pulled, and pulled, and his nose began to stretch. And

the Crocodile floundered into the water, making it all creamy with great sweeps of his tail, and *he* pulled, and pulled, and pulled.

And the Elephant's Child's nose kept on stretching; and the Elephant's Child spread all his little four legs and pulled, and pulled, and pulled, and his nose kept on stretching; and the Crocodile threshed his tail like an oar, and *he* pulled, and pulled, and pulled, and at each pull the Elephant's Child's nose grew longer and longer—and it hurt him hijjus!

Then the Elephant's Child felt his legs slipping, and he said through his nose, which was now nearly five feet long, "This is too butch for be!"

Then the Bi-Colored-Python-Rock-Snake came down from the bank, and knotted himself in a double-clove-hitch round the Elephant's Child's hind-legs, and said, "Rash and inexperienced traveler, we will now seriously devote ourselves to a little high tension, because if we do not, it is my impression that yonder self-propelling man-of-war with the armor-plated upper deck" (and by this, O Best Beloved, he meant the Crocodile) "will permanently vitiate your future career."

That is the way all Bi-Colored-Python-Rock-Snakes always talk.

So he pulled, and the Elephant's Child pulled, and the Crocodile pulled; but the Elephant's Child and the Bi-Colored-Python-Rock-Snake pulled hardest; and at last the Crocodile let go of the Elephant's Child's nose with a plop that you could hear all up and down the Limpopo.

Then the Elephant's Child sat down most hard and sudden; but first he was careful to say "Thank you" to the Bi-Colored-Python-Rock-Snake; and next he was kind to his poor pulled nose, and wrapped it all up in cool banana leaves, and hung it in the great gray-green, greasy Limpopo to cool.

"What are you doing that for?" said the Bi-Colored-Python-Rock-Snake.

"'Scuse me," said the Elephant's Child, "but my nose is badly out of shape, and I am waiting for it to shrink."

"Then you will have to wait a long time," said the Bi-Colored-Python-Rock-Snake. "Some people do not know what is good for them."

The Elephant's Child sat there for three days waiting for his nose to shrink. But it never grew any shorter, and, besides, it made him squint. For, O Best Beloved, you will see and understand that the Crocodile had pulled it out into a really truly trunk same as all Elephants have today.

At the end of the third day a fly came and stung him on the shoulder, and before he knew what he was doing he lifted up his trunk and hit that fly dead with the end of it.

"'Vantage number one!" said the Bi-Colored-Python-Rock-Snake. "You couldn't have done that with a mere-smear nose. Try and eat a little now."

Before he thought what he was doing the Elephant's Child put out his trunk and plucked a large bundle of grass, dusted it clean against his forelegs, and stuffed it into his own mouth.

"'Vantage number two!" said the Bi-Colored-Python-Rock-Snake. "You couldn't have done that with a mere-smear nose. Don't you think the sun is very hot here?"

"It is," said the Elephant's Child, and before he thought what he was doing he schlooped up a schloop of mud from the banks of the great gray-green, greasy Limpopo, and slapped it on his head, where it made a cool schloopy-sloshy mud-cap all trickly behind his ears.

"'Vantage number three!" said the Bi-Colored-Python-Rock-Snake. "You couldn't have done that with a mere-smear nose. Now how do you feel about being spanked again?"

"'Scuse me," said the Elephant's Child, "but I should not like it at all."

"How would you like to spank somebody?" said the Bi-Colored-Python-Rock-Snake.

"I should like it very much indeed," said the
Elephant's Child.

"Well," said the Bi-Colored-Python-Rock-Snake, "you will
find that new nose of yours very useful to spank people with."

"Thank you," said the Elephant's Child, "I'll remember that; and
now I think I'll go home to all my dear families and try."

So the Elephant's Child went home across Africa frisking and
whisking his trunk. When he wanted fruit to eat he pulled fruit down
from a tree, instead of waiting for it to fall as he used to do. When he
wanted grass he plucked grass up from the ground, instead of going on
his knees as he used to do. When the flies bit him he broke off the
branch of a tree and used it as a fly-whisk; and he made himself a new,
cool, slushy-squashy mud-cap whenever the sun was hot. When he felt
lonely walking through Africa he sang to himself down his trunk, and

the noise was louder than several brass bands. He went
specially out of his way to find a broad Hippopotamus (she was
no relation of his), and he spanked her very hard, to make sure
that the Bi-Colored-Python-Rock-Snake had spoken the truth
about his new trunk. The rest of the time he picked up the
melon-rinds that he had dropped on his way to the Limpopo—
for he was a Tidy Pachyderm.

One dark evening he came back to all his dear families, and he coiled up his trunk and said, "How do you do?" They were very glad to see him, and immediately said, "Come here and be spanked for your 'satiable curtiosity."

"Pooh," said the Elephant's Child. "I don't think you peoples know anything about spanking; but *I* do, and I'll show you."

Then he uncurled his trunk and knocked two of his dear brothers head over heels.

"O Bananas!" said they, "where did you learn that trick, and what have you done to your nose?"

"I got a new one from the Crocodile on the banks of the great gray-green, greasy Limpopo River," said Elephant's Child. "I asked him what he had for dinner, and he gave me this to keep."

"It looks very ugly," said his hairy uncle, the Baboon.

"It does," said the Elephant's Child. "But it's very useful," and he picked up his hairy uncle, the Baboon, by one hairy leg, and hove him into a hornets' nest.

Then that bad Elephant's Child spanked all his dear families for a long time, till they were very warm and greatly astonished. He pulled out his tall Ostrich aunt's tail-feathers; and he caught his tall uncle, the Giraffe, by the hind-leg, and dragged him through a thorn-bush; and he shouted at his broad aunt, the Hippopotamus, and blew bubbles into her ear when she was sleeping in the water after meals; but he never let anyone touch Kolokolo Bird.

At last things grew so exciting that his dear families went off one by one in a hurry to the banks of the great gray-green, greasy Limpopo River, all set about with fever-trees, to borrow new noses from the Crocodile. When they came back nobody spanked anybody any more; and ever since that day, O Best Beloved, all the Elephants you will ever see, besides all those that you won't, have trunks precisely like the trunk of the 'satiable Elephant's Child.

HOW THE RABBIT LOST HIS TAIL

A Native American Legend

WHEN GLOOSKAP FIRST created the animals in Canada, he took good care that they should all be friendly to himself and to his people. They could all talk like men, and like them they had one common speech. Each had a special duty to do for Glooskap, and each did his best to help him in his work. Of all the animals, the gentlest and most faithful was Bunny the Rabbit. Now, in those first days of his life, Rabbit was a very beautiful animal, more beautiful than he is today. He had a very long bushy tail like a fox; he always wore a thick brown coat; his body was large and round and sleek; his legs were straight and strong; he walked and ran like other animals and did not hop and jump about as he does now. He was always very polite and kind of heart. Because of his beauty and his good qualities, Glooskap chose him as his forest guide, his Scout of the Woods. He gave him power that enabled him to know well all the land, so that he could lead people and all the other animals wherever they wished to go without losing their way.

One day in the springtime it chanced that Bunny sat alone on a log in the forest, his long bushy tail trailing far behind him. He had just come back from a long scouting tour and he was very tired. As he sat resting in the sun, an Indian came along. The Indian was weary and stained with much travel, and he looked like a wayfarer who had come far. He threw himself on the ground close to the log on which Rabbit sat and began to weep bitterly. Bunny with his usual kindness asked, "Why do you weep?" And the man answered, "I have lost my way in the forest. I am on my way to marry this afternoon a beautiful girl whom her father pledged to me long ago. She is loved by a wicked forest Fairy and I have heard that perhaps she loves him. And I know that if I am late she will refuse to wait for me and that she will marry him instead." But Rabbit said: "Have no fear. I am Bunny, Glooskap's forest guide. I will show you the way and bring you to the wedding in good time." The man was comforted and his spirits rose, and they talked some time together and became good friends.

When the man had somewhat got back his strength, they began their journey to the wedding. But Rabbit, being nimble-footed, ran fast and was soon so far in advance of his companion that he was lost to view. The man followed slowly, catching here and there through the green trees a glimpse of his guide's brown coat. As he stumbled along, thinking of his troubles, he fell into a deep pit that lay close to the forest path. He was too weak to climb out, and he called loudly for help. Bunny soon missed his follower, but he heard the man's yells, and turning about he ran back to the pit. "Have no fear," said the Rabbit as he looked over the edge, "I will get you out without mishap." Then, turning his back to the pit, he let his long bushy tail hang to the bottom. "Catch hold of my tail," he ordered, "hold on tight and I will pull you out." The man did as he was told. Rabbit sprang forward, but as he jumped, the weight of the man, who was very heavy, was more than he could bear, and poor Bunny's tail broke off within an inch of the root. The man fell back into the pit with a thud, holding in his hand poor Rabbit's tail. But Bunny in all his work as a guide had never known defeat, and he determined not to know it now. Holding to a strong tree with his front feet, he put his hind legs into the pit and said to the man, "Take hold of my legs and hang on tight." The man did as he was told. Then Rabbit pulled and pulled until his hind legs stretched and he feared that they too would break off, but although the weight on them was great, he finally pulled the man out after great difficulty. He found to his dismay that his hind legs had lengthened greatly because of their heavy load. He was no longer able to walk straight, but he now had to hop along with a strange jumping gait. Even his body was much stretched, and his waist had become very slender because of his long heavy pull. The two travelers then went on their way, Bunny hopping along, and the man moving more cautiously.

Finally, they reached the end of their journey. The people were all gathered for the wedding, and eagerly awaiting the coming of the bridegroom. Sure enough, the forest Fairy was there, trying by his tricks to win the girl for himself. But the man was in good time, and he married the maiden as he had hoped. As he was very thankful to Bunny, he asked him to the marriage dance and told him he might dance with the bride. So Rabbit put rings on his heels and a bangle around his neck, after his usual custom at weddings, and joined the merry-makers. Through the forest green where they danced many tiny streams were flowing, and to the soft music of these the dance went on. As the bride jumped across one of these streams during her dance with Bunny, she accidentally let the end of her dress drop into the water so that it got very wet. When she moved again into the sun, her dress, because of its wetting, shrank and shrank until it reached her knees and made her much ashamed. But Rabbit's heart was touched as usual by her plight; he ran quickly and got a deer skin that he knew to be hidden in the trees not far away, and he wrapped the pretty skin around the bride. Then he twisted a cord with which to tie it on. He held one end of the cord in his teeth and twisted the other end with his front paws. But in his haste, he held it so tight and twisted it so hard that when a couple waltzing past carelessly bumped into him the cord split his upper lip right up to the nose. But Rabbit was not dismayed by his split lip. He fastened on the bride's new deer-skin gown, and then he danced all the evening until the moon was far up in the sky. Before he went away, the man and his bride wanted to pay him for his work, but he would not take payment. Then the bride gave him a new white fur coat and said, "In winter wear this white coat; it is the color of snow; your enemies cannot then see you so plainly against the white ground, and they cannot so easily do you harm; but in summer wear your old brown coat, the color of the leaves and grass." And Bunny gratefully took the coat and went his way.

He lingered many days in the new country, for he was ashamed to go back to his own people with his changed appearance. His lip was split; his tail was gone; and his hind legs were stretched and crooked. Finally, he mustered up his courage and returned home. His old friends wondered much at his changed looks, and some of them were cruel enough to laugh at him. But Bunny deceived them all. When they asked him where he had been so long, he answered, "I guided a man to a far-off land which you have never seen and of which you have never heard." Then he told them many strange tales of its beauty and its good people.

"How did you lose your fine tail?" they asked. And he answered, "In the land to which I have been, the animals wear no tails. It is an aristocratic country, and wishing to be in the fashion, I cut mine off."

"And why is your waist so slender?" they asked. "Oh," replied Bunny, "in that country it is not the fashion to be fat, and I took great trouble to make my waist slight and willowy." "Why do you hop about," they asked, "when you once walked so straight?" "In that land," answered Bunny, "it is not genteel to walk straight; only the vulgar and untrained do that. The best people have a walk of their own, and it took me many days under a good walking-teacher to learn it."

"But how did you split your upper lip?" they asked finally. "In the land to which I have been," said Bunny, "the people do not eat as we do. There they eat with knives and forks and not with their paws. I found it hard to get used to their new ways. One day I put food into my mouth with my knife—a very vulgar act in that land—and my knife slipped and cut my lip, and the wound has never healed."

And being deceived and envying Bunny because of the wonders he had seen, they asked him no more questions. But the descendants of Rabbit to this day wear a white coat in winter and a brown one in summer. They have also a split upper lip; their waist is still very slender; they have no tail; their hind legs are longer than their front ones; they hop and jump nimbly about, but they are unable to walk straight. And all these strange things are a result of old Bunny's accident at the man's wedding long ago.

MUTT MAKES HIS MARK

*Mutt was a real dog. He lived in Saskatoon with the
author when the author was just a boy. But Mutt was not
convinced that he was a dog—he thought that he was a human.
Some people sometimes seemed to think so, too. This story is
from* The Dog Who Wouldn't Be.

I T ALL BEGAN on one of those blistering July days when the prairie pants like a dying coyote, the dust lies heavy, and the air burns the flesh it touches. On such days those with good sense retire to the cellar caverns that are euphemistically known in Canada as beer parlors. These are all much the same across the country—ill-lit and crowded dens, redolent with the stench of sweat, spilled beer, and smoke—but they are, for the most part, moderately cool. And the insipid stuff that passes for beer is usually ice cold.

On this particular day five residents of the city, dog fanciers all, had forgathered in a beer parlor. They had just returned from witnessing some hunting-dog trials held in Manitoba, and they had brought a guest with them. He was a rather portly gentleman from the state of New York, and he had both wealth and ambition. He used his wealth lavishly to further his ambition, which was to raise and own the finest retrievers on the continent, if not in the world. Having watched his own dogs win the Manitoba trials, this man had come on to Saskatoon at the earnest invitation of the local men, in order to see what kind of dogs they bred, and to buy some if he fancied them.

He had not fancied them. Perhaps rightfully annoyed at having made the trip in the broiling summer weather to no good purpose, he had become a little overbearing in his manner. His comments when he viewed the local kennel dogs had been acidulous, and scornful. He had ruffled the local breeders' feelings, and as a result they were in a mood to do and say foolish things.

The visitor's train was due to leave at 4 P.M., and from 12:30 until 3 the six men sat cooling themselves internally, and talking dogs. The talk was as heated as the weather. Inevitably Mutt's name was mentioned, and he was referred to as an outstanding example of that rare breed, the Prince Albert retriever.

The stranger hooted. "Rare breed!" he cried. "I'll say it must be rare! I've never even heard of it."

The local men were incensed by this big-city skepticism. They immediately began telling tales of Mutt, and if they laid it on a little, who can blame them? But the more stories they told, the louder grew the visitor's mirth and the more pointed his disbelief. Finally someone was goaded a little too far.

"I'll bet you," Mutt's admirer said truculently, "I'll bet you a hundred dollars this dog can outretrieve any damn dog in the whole United States."

Perhaps he felt that he was safe, since the hunting season was not yet open. Perhaps he was too angry to think.

The stranger accepted the challenge, but it did not seem as if there was much chance of settling the bet. Someone said as much, and the visitor crowed.

"You've made your brag," he said. "Now show me."

There was nothing for it then but to seek out Mutt and hope for inspiration. The six men left the dark room and braved the blasting light of the summer afternoon as they made their way to the public library.

The library stood, four-square and ugly, just off the main thoroughfare of the city. The inevitable alley behind it was shared by two Chinese restaurants and by sundry other merchants. My father had his office in the rear of the library building overlooking the alley. A screened door gave access to whatever air was to be found trapped and roasted in the narrow space behind the building. It was through this rear door that the delegation came.

From his place under the desk Mutt barely raised his head to peer at the newcomers, then sank back into a comatose state of near oblivion engendered by the heat. He probably heard the mutter of talk, the introductions, and the slightly strident tone of voice of the stranger, but he paid no heed.

Father, however, listened intently. And he could hardly control his resentment when the stranger stooped, peered beneath the desk, and was heard to say, "*Now* I recognize the breed—Prince Albert rat-hound did you say it was?"

My father got stiffly to his feet. "You gentlemen wish a demonstration of Mutt's retrieving skill—is that it?" he asked.

A murmur of agreement from the local men was punctuated by a derisive comment from the visitor. "Test him," he said offensively. "How about that alley there—it must be full of rats."

Father said nothing. Instead he pushed back his chair and, going to the large cupboard where he kept some of his shooting things so that they would be available for after-work excursions, he swung wide the door and got out his gun case. He drew out the barrels, fore and end, and stock and assembled the gun. He closed the breech and tried the triggers, and at that familiar sound Mutt was galvanized into life and came scuffling out from under the desk to stand with twitching nose and a perplexed air about him.

He had obviously been missing something. This wasn't the hunting season. But—the gun was out.

He whined interrogatively and my father patted his head. "Good boy," he said, and then walked to the screen door with Mutt crowding against his heels.

By this time the group of human watchers was as perplexed as Mutt. The six men stood in the office doorway and watched curiously as my father stepped out on the porch, raised the unloaded gun, leveled it down the alley toward the main street, pressed the triggers, and said in a quiet voice, "Bang—bang—go get 'em boy!"

To this day Father maintains a steadfast silence as to what his intentions really were. He will not say that he expected the result that followed, and he will not say that he did not expect it.

Mutt leaped from the stoop and fled down that alleyway at his best speed. They saw him turn the corner into the main street, almost causing two elderly women to collide with one another. The watchers saw the people on the far side of the street stop, turn to stare, and then stand as if petrified. But Mutt himself they could no longer see.

He was gone only about two minutes, but to the group upon the library steps it must have seemed much longer. The man from New York had just cleared his throat preparatory to a new and even more amusing sally, when he saw something that made the words catch in his gullet.

They all saw it—and they did not believe.

Mutt was coming back up the alley. He was trotting. His head and tail were high—and in his mouth was a magnificent ruffed grouse. He came up the porch stairs nonchalantly, laid the bird down at my father's feet, and with a satisfied sigh crawled back under the desk.

There was silence except for Mutt's panting. Then one of the local men stepped forward as if in a dream, and picked up the bird.

"Already stuffed, by God!" he said, and his voice was hardly more than a whisper.

It was then that the clerk from Ashbridge's Hardware arrived. The clerk was disheveled and mad. He came bounding up the library steps, accosted Father angrily, and cried:

"That damn dog of yours—you ought to keep him locked up. Come bustin' into the shop a moment ago and snatched the stuffed grouse right out of the window. Mr. Ashbridge's fit to be tied. Was the best bird in his whole collection. . . ."

I do not know if the man from New York ever paid his debt. I do know that the story of that day's happening passed into the nation's history, for the Canadian press picked it up from the *Star-Phoenix*, and Mutt's fame was carried from coast to coast across the land.

That surely was no more than his due.

TALE OF A TORTOISE AND OF A MISCHIEVOUS MONKEY

A Brazilian Fairytale

ONCE UPON A time there was a country where the rivers were larger, and the forests deeper, than anywhere else. Hardly any men came there, and the wild creatures had it all to themselves, and used to play all sorts of strange games with each other. The great trees, chained one to the other by thick flowering plants with bright scarlet or yellow blossoms, were famous hiding-places for the monkeys, who could wait unseen, till a puma or an elephant passed by, and then jump on their backs and go for a ride, swinging themselves up by the creepers when they had had enough. Near the rivers huge tortoises were to be found, and though to our eyes a tortoise seems a dull, slow thing, it is wonderful to think how clever they were, and how often they outwitted many of their livelier friends.

There was one tortoise in particular that always managed to get the better of everybody, and many were the tales told in the forest of his great deeds. They began when he was quite young, and tired of staying at home with his father and mother. He left them one day, and walked off in search of adventures. In a wide open space surrounded by trees he met with an elephant, who was having his supper before taking his evening bath in the river which ran close by. "Let us see which of us two is strongest," said the young tortoise, marching up to the elephant. "Very well," replied the elephant, much amused at the impertinence of the little creature; "when would you like the trial to be?"

"In an hour's time; I have some business to do first," answered the tortoise. And he hastened away as fast as his short legs would carry him.

In a pool of the river a whale was resting, blowing water into the air and making a lovely fountain. The tortoise, however, was too young and too busy to admire such things, and he called to the whale to stop, as he wanted to speak to him. "Would you like to try which of us is the stronger?" said he. The whale looked at him, sent up another fountain, and answered: "Oh, yes; certainly. When do you wish to begin? I am quite ready."

"Then give me one of your longest bones, and I will fasten it to my

leg. When I give the signal, you must pull, and we will see which can pull the hardest."

"Very good," replied the whale; and he took out one of his bones and passed it to the tortoise.

The tortoise picked up the end of the bone in his mouth and went back to the elephant. "I will fasten this to your leg," said he, "in the same way as it is fastened to mine, and we must both pull as hard as we can. We shall soon see which is the stronger." So he wound it carefully round the elephant's leg, and tied it in a firm knot. "Now!" cried he, plunging into a thick bush behind him.

The whale tugged at one end, and the elephant tugged at the other, and neither had any idea that he had not the tortoise for his foe. When the whale pulled hardest the elephant was dragged into the water; and when the elephant pulled the hardest the whale was hauled onto the land. They were very evenly matched, and the battle was a hard one.

At last they were quite tired, and the tortoise, who was watching, saw that they could play no more. So he crept from his hiding-place, and dipping himself in the river, he went to the elephant and said: "I see that you really are stronger than I thought. Suppose we give it up

for today?" Then he dried himself on some moss and went to the whale and said: "I see that you really are stronger than I thought. Suppose we give it up for today?"

The two adversaries were only too glad to be allowed to rest, and believed to the end of their days that, after all, the tortoise was stronger than either of them.

A day or two later the young tortoise was taking a stroll, when he met a fox, and stopped to speak to him. "Let us try," said he in a careless manner, "which of us can lie buried in the ground during seven years."

"I shall be delighted," answered the fox, "only I would rather that you began."

"It is all the same to me," replied the tortoise; "if you come round this way tomorrow you will see that I have fulfilled my part of the bargain."

So he looked about for a suitable place, and found a convenient hole at the foot of an orange tree. He crept into it, and the next morning the fox heaped up the earth round him, and promised to feed him every day with fresh fruit. The fox so far kept his word that each morning when the sun rose he appeared to ask how the tortoise was getting on. "Oh, very well; but I wish you would give me some fruit," replied he.

"Alas! the fruit is not ripe enough yet for you to eat," answered the fox, who hoped that the tortoise would die of hunger long before the seven years were over.

"Oh dear, oh dear! I am so hungry!" cried the tortoise.

"I am sure you must be; but it will be all right tomorrow," said the fox, trotting off, not knowing that the oranges dropped down the hollow trunk, straight into the tortoise's hole, and that he had as many as he could possibly eat.

So the seven years went by; and when the tortoise came out of his hole he was as fat as ever.

Now it was the fox's turn, and he chose his hole, and the tortoise heaped the earth round, promising to return every day or two with a nice young bird for his dinner. "Well, how are you getting on?" he would ask cheerfully when he paid his visits.

"Oh, all right; only I wish you had brought a bird with you," answered the fox.

"I have been so unlucky, I have never been able to catch one," replied the tortoise. "However, I shall be more fortunate tomorrow, I am sure."

But not many tomorrows after, when the tortoise arrived with his usual question: "Well, how are you getting on?" he received no answer, for the fox was lying in his hole quite still, dead of hunger.

By this time the tortoise was grown up, and was looked up to throughout the forest as a person to be feared for his strength and wisdom. But he was not considered a very swift runner, until an adventure with a deer added to his fame.

One day, when he was basking in the sun, a stag passed by, and stopped for a little conversation. "Would you care to see which of us can run fastest?" asked the tortoise, after some talk. The stag thought the question so silly that he only shrugged his shoulders. "Of course, the victor would have the right to kill the other," went on the tortoise. "Oh, on that condition I agree," answered the deer; "but I am afraid you are a dead man."

"It is no use trying to frighten me," replied the tortoise. "But I should like three days for training; then I shall be ready to start when the sun strikes on the big tree at the edge of the great clearing."

The first thing the tortoise did was to call his brothers and his cousins together, and he posted them carefully under ferns all along the line of the great clearing, making a sort of ladder which stretched for many miles. This done to his satisfaction, he went back to the starting place.

The stag was quite punctual, and as soon as the sun's rays struck the trunk of the tree the stag started off, and was soon far out of the sight of the tortoise. Every now and then he would turn his head as he ran, and call out: "How are you getting on?" and the tortoise who happened to be nearest at that moment would answer: "All right, I am close up to you."

Full of astonishment, the stag would redouble his efforts, but it was no use. Each time he asked: "Are you there?" the answer would come: "Yes, of course, where else should I be?" And the stag ran, and ran, and ran, till he could run no more, and dropped down dead on the grass.

And the tortoise, when he thinks about it, laughs still.

But the tortoise was not the only creature of whose tricks stories were told in the forest. There was a famous monkey who was just as clever and more mischievous, because he was so much quicker on his feet and with his hands. It was quite impossible to catch him and give him the thrashing he so often deserved, for he just swung himself up into a tree and laughed at the angry victim who was sitting below. Sometimes, however, the inhabitants of the forest were so foolish as to provoke him, and then they got the worst of it. This was what happened to the barber, whom the monkey visited one morning, saying that he wished to be shaved. The barber bowed politely to his customer, and begging him to be seated, tied a large cloth round his neck, and rubbed his chin with soap; but instead of cutting off his beard, the barber made a snip at the end of his tail. It was only a very little bit, and the monkey started up more in rage than in pain. "Give me back the end of my tail," he roared, "or I will take one of your razors." The barber refused to give back the missing piece, so the monkey caught up a razor from the table and ran away with it, and no one in the forest could be shaved for days, as there was not another to be got for miles and miles.

As he was making his way to his own particular palm-tree, where the cocoanuts grew, which were so useful for pelting passers-by, he met a woman who was scaling a fish with a bit of wood, for in this side of the forest a few people lived in huts near the river.

"That must be hard work," said the monkey, stopping to look; "try my knife—you will get on quicker." And he handed her the razor as he spoke. A few days later he came back and rapped at the door of the hut. "I have called for my razor," he said, when the woman appeared.

"I have lost it," answered she.

"If you don't give it to me at once I will take your sardine," replied the monkey, who did not believe her. The woman protested she had not got the knife, so he took the sardine and ran off.

A little further along he saw a baker who was standing at the door, eating one of his loaves. "That must be rather dry," said the monkey, "try my fish;" and the man did not need twice telling. A few days later the monkey stopped again at the baker's hut. "I've called for that fish," he said.

"That fish? But I have eaten it!" exclaimed the baker in dismay.

"If you have eaten it I shall take this barrel of meal in exchange," replied the monkey; and he walked off with the barrel under his arm.

As he went he saw a woman with a group of little girls round her, teaching them how to dress hair. "Here is something to make cakes for the children," he said, putting down his barrel, which by this time he found rather heavy. The children were delighted, and ran directly to find some flat stones to bake their cakes on, and when they had made and eaten them, they thought they had never tasted anything so nice. Indeed, when they saw the monkey approaching not long after, they rushed to meet him, hoping that he was bringing them some more presents. But he took no notice of their questions, he only said to their mother: "I've called for my barrel of meal."

"Why, you gave it to me to make cakes of!" cried the mother.

"If I can't get my barrel of meal, I shall take one of your children," answered the monkey. "I am in want of somebody who can bake me bread when I am tired of fruit, and who knows how to make cocoanut cakes."

"Oh, leave me my child, and I will find you another barrel of meal," wept the mother.

"I don't *want* another barrel, I want *that* one," answered the monkey sternly. And as the woman stood wringing her hands, he caught up the little girl that he thought the prettiest and took her to his home in the palm-tree.

She never went back to the hut, but on the whole she was not much to be pitied, for monkeys are nearly as good as children to play with, and they taught her how to swing, and to climb, and to fly from tree to tree, and everything else they knew, which was a great deal.

Now the monkey's tiresome tricks had made him many enemies in the forest, but no one hated him so much as the puma. The cause of their quarrel was known only to themselves, but everybody was aware of the fact, and took care to be out of the way when there was any chance of these two meeting. Often and often the puma had laid traps for the monkey, which he felt sure his foe could not escape; and the monkey would pretend that he saw nothing, and rejoice the hidden puma's heart by seeming to walk straight into the snare, when, lo! a loud laugh would be heard, and the monkey's grinning face would peer out of a mass of creepers and disappear before his foe could reach him.

This state of things had gone on for quite a long while, when at last there came a season such as the oldest parrot in the forest could never remember. Instead of two or three hundred inches of rain falling, which they were all accustomed to, month after month passed without a cloud, and the rivers and springs dried up, till there was only one small pool left for everyone to drink from. There was not an animal for miles round that did not grieve over this shocking condition of affairs, not one at least except the puma. His only thought for years had been how to get the monkey into his power, and this time he imagined his chance had really arrived. He would hide himself in a thicket, and when the monkey came down to drink—and come he must—the puma would spring out and seize him. Yes, on this occasion there could be no escape!

And no more there would have been if the puma had had greater patience; but in his excitement he moved a little too soon. The monkey, who was stooping to drink, heard a rustling, and turning caught the gleam of two yellow, murderous eyes. With a mighty spring he grasped a creeper which was hanging above him, and landed himself on the branch of a tree, feeling the breath of the puma on his feet as the animal bounded from his cover. Never had the monkey been so near death, and it was some time before he recovered enough courage to venture on the ground again.

Up there in the shelter of the trees, he began to turn over in his head plans for escaping the snares of the puma. And at length chance helped him. Peeping down to the earth, he saw a man coming along the path carrying on his head a large gourd filled with honey.

He waited till the man was just underneath the tree, then he hung from a bough, and caught the gourd while the man looked up wondering, for he was no tree-climber. Then the monkey rubbed the honey all over him, and a quantity of leaves from a creeper that was hanging close by; he stuck them all close together into the honey, so that he looked like a walking bush. This finished, he ran to the pool to see the result, and, quite pleased with himself, set out in search of adventures.

Soon the report went through the forest that a new animal had appeared from no one knew where, and that when somebody had asked his name, the strange creature had answered that it was Jack-in-the-Green. Thanks to this, the monkey was allowed to drink at the pool as often as he liked, for neither beast nor bird had the faintest notion who he was. And if they made any inquiries the only answer they got was that the water of which he had drunk deeply had turned his hair into leaves, so that they all knew what would happen in case they became too greedy.

By-and-by the great rains began again. The rivers and streams filled up, and there was no need for him to go back to the pool, near the home of his enemy, the puma, as there was a large number of places for him to choose from. So one night, when everything was still and silent, and even the chattering parrots were asleep on one leg, the monkey stole down softly from his perch, and washed off the honey and the leaves, and came out from his bath in his own proper skin. On his way to breakfast he met a rabbit, and stopped for a little talk.

"I am feeling rather dull," he remarked; "I think it would do me good to hunt a while. What do you say?"

"Oh, I am quite willing," answered the rabbit, proud of being spoken to by such a large creature. "But the question is, what shall we hunt?"

"There is no credit in going after an elephant or a tiger," replied the monkey stroking his chin, "they are so big they could not possibly get out of your way. It shows much more skill to be able to catch a small thing that can hide itself in a moment behind a leaf. I'll tell you what! Suppose I hunt butterflies, and you, serpents."

The rabbit, who was young and without experience, was delighted with this idea, and they both set out on their various ways.

The monkey quietly climbed up the nearest tree, and ate fruit most of the day, but the rabbit tired himself to death poking his nose into every heap of dried leaves he saw, hoping to find a serpent among them. Luckily for himself the serpents were all away for the afternoon, at a meeting of their own, for there is nothing a serpent likes so well for dinner as a nice plump rabbit. But, as it was, the dried leaves were all empty, and the rabbit at last fell asleep where he was. Then the monkey, who had been watching him, fell down and pulled his ears, to the rage of the rabbit, who vowed vengeance.

It was not easy to catch the monkey off his guard, and the rabbit waited long before an opportunity arrived. But one day Jack-in-the-Green was sitting on a stone, wondering what he should do next, when the rabbit crept softly behind him, and gave his tail a sharp pull. The monkey gave a shriek of pain, and darted up into a tree, but when he saw that it was only the rabbit who had dared to insult him so, he chattered so fast in his anger, and looked so fierce, that the rabbit fled into the nearest hole, and stayed there for several days, trembling with fright.

Soon after this adventure the monkey went away into another part of the country, right on the outskirt of the forest, where there was a beautiful garden full of oranges hanging ripe from the trees. This garden was a favorite place for birds of all kinds, each hoping to secure an orange for dinner, and in order to frighten the birds away and keep a little fruit for himself, the master had fastened a waxen figure on one of the boughs.

Now the monkey was as fond of oranges as any of the birds, and when he saw a man standing in the tree where the largest and sweetest oranges grew, he spoke to him at once. "You man," he said rudely, "throw me down that big orange up there, or I will throw a stone at you." The wax figure took no notice of this request, so the monkey, who was easily made angry, picked up a stone, and flung it with all his force. But instead of falling to the ground again, the stone stuck to the soft wax.

At this moment a breeze shook the tree, and the orange on which the monkey had set his heart dropped from the bough. He picked it up and ate it every bit, including the rind, and it was so good he thought he should like another. So he called again to the wax figure to throw him an orange, and as the figure did not move, he hurled another stone, which stuck to the wax as the first had done. Seeing that the man was quite indifferent to stones, the monkey grew more angry still, and climbing the tree hastily, gave the figure a violent kick. But like the two stones his leg remained stuck to the wax, and he was held fast. "Let me go at once, or I will give you another kick," he cried, suiting the action to the word, and this time also his foot remained in the grasp of the man. Not knowing what he did, the monkey hit out, first with one hand and then with the other, and when he found that he was literally bound hand and foot, he became so mad with anger and terror that in his struggles he fell to the ground, dragging the figure after him. This freed his hands and feet, but besides the shock of the fall, they had tumbled into a bed of thorns, and he limped away broken and bruised, and groaning loudly; for when monkeys *are* hurt, they take pains that everybody shall know it.

It was a long time before Jack was well enough to go about again; but when he did, he had an encounter with his old enemy the puma. And this was how it came about.

One day the puma invited his friend the stag to go with him and see a comrade, who was famous for the good milk he got from his cows. The stag loved milk, and gladly accepted the invitation, and when the sun began to get a little low the two started on their walk. On the way they arrived on the banks of a river, and as there were no bridges in those days it was necessary to swim across it. The stag was not fond of swimming, and began to say that he was tired, and thought that after all it was not worth going so far to get milk, and that he would return home. But the puma easily saw through these excuses, and laughed at him.

"The river is not deep at all," he said; "why, you will never be off your feet. Come, pluck up your courage and follow me."

The stag was afraid of the river; still, he was much more afraid of being laughed at, and he plunged in after the puma; but in an instant the current had swept him away, and if it had not borne him by accident to a shallow place on the opposite side, where he managed to scramble up the bank, he would certainly have been drowned. As it was, he scrambled out, shaking with terror, and found the puma waiting for him. "You had a narrow escape that time," said the puma.

After resting for a few minutes, to let the stag recover from his fright, they went on their way till they came to a grove of bananas.

"They look very good," observed the puma with a longing glance, "and I am sure you must be hungry, friend stag? Suppose you were to climb the tree and get some. You shall eat the green ones, they are the best and sweetest; and you can throw the yellow ones down to me. I dare say they will do quite well?" The stag did as he was bid, though not being used to climbing, it gave him a deal of trouble and sore knees, and besides, his horns were continually getting entangled in the creepers. What was worse, when once he had tasted the bananas, he found them not at all to his liking, so he threw them all down, green and yellow alike, and let the puma take his choice. And what a dinner he made! When he had *quite* done, they set forth once more.

The path lay through a field of maize, where several men were working. As they came up to them, the puma whispered: "Go on in front, friend stag, and just say 'Bad luck to all workers!'" The stag obeyed, but the men were hot and tired, and did not think this a good joke. So they set their dogs at him, and he was obliged to run away as fast as he could.

"I hope your industry will be rewarded as it deserves," said the puma as he passed along; and the men were pleased, and offered him some of their maize to eat.

By-and-by the puma saw a small snake with a beautiful shining skin, lying coiled up at the foot of a tree. "What a lovely bracelet that would make for your daughter, friend stag!" said he. The stag stooped and picked up the snake, which bit him, and he turned angrily to the puma. "Why did you not tell me it would bite?" he asked.

"Is it my fault if you are an idiot?" replied the puma.

At last they reached their journey's end, but by this time it was late, and the puma's comrade was ready for bed, so they slung their hammocks in convenient places, and went to sleep. But in the middle of the night the puma rose softly and stole out of the door to the sheepfold, where he killed and ate the fattest sheep he could find, and taking a bowl full of its blood, he sprinkled the sleeping stag with it. This done, he returned to bed.

In the morning the shepherd went as usual to let the sheep out of the fold, and found one of them missing. He thought directly of the puma, and ran to accuse him of having eaten the sheep. "I, my good man? What has put it into your head to think of such a thing? Have *I* got any blood about me? If anyone has eaten a sheep it must be my friend the stag." Then the shepherd went to examine the sleeping stag, and of course he saw the blood. "Ah! I will teach you how to steal!" cried he, and he hit the stag such a blow on his skull that he died in a moment. The noise awakened the comrade above, and he came downstairs. The puma greeted him with joy, and begged he might have some of the famous milk as soon as possible, for he was very thirsty. A large bucket was set before the puma directly. He drank it to the last drop, and then took leave.

On his way home he met the monkey. "Are you fond of milk?" asked he. "I know a place where you get it very nice. I will show you it if you like." The monkey knew that the puma was not so good-natured for nothing, but he felt quite able to take care of himself, so he said he should have much pleasure in accompanying his friend.

They soon reached the same river, and, as before, the puma remarked: "Friend monkey, you will find it very shallow; there is no cause for fear. Jump in, and I will follow."

"Do you think you have the stag to deal with?" asked the monkey, laughing. "I should prefer to follow; if not I shall go no further." The puma understood that it was useless trying to make the monkey do as he wished, so he chose a shallow place and began to swim across. The monkey waited till the puma had got to the middle, then he gave a great spring and jumped on his back, knowing quite well that the puma would be afraid to shake him off, lest he should be swept away into deep water. So in this manner they reached the bank.

The banana grove was not far distant, and here the puma thought he would pay the monkey out for forcing him to carry him over the river. "Friend monkey, look what fine bananas," cried he. "You are fond of climbing; suppose you run up and throw me down a few. You can eat the green ones, which are the nicest, and I will be content with the yellow."

"Very well," answered the monkey, swinging himself up; but he ate all the yellow ones himself, and only threw down the green ones that were left. The puma was furious and cried out: "I will punch your head for that." But the monkey only answered: "If you are going to talk such nonsense I won't walk with you." And the puma was silent.

In a few minutes more they arrived at the field where the men were reaping the maize, and the puma remarked as he had done before:

"Friend monkey, if you wish to please these men, just say as you go by: 'Bad luck to all workers.'"

"Very well," replied the monkey; but, instead, he nodded and smiled, and said: "I hope your industry may be rewarded as it deserves." The men thanked him heartily, let him pass on, and the puma followed behind him.

Further along the path they saw the shining snake lying on the moss. "What a lovely necklace for your daughter," exclaimed the puma. "Pick it up and take it with you."

"You are very kind, but I will leave it for you," answered the monkey, and nothing more was said about the snake.

Not long after this they reached the comrade's house, and found him just ready to go to bed. So, without stopping to talk, the guests slung their hammocks, the monkey taking care to place his so high that no one could get at him. Besides, he thought it would be more prudent not to fall asleep, so he only lay still and snored loudly. When it was quite dark and no sound was to be heard, the puma crept out to the sheepfold, killed the sheep, and carried back a bowl full of its blood with which to sprinkle the monkey. But the monkey, who had been watching him out of the corner of his eye, waited until the puma drew near, and with a violent kick upset the bowl all over the puma himself.

When the puma saw what had happened, he turned in a great hurry to leave the house, but before he could do so, he saw the shepherd coming, and hastily lay down again.

"This is the second time I have lost a sheep," the man said to the monkey; "it will be the worse for the thief when I catch him, I can tell you." The monkey did not answer, but silently pointed to the puma who was pretending to be asleep. The shepherd stooped and saw the blood, and cried out: "Ah! so it is you, is it? Then take that!" and with his stick he gave the puma such a blow on the head that he died then and there.

Then the monkey got up and went to the dairy, and drank all the milk he could find. Afterwards he returned home and married, and that is the last we heard of him.

BELLING THE CAT

LONG AGO, THE mice held a general council to consider what measures they could take to outwit their common enemy, the cat. Some said this, and some said that; but at last a young mouse got up and said he had a proposal to make, which he thought would meet the case. "You will all agree," said he, "that our chief danger consists in the sly and treacherous manner in which the enemy approaches us. Now, if we could receive some signal of her approach, we could easily escape from her. I venture, therefore, to propose that a small bell be procured, and attached by a ribbon round the neck of the cat. By this means we should always know when she was about, and could easily retire while she was in the neighborhood."

This proposal met with general applause, until an old mouse got up and said: "That is all very well, but who is to bell the cat?" The mice looked at one another and nobody spoke. Then the old mouse said:

It is easy to propose impossible remedies.

THE
WONDERFUL OX

*There are many tall tales about the mighty logger Paul
Bunyan, but none more remarkable than those about Babe,
Paul's gigantic blue ox.*

THE GREAT BLUE OX was so strong that he could pull anything
that had two ends and some things that had no ends at all, which made
him very valuable at times, as one can easily understand.

Babe was remarkable in a number of ways besides that of his color,
which was a bright blue. His size is rather a matter of doubt, some people
holding that he was twenty-four ax-handles and a plug of tobacco wide
between the eyes, and others saying that he was forty-two ax-handles
across the forehead. It may be that both are wrong, for the story goes
that Jim, the pet crow, who always roosted on Babe's left horn, one day
decided to fly across to the tip of the other horn. He got lost on the
way, and didn't get to the other horn until after the spring thaw, and he
had started in the dead of winter.

The Great Blue Ox was so long in the body that an ordinary person, standing at his head, would have had to use a pair of field glasses
in order to see what the animal was doing with his hind feet.

Babe had a great love for Paul, and a peculiar way of showing it
which discovered the great logger's only weakness. Paul was ticklish,
especially around the neck, and the Ox had a strong passion for licking

him there with his tongue. His master good-naturedly avoided such outbursts of affection from his pet whenever possible.

One day Paul took the Blue Ox with him to town, and there he loaded him with all the supplies that would be needed for the camp and crew during the winter. When everything had been packed on Babe's back, the animal was so heavily laden that on the way back to camp he sank to his knees in the solid rock at nearly every step. These footprints later filled with water and became the countless lakes which are to be found today scattered throughout the state of Maine.

Babe was compelled to go slowly, of course, on account of the great load he carried, and so Paul had to camp overnight along the way. He took the packs from the Ox's back, turned the big animal out to graze, and after eating supper he and Ole lay down to sleep.

The Blue Ox, however, was for some strange reason in a restless mood that night, and after feeding all that he cared to, he wandered away for many miles before he finally found a place that suited his particular idea of what a bedding ground should be. There he lay down, and it is quite possible that he was very much amused in thinking of the trouble which his master would have in finding him the next morning. The Ox was a very wise creature, and every now and then he liked to play a little joke on Paul.

Along about dawn Paul Bunyan awoke and looked about for his pet. Not a glimpse of him could he get in any direction, though he whistled so loudly for him that the nearby trees were shattered into bits. At last, after he and Ole had eaten their breakfast and Babe still did not appear, Paul knew that the joke was on him. "He thinks he has put up a little trick on me," he said to Ole with a grin. "You go ahead and make up the packs again, while I play hide-and-seek for a while," and as the Big Swede started gathering everything together again he set off trailing the missing animal.

Babe's tracks were so large that it took three men, standing close together, to see across one of them, and they were so far apart that no one could follow them but Paul, who was an expert trailer, no one else ever being able to equal him in this ability. So remarkable was he in this respect that he could follow any tracks that were ever made, no matter how old or how faint they were. It is told of him that he once came across the carcass of a bull moose that had died of old age, and having a couple of hours to spare, and being also of an inquiring turn of mind, he followed the tracks of the moose back to the place where it had been born.

Being such an expert, therefore, it did not take him very long to locate Babe. The Great Blue Ox, when he at last came across him, was lying down contentedly chewing his cud, and waiting for his master to come and find him. "You worthless critter!" Paul said to him, and thwacked him good-naturedly with his hand. "Look at the trouble you have put me to, and just look at the damage you have done here," and he pointed to the great hollow place in the ground which Babe had wallowed out while lying there. The Ox's only reply was to smother Paul for a moment with a loving, juicy lick of his great tongue, and then together they set off to where Ole was waiting for them.

Anyone, by looking at a map of the state of Maine, can easily locate Moosehead Lake, which is, as history shows, the place where the Great Blue Ox lay down.

No one, certainly, could be expected to copy him in the matter of straightening out crooked logging trails. It was all wild country where Paul did his logging, and about the only roads which he found through the woods were the trails and paths made by the wild animals that had traveled over them for hundreds of years. Paul decided to use these game trails as logging roads, but they twisted and turned in every direction and were all so crooked that they had to be straightened before any use could be made of them. It is well known that the Great Blue Ox was so powerful that he could pull anything that had two ends, and so when Paul wanted a crooked logging trail straightened out, he would just hitch Babe up to one end of it, tell his pet to go ahead, and, lo and behold! the crooked trail would be pulled out perfectly straight.

There was one particularly bad stretch of road, about twenty or thirty miles long, that gave Babe and Paul a lot of trouble before they

finally
got all the
crooks pulled
out of it. It cer-
tainly must have been the crookedest
road in the world—it twisted and turned so much that it
spelled out every letter of the alphabet, some of the letters two or
three times. Paul taught Babe how to read just by leading him over it a
few times, and men going along it met themselves coming from the
other direction so often that the whole camp was near crazy before long.

So Paul decided that the road would have to be straightened out without any further delay, and with that end in view he ordered Ole to make
for him the strongest chain he knew how. The Big Swede set to work with
a will, and when the chain was completed it had links four feet long and
two feet across and the steel they were made of was thirteen inches thick.

The chain being ready, Paul hitched Babe up to one end of the road with it. At his master's word the Great Blue Ox began to puff and pull and strain away as he had never done before, and at last he got the end pulled out a little ways. Paul chirped to him again, and he pulled away harder than ever. With every tug he made one of the twists in the road would straighten out, and then Babe would pull away again, hind legs straight out behind and belly to the ground. It was the hardest job Babe had ever been put up against, but he stuck to it most admirably.

When the task was finally done the Ox was nearly fagged out, a condition that he had never known before, and that big chain had been pulled on so hard that it was pulled out into a solid steel bar. The road was straightened out, however, which was the thing Paul wanted, and he considered the time and energy expended as well worth while, since the nuisance had been transformed into something useful. He found, though, that since all the kinks and twists had been pulled out, there was now a whole lot more of the road than was needed, but—never being a person who could stand to waste anything which might be useful—he rolled up all the extra length and laid it down in a place where there had never been a road before but where one might come in handy sometime.

Nor was the straightening of crooked roads the only useful work which the Great Blue Ox did. It was also his task to skid or drag the logs from the stumps to the rollways by the streams, where they were stored for the drives. Babe was always obedient, and a tireless and patient worker. It is said that the timber of nineteen states, except a few scant sections here and there which Paul Bunyan did not touch, was skidded from the stumps by the all-powerful Great Blue Ox. He was docile and willing, and could be depended upon for the performance of almost any task set him, except that once in a while he would develop a sudden streak of mischief and drink a river dry behind a drive or run off into the woods. Sometimes he would step on a ridge that formed the bank of the river, and smash it down so that the river would start running out through his tracks, thus changing its course entirely from what Paul had counted on.

THE COWARDLY
LION

*Dorothy has been swept up into a tornado and transported
to the magical land of Oz. Once in Oz, Dorothy is told
that she will find the wizard who can return her to Kansas by
following the yellow brick road. As she travels up the road,
she meets new friends.*

ALL THIS TIME Dorothy and her companions had been walking through the thick woods. The road was still paved with yellow brick, but these were much covered by dried branches and dead leaves from the trees and the walking was not at all good.

There were few birds in this part of the forest, for birds love the open country where there is plenty of sunshine, but now and then there came a deep growl from some wild animal hidden among the trees. These sounds made the little girl's heart beat fast, for she did not know what made them; but Toto knew, and he walked close to Dorothy's side, and did not even bark in return.

"How long will it be," the child asked of the Tin Woodman, "before we are out of the forest?"

"I cannot tell," was the answer, "for I have never been to the Emerald City. But my father went there once, when I was a boy, and he said it was a long journey through a dangerous country, although nearer to the city where Oz dwells the country is beautiful. But I am not afraid so long as I have my oil-can, and nothing can hurt the Scarecrow, while you bear upon your forehead the mark of the good Witch's kiss, and that will protect you from harm."

"But Toto!" said the girl, anxiously; "what will protect him?"

"We must protect him ourselves, if he is in danger," replied the Tin Woodman.

Just as he spoke there came from the forest a terrible roar, and the next moment a great Lion bounded into the road. With one blow of his paw he sent the Scarecrow spinning over and over to the edge of the road, and then he struck at the Tin Woodman with his sharp claws. But, to the Lion's surprise, he could make no impression on the tin, although the Woodman fell over in the road and lay still.

Little Toto, now that he had an enemy to face, ran barking toward the Lion, and the great beast had opened his mouth to bite the dog, when Dorothy, fearing Toto would be killed, and heedless of danger, rushed forward and slapped the Lion upon his nose as hard as she could, while she cried out:

"Don't you dare to bite Toto! You ought to be ashamed of yourself, a big beast like you, to bite a poor little dog!"

"I didn't bite him," said the Lion, as he rubbed his nose with his paw where Dorothy had hit it.

"No, but you tried to," she retorted. "You are nothing but a big coward."

"I know it," said the Lion, hanging his head in shame; "I've always known it. But how can I help it?"

"I don't know, I'm sure. To think of your striking a stuffed man, like the poor Scarecrow!"

"Is he stuffed?" asked the Lion, in surprise, as he watched her pick up the Scarecrow and set him upon his feet, while she patted him into shape again.

"Of course he's stuffed," replied Dorothy, who was still angry.

"That's why he went over so easily," remarked the Lion. "It astonished me to see him whirl around so. Is the other one stuffed, also?"

"No," said Dorothy, "he's made of tin." And she helped the Woodman up again.

"That's why he nearly blunted my claws," said the Lion. "When they scratched against the tin it made a cold shiver run down my back. What is that little animal you are so tender of?"

"He is my dog, Toto," answered Dorothy.

"Is he made of tin, or stuffed?" asked the Lion.

"Neither. He's a—a—a meat dog," said the girl.

"Oh. He's a curious animal, and seems remarkably small, now that I look at him. No one would think of biting such a little thing except a coward like me," continued the Lion, sadly.

"What makes you a coward?" asked Dorothy, looking at the great beast in wonder, for he was as big as a small horse.

"It's a mystery," replied the Lion. "I suppose I was born that way. All the other animals in the forest naturally expect me to be brave, for the Lion is everywhere thought to be the King of Beasts. I learned that if I roared very loudly every living thing was frightened and got out of my way. Whenever I've met a man I've been awfully scared; but I just roared at him, and he has always run away as fast as he could go. If the elephants and the tigers and the bears had ever tried to fight me I should have run myself—I'm such a coward; but just as soon as they hear me roar they all try to get away from me, and of course I let them go."

"But that isn't right. The King of Beasts shouldn't be a coward," said the Scarecrow.

"I know it," returned the Lion, wiping a tear from his eye with the tip of his tail; "it is my great sorrow, and makes my life very unhappy. But whenever there is danger my heart begins to beat fast."

"Perhaps you have heart disease," said the Tin Woodman.

"It may be," said the Lion.

"If you have," continued the Tin Woodman, "you ought to be glad, for it proves you have a heart. For my part, I have no heart; so I cannot have heart disease."

"Perhaps," said the Lion, thoughtfully, "if I had no heart I should not be a coward."

"Have you brains?" asked the Scarecrow.

"I suppose so. I've never looked to see," replied the Lion.

"I am going to the great Oz to ask him to give me some," remarked the Scarecrow, "for my head is stuffed with straw."

"And I am going to ask him to give me a heart," said the Woodman.

"And I am going to ask him to send Toto and me back to Kansas," added Dorothy.

"Do you think Oz could give me courage?" asked the Cowardly Lion.

"Just as easily as he could give me brains," said the Scarecrow.

"Or give me a heart," said the Tin Woodman.

"Or send me back to Kansas," said Dorothy.

"Then, if you don't mind, I'll go with you," said the Lion, "for my life is simply unbearable without a bit of courage."

"You will be very welcome," answered Dorothy, "for you will help to keep away the other wild beasts. It seems to me they must be more cowardly than you are if they allow you to scare them so easily."

"They really are," said the Lion; "but that doesn't make me any braver, and as long as I know myself to be a coward I shall be unhappy."

So once more the little company set off upon the journey, the Lion walking with stately strides at Dorothy's side. Toto did not approve this new comrade at first, for he could not forget how nearly he had been crushed between the Lion's great jaws; but after a time he became more at ease, and presently Toto and the Cowardly Lion had grown to be good friends.

During the rest of that day there was no other adventure to mar the peace of their journey. Once, indeed, the Tin Woodman stepped upon a beetle that was crawling along the road, and killed the poor little thing. This made the Tin Woodman very unhappy, for he was always careful not to hurt any living creature; and as he walked along he wept several tears of sorrow and regret. These tears ran slowly down his face and over the hinges of his jaw, and there they rusted. When Dorothy presently asked him a question the Tin Woodman could not open his mouth, for his jaws were tightly rusted together. He became greatly frightened at this and made many motions to Dorothy to relieve him, but she could not understand. The Lion was also puzzled to know what was wrong. But the Scarecrow seized the oil-can from Dorothy's basket and oiled the Woodman's jaws, so that after a few moments he could talk as well as before.

"This will serve me a lesson," said he, "to look where I step. For if I should kill another bug or beetle I should surely cry again, and crying rusts my jaw so that I cannot speak."

Thereafter he walked very carefully, with his eyes on the road, and when he saw a tiny ant toiling by he would step over it, so as not to harm it. The Tin Woodman knew very well he had no heart, and therefore he took great care never to be cruel or unkind to anything.

"You people with hearts," he said, "have something to guide you, and need never do wrong; but I have no heart, and so I must be very careful. When Oz gives me a heart of course I needn't mind so much."

THE TOWN MOUSE AND THE COUNTRY MOUSE

A COUNTRY MOUSE was very happy that his city cousin, the town mouse, had accepted his invitation to dinner. He gave his city cousin all the best food he had, such as dried beans, peas, and crusts of bread. The town mouse tried not to show how he disliked the food and picked a little here and tasted a little there to be polite. After dinner, however, he said, "How can you stand such food all the time? Still I suppose here in the country you don't know about any better. Why don't you go home with me? When you have once tasted the delicious things I eat, you will never want to come back here." The country mouse not only kindly forgave the town mouse for not liking his dinner, but even consented to go that very evening to the city with his cousin. They arrived late at night; and the city mouse, as host, took his country cousin at once to a room where there had been a big dinner. "You are tired," he said. "Rest here, and I'll bring you some real food." And he brought the country mouse such things as nuts, dates, cakes, and fruit. The country mouse thought it was all so good, he would like to stay there. But before he had a chance to say so, he heard a terrible roar, and looking up, he saw a huge creature dash into the room. Frightened half out of his wits, the country mouse ran from the table, and round and round the room, trying to find a hiding-place. At last he found a place of safety. While he stood there trembling he made up his mind to go home as soon as he could get safely away; for, to himself, he said, "I'd rather have common food in safety than dates and nuts in the midst of danger."

The troubles you know are easiest to bear.

THE RIVERBANK

*If you have ever felt that animals have thoughts, feelings, and
jokes to share, just as people do, then you will build lasting
friendships when you read* The Wind in the Willows *by Kenneth
Grahame. In the first chapter, which is printed here, you will
meet Mole and Water Rat. When you finish reading, you will
probably be curious to find out more about Ratty's companions,
Badger and Toad, the other important characters in the story.*

THE MOLE HAD been working very hard all the morning,
spring cleaning his little home. First with brooms, then with
dusters; then on ladders and steps and chairs, with a brush and
a pail of whitewash; till he had dust in his throat and eyes, and
splashes of whitewash all over his black fur, and an aching back
and weary arms. Spring was moving in the air above and in the earth
below and around him, penetrating even his dark and lowly little house
with its spirit of divine discontent and longing. It was small wonder,
then, that he suddenly flung down his brush on the floor, said
"Bother!" and "Oh blow!" and also "Hang spring cleaning!" and
bolted out of the house without even waiting to put on his coat.
Something up above was calling him imperiously, and he made for the
steep little tunnel which answered in his case to the graveled carriage-
drive owned by animals whose residences are nearer to the sun and air.
So he scraped and scratched and scrabbled and scrooged, and then he
scrooged again and scrabbled and scratched and scraped, working

busily with his little paws and muttering to himself, "Up we go! Up we go!" till at last, pop! his snout came out into the sunlight, and he found himself rolling in the warm grass of a great meadow.

"This is fine!" he said to himself. "This is better than whitewashing!" The sunshine struck hot on his fur, soft breezes caressed his heated brow, and after the seclusion of the cellarage he had lived in so long the carol of happy birds fell on his dulled hearing almost like a shout. Jumping off all his four legs at once, in the joy of living and the delight of spring without its cleaning, he pursued his way across the meadow till he reached the hedge on the further side.

"Hold up!" said an elderly rabbit at the gap. "Sixpence for the privilege of passing by the private road!" He was bowled over in an instant by the impatient and contemptuous Mole, who trotted along the side of the hedge chaffing the other rabbits as they peeped hurriedly from their holes to see what the row was about. "Onion-sauce! Onion-sauce!" he remarked jeeringly, and was gone before they could think of a thoroughly satisfactory reply. Then they all started grumbling at each other. "How *stupid* you are! Why didn't you tell him—" "Well, why didn't *you* say—" "You might have reminded him—" and so on, in the usual way; but, of course, it was then much too late, as is always the case.

It all seemed too good to be true. Hither and thither through the meadows he rambled busily, along the hedge-rows, across the copses, finding everywhere birds building, flowers budding, leaves thrusting—everything happy, and progressive, and occupied. And instead of having an uneasy conscience pricking him and whispering, "Whitewash!" he somehow could only feel how jolly it was to be the only idle dog among all these busy citizens. After all, the best part of a holiday is perhaps not so much to be resting yourself, as to see all the other fellows busy working.

He thought his happiness was complete when, as he meandered aimlessly along, suddenly he stood by the edge of a full-fed river. Never in his life had he seen a river before—this sleek, sinuous, full-bodied animal, chasing and chuckling, gripping things with a gurgle and leaving them with a laugh, to fling itself on fresh playmates that shook themselves free, and were caught and held again. All was a-shake and a-shiver—glints and gleams and sparkles, rustle and swirl, chatter and bubble. The Mole was bewitched, entranced, fascinated. By the side of the river he trotted as one trots, when very small, by the side of a man who holds one spellbound by exciting stories; and when tired at last, he sat on the bank, while the river still chattered on to him, a babbling procession of the best stories in the world, sent from the heart of the earth to be told at last to the insatiable sea.

As he sat on the grass and looked across the river, a dark hole in the bank opposite, just above the water's edge, caught his eye, and dreamily he fell to considering what a nice snug dwelling place it would make for an animal with few wants and fond of a bijou riverside residence, above flood level and remote from noise and dust. As he gazed, something bright and small seemed to twinkle down in the heart of it, vanished, then twinkled once more like a tiny star. But it could hardly be a star in such an unlikely situation; and it was too glittering and small for a glowworm. Then, as he looked, it winked at him, and so declared itself to be an eye; and a small face began gradually to grow up round it, like a frame round a picture.

A brown little face, with whiskers.

A grave round face, with the same twinkle in its eye that had first attracted his notice.

Small neat ears and thick silky hair.

It was the Water Rat!

Then the two animals stood and regarded each other cautiously.

"Hullo, Mole!" said the Water Rat.

"Hullo, Rat!" said the Mole.

"Would you like to come over?" inquired the Rat presently.

"Oh, it's all very well to *talk*," said the Mole rather pettishly, he being new to a river and riverside life and its ways.

The Rat said nothing, but stooped and unfastened a rope and hauled on it; then lightly stepped into a little boat which the Mole had

not observed. It was painted blue outside and white within, and was just the size for two animals; and the Mole's whole heart went out to it at once, even though he did not yet fully understand its uses.

The Rat sculled smartly across and made fast. Then he held up his forepaw as the Mole stepped gingerly down. "Lean on that!" he said. "Now then, step lively!" and the Mole to his surprise and rapture found himself actually seated in the stern of a real boat.

"This has been a wonderful day!" said he, as the Rat shoved off and took to the sculls again. "Do you know, I've never been in a boat before in all my life."

"What?" cried the Rat, openmouthed: "Never been in a—you never—well, I—what have you been doing, then?"

"Is it so nice as all that?" asked the Mole shyly, though he was quite prepared to believe it as he leaned back in his seat and surveyed the cushions, the oars, the rowlocks, and all the fascinating fittings, and felt the boat sway lightly under him.

"Nice? It's the *only* thing," said the Water Rat solemnly, as he leaned forward for his stroke. "Believe me, my young friend, there is *nothing*—absolutely nothing—half so much worth doing as simply messing about in boats. Simply messing," he went on dreamily: "messing—about—in—boats; messing—"

"Look ahead, Rat!" cried the Mole suddenly.

It was too late. The boat struck the bank full tilt. The dreamer, the joyous oarsman lay on his back at the bottom of the boat, his heels in the air.

"—about in boats—or *with* boats," the Rat went on composedly, picking himself up with a pleasant laugh. "In or out of 'em, it doesn't matter. Nothing seems really to matter, that's the charm of it. Whether you get away, or whether you don't; whether you arrive at your desti-

nation or whether you reach somewhere else, or whether you never get anywhere at all, you're always busy, and you never do anything in particular; and when you've done it there's always something else to do, and you can do it if you like, but you'd much better not. Look here! If you've really nothing else on hand this morning, supposing we drop down the river together, and have a long day of it?"

The Mole waggled his toes from sheer happiness, spread his chest with a sigh of full contentment, and leaned back blissfully into the soft cushions. "*What* a day I'm having!" he said. "Let us start at once!"

"Hold hard a minute, then!" said the Rat. He looped the painter through a ring in his landing-stage, climbed up into his hole above, and after a short interval reappeared staggering under a fat, wicker luncheon-basket.

"Shove that under your feet," he observed to the Mole, as he passed it down into the boat. Then he untied the painter and took the sculls again.

"What's inside it?" asked the Mole, wiggling with curiosity.

"There's cold chicken inside it," replied the Rat briefly; "cold-tonguecoldhamcoldbeefpickledgherkinssaladfrenchrollscresssand-widgespottedmeatgingerbeerlemonadesodawater—"

"Oh stop, stop," cried the Mole in ecstasies: "This is too much!"

"Do you really think so?" inquired the Rat seriously. "It's only what I always take on these little excursions; and the other animals are always telling me that I'm a mean beast and cut it *very* fine!"

The Mole never heard a word he was saying. Absorbed in the new life he was entering upon, intoxicated with the sparkle, the ripple, the scents and the sounds and the sunlight, he trailed a paw in the water and dreamed long waking dreams. The Water Rat, like the good little fellow he was, sculled steadily on and forbore to disturb him.

"I like your clothes awfully, old chap," he remarked after some half an hour or so had passed. "I'm going to get a black velvet smoking suit myself someday, as soon as I can afford it."

"I beg your pardon," said the Mole, pulling himself together with an effort. "You must think me very rude; but all this is so new to me. So—this—is—a—River!"

"*The* River," corrected the Rat.

"And you really live by the river? What a jolly life!"

"By it and with it and on it and in it," said the Rat. "It's brother and sister to me, and aunts, and company, and food and drink, and (naturally) washing. It's my world, and I don't want any other. What it hasn't got is not worth having, and what it doesn't know is not worth knowing. Lord! the times we've had together! Whether in winter or summer, spring or autumn, it's always got its fun and its excitements. When the floods are on in February, and my cellars and basement are brimming with drink that's no good to me, and the brown water runs by my best bedroom window; or again when it all drops away and shows patches of mud that smells like plum cake, and the rushes and weed clog the channels, and I can potter about dry-shod over most of the bed of it and find fresh food to eat, and things careless people have dropped out of boats!"

"But isn't it a bit dull at times?" the Mole ventured to ask. "Just you and the river, and no one else to pass a word with?"

"No one else to—well, I mustn't be hard on you," said the Rat with forbearance. "You're new to it, and of course you don't know. The bank is so crowded nowadays that many people are moving away altogether. Oh no, it isn't what it used to be, at all. Otters, kingfishers, dabchicks, moorhens, all of them about all day long and always wanting you to *do* something—as if a fellow had no business of his own to attend to!"

"What lies over *there?*" asked the Mole, waving a paw towards a background of woodland that darkly framed the water meadows on one side of the river.

"That? Oh that's just the Wild Wood," said the Rat shortly. "We don't go there very much, we riverbankers."

"Aren't they—aren't they very *nice* people in there?" said the Mole a trifle nervously.

"W-e-ll," replied the Rat, "let me see. The squirrels are all right. *And* the rabbits—some of 'em, but rabbits are a mixed lot. And then there's Badger, of course. He lives right in the heart of it; wouldn't live any- where else, either, if you paid him to do it. Dear old Badger! Nobody interferes with *him*. They'd better not," he added significantly.

"Why, who *should* interfere with him?" asked the Mole.

"Well, of course—there—are others," explained the Rat in a hesi- tating sort of way. "Weasels—and stoats—and foxes—and so on. They're all right in a way—I'm very good friends with them—pass the time of day when we meet, and all that—but they break out some- times, there's no denying it, and then—well, you can't really trust them, and that's the fact."

The Mole knew well that it is quite against animal etiquette to dwell on possible trouble ahead, or even to allude to it; so he dropped the subject.

"And beyond the Wild Wood again?" he asked: "Where it's all blue and dim, and one sees what may be hills or perhaps they mayn't and something like the smoke of towns, or is it only cloud-drift?"

"Beyond the Wild Wood comes the Wide World," said the Rat. "And that's something that doesn't matter, either to you or to me. I've never been there, and I'm never going, nor you either, if you've got any sense at all. Don't ever refer to it again, please. Now then! Here's our backwater at last, where we're going to lunch."

Leaving the main stream, they now passed into what seemed at first sight like a little landlocked lake. Green turf sloped down to either edge, brown snaky tree-roots gleamed below the surface of the quiet water, while ahead of them the silvery shoulder and foamy tumble of a weir, arm-in-arm with a restless dripping mill wheel, that held up in its turn a gray-gabled mill house, filled the air with a soothing murmur of sound, dull and smothery, yet with little clear voices speaking up cheerfully out of it at intervals. It was so very beautiful that the Mole could only hold up both forepaws and gasp, "Oh my! Oh my! Oh my!"

The Rat brought the boat alongside the bank, made her fast, helped the still awkward Mole safely ashore, and swung out the luncheon-basket.

The Mole begged as a favor to be allowed to unpack it all by himself; and the Rat was very pleased to indulge him, and to sprawl at full length on the grass and rest, while his excited friend shook out the tablecloth and spread it, took out all the mysterious packets one by one and arranged their contents in due order, still gasping, "Oh my! Oh my!" at each fresh revelation. When all was ready, the Rat said, "Now, pitch in, old fellow!" and the Mole was indeed very glad to obey, for he had started his spring cleaning at a very early hour that morning, as people *will* do, and had not paused for bite or sup; and he had been through a very great deal since that distant time which now seemed so many days ago.

"What are you looking at?" said the Rat presently, when the edge of their hunger was somewhat dulled, and the Mole's eyes were able to wander off the tablecloth a little.

"I am looking," said the Mole, "at a streak of bubbles that I see traveling along the surface of the water. That is a thing that strikes me as funny."

"Bubbles? Oho!" said the Rat, and chirruped cheerily in an inviting sort of way.

A broad glistening muzzle showed itself above the edge of the bank, and the Otter hauled himself out and shook the water from his coat.

"Greedy beggars!" he observed, making for the provender. "Why didn't you invite me, Ratty?"

"This was an impromptu affair," explained the Rat. "By the way— my friend Mr. Mole."

"Proud, I'm sure," said the Otter, and the two animals were friends forthwith.

"Such a rumpus everywhere!" continued the Otter. "All the world seems out on the river today. I come up this backwater to try and get a moment's peace, and then stumble upon you fellows!—At least—I beg pardon—I don't exactly mean that, you know."

There was a rustle behind them, proceeding from a hedge wherein last year's leaves still clung thick, and a stripy head, with high shoulders behind it, peered forth on them.

"Come on, old Badger," shouted the Rat.

The Badger trotted forward a pace or two; then grunted, "H'm! Company," and turned his back and disappeared from view.

"That's *just* the sort of fellow he is!" observed the disappointed Rat. "Simply hates Society! Now we shan't see any more of him today. Well, tell us *who's* out on the river?"

"Toad's out, for one," replied the Otter. "In his brand-new wager-boat; new togs, new everything!"

The two animals looked at each other and laughed.

"Once, it was nothing but sailing," said the Rat. "Then he tired of that and took to punting. Nothing would please him but to punt all day and every day, and a nice mess he made of it. Last year it was houseboating, and we all had to go and stay with him in his houseboat, and pretend we liked it. He was going to spend the rest of his life in a houseboat. It's all the same whatever he takes up; he gets tired of it, and starts on something fresh."

"Such a good fellow, too," remarked the Otter reflectively: "But no stability—especially in a boat!"

From where they sat they could get a glimpse of the main stream across the island that separated them; and just then a wager-boat flashed into view, the rower—a short, stout figure—splashing badly and rolling a good deal, but working his hardest. The Rat stood up and hailed him, but Toad—for it was he—shook his head and settled sternly to his work.

"He'll be out of the boat in a minute if he rolls like that," said the Rat, sitting down again.

"Of course he will," chuckled the Otter. "Did I ever tell you that good story about Toad and the lock keeper? It happened this way. Toad . . ."

An errant mayfly swerved unsteadily athwart the current in the intoxicated fashion affected by young bloods of mayflies seeing life. A swirl of water and a "cloop!" and the mayfly was visible no more.

Neither was the Otter.

The Mole looked down. The voice was still in his ears, but the turf

whereon he had sprawled was clearly vacant. Not an Otter to be seen, as far as the distant horizon.

But again there was a streak of bubbles on the surface of the river.

The Rat hummed a tune, and the Mole recollected that animal etiquette forbade any sort of comment on the sudden disappearance of one's friends at any moment, for any reason or no reason whatever.

"Well, well," said the Rat, "I suppose we ought to be moving. I wonder which of us had better pack the luncheon-basket?" He did not speak as if he was frightfully eager for the treat.

"Oh please let me," said the Mole. So, of course, the Rat let him.

Packing the basket was not quite such pleasant work as unpacking the basket. It never is. But the Mole was bent on enjoying everything, and although just when he had got the basket

packed and strapped up tightly he saw a plate
staring up at him from the grass, and when the job had been
done again the Rat pointed out a fork which anybody ought to
have seen, and last of all, behold! the mustard pot, which he had
been sitting on without knowing it—still, somehow, the thing got finished at last, without much loss of temper.

The afternoon sun was getting low as the Rat sculled gently home-
wards in a dreamy mood, murmuring poetry-things over to himself,
and not paying much attention to Mole. But the Mole was very full of
lunch, and self-satisfaction, and pride, and already quite at home in a
boat (so he thought) and was getting a bit restless besides: and
presently he said, "Ratty! Please, *I* want to row, now!"

The Rat shook his head with a smile. "Not yet, my young friend,"
he said—"wait till you've had a few lessons. It's not so easy as it looks."

The Mole was quiet for a minute or two. But he began to feel more and more jealous of Rat, sculling so strongly and so easily along, and his pride began to whisper that he could do it every bit as well. He jumped up and seized the sculls so suddenly that the Rat, who was gazing out over the water and saying more poetry-things to himself, was taken by surprise and fell backwards off his seat with his legs in the air for the second time, while the triumphant Mole took his place and grabbed the sculls with entire confidence.

"Stop it, you *silly* ass!" cried the Rat, from the bottom of the boat. "You can't do it! You'll have us over!"

The Mole flung his sculls back with a flourish, and made a great dig at the water. He missed the surface altogether, his legs flew up above his head, and he found himself lying on the top of the prostrate Rat. Greatly alarmed, he made a grab at the side of the boat, and the next moment—sploosh!

Over went the boat, and he found himself struggling in the river.

Oh my, how cold the water was, and Oh, how *very* wet it felt. How it sang in his ears as he went down, down, down! How bright and welcome the sun looked as he rose to the surface coughing and spluttering! How black was his despair when he felt himself sinking again! Then a firm paw gripped him by the back of his neck. It was the Rat, and he was evidently laughing—the Mole could *feel* him laughing, right down his arm and through his paw, and so into his—the Mole's—neck.

The Rat got hold of a scull and shoved it under the Mole's arm; then he did the same by the other side of him and, swimming behind, propelled the helpless animal to shore, hauled him out, and set him down on the bank, a squashy, pulpy lump of misery.

When the Rat had rubbed him down a bit, and wrung some of the wet out of him, he said, "Now, then, old fellow! Trot up and down the towing-path as hard as you can, till you're warm and dry again, while I dive for the luncheon-basket."

So the dismal Mole, wet without and ashamed within, trotted

about till he was fairly dry, while the Rat plunged into the water again, recovered the boat, righted her and made her fast, fetched his floating property to shore by degrees, and finally dived successfully for the luncheon-basket and struggled to land with it.

When all was ready for a start once more, the Mole, limp and dejected, took his seat in the stern of the boat; and as they set off, he said in a low voice, broken with emotion, "Ratty, my generous friend! I am very sorry indeed for my foolish and ungrateful conduct. My heart quite fails me when I think how I might have lost that beautiful luncheon-basket. Indeed, I have been a complete ass, and I know it. Will you over-look it this once and forgive me, and let things go on as before?"

"That's all right, bless you!" responded the Rat cheerily. "What's a little wet to a Water Rat? I'm more in the water than out of it most days. Don't you think any more about it; and, look here! I really think you had better come and stop with me for a little time. It's very plain and rough, you know—not like Toad's house at all—but you haven't seen that yet; still, I can make you comfortable. And I'll teach you to row, and to swim, and you'll soon be as handy on the water as any of us."

The Mole was so touched by his kind manner of speaking that he could find no voice to answer him; and he had to brush away a tear or two with the back of his paw. But the Rat kindly looked in another direction, and presently the Mole's spirits revived again, and he was even able to give some straight back-talk to a couple of moorhens who were sniggering to each other about his bedraggled appearance.

When they got home, the Rat made a bright fire in the parlor, and planted the Mole in an armchair in front of it, having fetched down a dressing gown and slippers for him, and told him river stories till sup-pertime. Very thrilling stories they were, too, to an earth-dwelling ani-mal like Mole. Stories about weirs, and sudden floods, and leaping pike, and steamers that flung hard bottles—at least bottles were cer-tainly flung, and *from* steamers, so presumably *by* them; and about herons, and how particular they were whom they spoke to; and about adventures down drains, and night fishings with Otter, or excursions far afield with Badger. Supper was a most cheerful meal; but very shortly afterwards a terribly sleepy Mole had to be escorted upstairs by his considerate host, to the best bedroom, where he soon laid his head on his pillow in great peace and contentment, knowing that his new-found friend the River was lapping the sill of his window.

This day was only the first of many similar ones for the emancipated Mole, each of them longer and fuller of interest as the ripening summer moved onward. He learned to swim and to row, and entered into the joy of running water; and with his ear to the reed-stems he caught, at intervals, something of what the wind went whispering so constantly among them.

THE DANCE OF THE ROYAL ANTS

The Little Black Ant *reveals the bustling life and variety of an ant colony through the adventures of one special little black ant.*

BIRDS WERE SINGING, bees were humming, and dewdrops sparkled on every bush and tree. Another summer day had come. And inside the mound of sand at the edge of the thicket the ant people were going about their morning tasks.

Little Black Ant liked the early morning hour when the hill began to stir, but this morning there was an unusual thrill about it. This was no ordinary day. Something strange was about to happen.

The halls and corridors were humming with excitement, for news travels swiftly among the ant people, and there was not an ant in all the hill who did not know that today the royal princes and princesses were going away. They were going to leave the hill and go on a mysterious journey. And some of them would never come back.

Little Black Ant was thinking about this as she walked along the winding corridor. She had often felt sorry for these royal ants who must stay in their small dark rooms all day long and could not wander through the green grass forest. They were not allowed to do any work at all; no digging, no carrying, no foraging for food. They were not even allowed to help with the cleaning. Little Black Ant did not understand this but she knew it must be right, for it had always been a law among her people that the royal ants should do no work.

And now they were going away! The thought of this made her a little sad. She would miss them, she knew, for they had lived at the hill all their lives and she had seen them almost every day.

"I am glad I am not a royal princess," she said to herself. "I should not like to be going away on a mysterious journey. I should much rather visit the white blossoms where the wells of honey are."

Quickening her pace, she overtook one of the royal princesses. "Good morning, Princess," she said. "You are going away today, aren't you? Won't you tell me about your journey? Where will you go?"

"I do not know," the royal princess said, "but I know that I shall be very merry for this is my wedding day. Did you know that, little Ant?"

"Yes," answered the little ant. "All the hill knows that this is to be a day of weddings for the royal ants."

"It is wonderful," the princess went on eagerly, "for it is said that we will dance all day long in the sunshine, high above the treetops. Just think! I have never used my beautiful wings before, but today I shall fly!"

"Wings are strange things, aren't they?" Little Black Ant said.

"Yes," replied the princess, "and I am glad I have them." She paused for a moment and then added: "I am sorry that you workers have no wings. I wish you were going to fly, too, little Ant."

"Oh, I do not want to fly," Little Black Ant told her. "I would much rather travel on the ground, through the crooked pathways in the grass and among the tangled roots."

They had reached the gateway and the outside world lay before them, sparkling in the sunlight. "Goodbye, Princess," said Little Black Ant. "I must be off now to look for food."

"Goodbye," replied the princess. "I, too, must be off on my journey high in the air."

"Above the treetops," Little Black Ant said wonderingly.

"Yes, above the treetops," the princess answered. "But I shall not forget you, little Ant, and I shall not forget the good food you so often brought me. Last night it was three drops of honey—the sweetest honey. Do you remember?"

"Yes," said Little Black Ant, "I remember. And now perhaps I shall never bring you honey any more. Perhaps I shall never see you again."

"Who knows?" replied the princess. "Who knows, little Ant?"

There was much more that Little Black Ant would have liked to say, but the sentinel told them to move on so that the other ants could go through the gateway and, without another word, they parted.

The royal princess had seldom before been outside the gates of the hill. Sometimes she had been allowed to walk out here for a little while, accompanied by her attendants; but she had never been free as she was today.

A number of her royal sisters were gathered on the hillside. Some of them had already risen from the ground, their silvery wings glistening as they flew away. The princess moved her own wings restlessly. They felt firm and strong. "They will bear me up," she thought, moving them faster and faster until at last she rose in the air.

She was flying!

Others were flying now, hundreds of them; and, high above the treetops, the royal princesses found their mates as they wheeled and circled in a merry dance. The dance of the royal ants.

But of those who flew that day, few ever found their way back to their home. In this new freedom their wings had given them, most of them flew farther and farther away, letting the breeze carry them where it would.

The royal princess was one of these. She flew high and far. And when evening came she drifted slowly to the ground and found shelter under a blade of grass. The dance was over. Her wings had carried her far from the thicket and her own little mound of sand.

She was alone now. Alone in a strange new world.

"IF YOU TALK TO ANIMALS..."

I F YOU TALK to animals they will talk with you and you will know each other.

If you do not talk to them you will not know them and what you do not know you will fear.

What one fears one destroys.

THE TRAIN DOGS

OUT OF THE night and the north;
Savage of breed and of bone,
Shaggy and swift comes the yelping band,
Freighters of fur from the voiceless land
That sleeps in the Arctic zone.

Laden with skins from the north,
Beaver and bear and raccoon,
Marten and mink from the polar belts,
Otter and ermine and sable pelts—
The spoils of the hunter's moon.

Out of the night and the north,
Sinewy, fearless and fleet,
Urging the pack through the pathless snow,
The Indian driver, calling low,
Follows with moccasined feet.

Ships of the night and the north,
Freighters on prairies and plains,
Carrying cargoes from field and flood
They scent the trail through their wild red blood,
The wolfish blood in their veins.

THE FIRE-BIRD, THE HORSE OF POWER, AND THE PRINCESS VASILISSA

A Russian Fairytale

ONCE UPON A time a strong and powerful Tzar ruled in a country far away. And among his servants was a young archer, and this archer had a horse—a horse of power—such a horse as belonged to the wonderful men of long ago—a great horse with a broad chest, eyes like fire, and hoofs of iron. There are no such horses nowadays. They sleep with the strong men who rode them, the bogatirs, until the time comes when Russia has need of them. Then the great horses will thunder up from under the ground, and the valiant men leap from the graves in the armor they have worn so long. The strong men will sit on those horses of power, and there will be swinging of clubs and thunder of hoofs, and the earth will be swept clean from the enemies of God and the Tzar. So my grandfather used to say, and he was as much older than I as I am older than you, little ones, and so he should know.

Well, one day long ago, in the green time of the year, the young archer rode through the forest on his horse of power. The trees were green; there were little blue flowers on the ground under the trees; the squirrels ran in the branches, and the hares in the undergrowth; but no birds sang. The young archer rode along the forest path and listened for the singing of the birds, but there was no singing. The forest was silent, and the only noises in it were the scratching of four-footed beasts, the dropping of fir cones, and the heavy stamping of the horse of power in the soft path.

"What has come to the birds?" said the young archer.

He had scarcely said this before he saw a big curving feather lying in the path before him. The feather was larger than a swan's, larger than an eagle's. It lay in the path, glittering like a flame; for the sun was on it, and it was a feather of pure gold. Then he knew why there was no singing in the forest. For he knew that the fire-bird had flown that way, and that the feather in the path before him was a feather from its burning breast.

The horse of power spoke and said:

"Leave the golden feather where it lies. If you take it you will be sorry for it, and know the meaning of fear."

But the brave young archer sat on the horse of power and looked at the golden feather, and wondered whether to take it or not. He had no wish to learn what it was to be afraid, but he thought, "If I take it and bring it to the Tzar my master, he will be pleased; and he will not send me away with empty hands, for no tzar in the world has a feather from the burning breast of the fire-bird." And the more he thought, the more he wanted to carry the feather to the Tzar. And in the end he did not listen to the words of the horse of power. He leapt from the saddle, picked up the golden feather of the fire-bird, mounted his horse again, and galloped back through the green forest till he came to the palace of the Tzar.

He went into the palace, and bowed before the Tzar and said:

"O Tzar, I have brought you a feather of the fire-bird."

The Tzar looked gladly at the feather, and then at the young archer.

"Thank you," says he; "but if you have brought me a feather of the fire-bird, you will be able to bring me the bird itself. I should like to see it. A feather is not a fit gift to bring to the Tzar. Bring the bird itself, or, I swear by my sword, your head shall no longer sit between your shoulders."

The young archer bowed his head and went out. Bitterly he wept, for he knew now what it was to be afraid. He went out into the court-yard, where the horse of power was waiting for him, tossing its head and stamping on the ground.

"Master," says the horse of power, "why do you weep?"

"The Tzar has told me to bring him the fire-bird, and no man on earth can do that," says the young archer, and he bowed his head on his breast.

"I told you," says the horse of power, "that if you took the feather you would learn the meaning of fear. Well, do not be frightened yet, and do not weep. The trouble is not now; the trouble lies before you. Go to the Tzar and ask him to have a hundred sacks of maize scattered over the open field, and let this be done at midnight."

The young archer went back into the palace and begged the Tzar for this, and the Tzar ordered that at midnight a hundred sacks of maize should be scattered in the open field.

Next morning, at the first redness in the sky, the young archer rode out on the horse of power, and came to the open field. The ground was scattered all over with maize. In the middle of the field stood a great oak with spreading boughs. The young archer leapt to the ground, took off the saddle, and let the horse of power loose to wander as he pleased about the field. Then he climbed up into the oak and hid him-self among the green boughs.

The sky grew red and gold, and the sun rose. Suddenly there was a noise in the forest round the field. The trees shook and swayed, and almost fell. There was a mighty wind. The sea piled itself into waves with crests of foam, and the fire-bird came flying from the other side of the world. Huge and golden and flaming in the sun, it flew, dropped down with open wings into the field, and began to eat the maize.

The horse of power wandered in the field. This way he went, and that, but always he came a little nearer to the fire-bird. Nearer and nearer came the horse. He came close up to the fire-bird, and then suddenly stepped on one of its spreading fiery wings and pressed it heavily to the ground. The bird struggled, flapping mightily with its fiery wings, but it could not get away. The young archer slipped down from the tree, bound the fire-bird with three strong ropes, swung it on his back, saddled the horse, and rode to the palace of the Tzar.

The young archer stood before the Tzar, and his back was bent under the great weight of the fire-bird, and the broad wings of the bird hung on either side of him like fiery shields, and there was a trail of golden feathers on the floor. The young archer swung the magic bird to the foot of the throne before the Tzar; and the Tzar was glad, because since the beginning of the world no Tzar had seen the fire-bird flung before him like a wild duck caught in a snare.

The Tzar looked at the fire-bird and laughed with pride. Then he lifted his eyes and looked at the young archer, and says he:

"As you have known how to take the fire-bird, you will know how to bring me my bride, for whom I have long been waiting. In the land of Never, on the very edge of the world, where the red sun rises in flame from behind the sea, lives the Princess Vasilissa. I will marry none but her. Bring her to me, and I will reward you with silver and gold. But if you do not bring her, then, by my sword, your head will no longer sit between your shoulders!"

The young archer wept bitter tears, and went out into the courtyard where the horse of power was stamping the ground with its hoofs of iron and tossing its thick mane.

"Master, why do you weep?" asked the horse of power.

"The Tzar has ordered me to go to the land of Never, and to bring back the Princess Vasilissa."

"Do not weep—do not grieve. The trouble is not yet; the trouble is to come. Go to the Tzar and ask him for a silver tent with a golden roof, and for all kinds of food and drink to take with us on the journey."

The young archer went in and asked the Tzar for this, and the Tzar gave him a silver tent with silver hangings and a gold-embroidered roof, and every kind of rich wine and the tastiest of foods.

Then the young archer mounted the horse of power and rode off to the land of Never. On and on he rode, many days and nights, and came at last to the edge of the world, where the red sun rises in flame from behind the deep blue sea.

On the shore of the sea the young archer reined in the horse of power, and the heavy hoofs of the horse sank in the sand. He shaded his eyes and looked out over the blue water, and there was the Princess Vasilissa in a little silver boat, rowing with golden oars.

The young archer rode back a little way to where the sand ended and the green world began. There he loosed the horse to wander where he pleased, and to feed on the green grass. Then on the edge of the shore, where the green grass ended and grew thin and the sand began, he set up the shining tent, with its silver hangings and its gold-embroidered roof. In the tent he set out the tasty dishes and the rich flagons of wine which the Tzar had given him, and he sat himself down in the tent and began to regale himself, while he waited for the Princess Vasilissa.

The Princess Vasilissa dipped her golden oars in the blue water, and the little silver boat moved lightly through the dancing waves. She sat in the little boat and looked over the blue sea to the edge of the world, and there, between the golden sand and the green earth, she saw the tent standing, silver and gold in the sun. She dipped her oars, and came nearer to see it better. The nearer she came the fairer seemed the tent,

and at last she rowed to the shore and grounded her little boat on the golden sand, and stepped out daintily and came up to the tent. She was a little frightened, and now and again she stopped and looked back to where the silver boat lay on the sand with the blue sea beyond it. The young archer said not a word, but went on regaling himself on the pleasant dishes he had set out there in the tent.

At last the Princess Vasilissa came up to the tent and looked in.

The young archer rose and bowed before her. Says he:

"Good day to you, Princess! Be so kind as to come in and take bread and salt with me, and taste my foreign wines."

And the Princess Vasilissa came into the tent and sat down with the young archer, and ate sweetmeats with him, and drank his health in a golden goblet of the wine the Tzar had given him. Now this wine was heavy, and the last drop from the goblet had no sooner trickled down her little slender throat than her eyes closed against her will, once, twice, and again.

"Ah me!" says the Princess, "it is as if the night itself had perched on my eyelids, and yet it is but noon."

And the golden goblet dropped to the ground from her little fingers, and she leant back on a cushion and fell instantly asleep. If she had been beautiful before, she was lovelier still when she lay in that deep sleep in the shadow of the tent.

Quickly the young archer called to the horse of power. Lightly he lifted the Princess in his strong young arms. Swiftly he leapt with her into the saddle. Like a feather she lay in the hollow of his left arm, and slept while the iron hoofs of the great horse thundered over the ground.

They came to the Tzar's palace, and the young archer leapt from the horse of power and carried the Princess into the palace. Great was the joy of the Tzar; but it did not last for long.

"Go, sound the trumpets for our wedding," he said to his servants, "let all the bells be rung."

The bells rang out and the trumpets sounded, and at the noise of the horns and the ringing of the bells the Princess Vasilissa woke up and looked about her.

"What is this ringing of bells," says she, "and this noise of trumpets? And where, oh, where is the blue sea, and my little silver boat with its golden oars?" And the Princess put her hand to her eyes.

"The blue sea is far away," says the Tzar, "and for your little silver boat I give you a golden throne. The trumpets sound for our wedding, and the bells are ringing for our joy."

But the Princess turned her face away from the Tzar; and there was no wonder in that, for he was old, and his eyes were not kind.

And she looked with love at the young archer; and there was no wonder in that either, for he was a young man fit to ride the horse of power.

The Tzar was angry with the Princess Vasilissa, but his anger was as useless as his joy.

"Why, Princess," says he, "will you not marry me, and forget your blue sea and your silver boat?"

"In the middle of the deep blue sea lies a great stone," says the Princess, "and under that stone is hidden my wedding-dress. If I cannot wear that dress I will marry nobody at all."

Instantly the Tzar turned to the young archer, who was waiting before the throne.

"Ride swiftly back," says he, "to the land of Never, where the red sun rises in flame. There—do you hear what the Princess says?—a great stone lies in the middle of the sea. Under that stone is hidden her wedding-dress. Ride swiftly. Bring back that dress, or, by my sword, your head shall no longer sit between your shoulders!"

The young archer wept bitter tears, and went out into the court-yard, where the horse of power was waiting for him, champing its golden bit.

"There is no way of escaping death this time," he said.

"Master, why do you weep?" asked the horse of power.

"The Tzar has ordered me to ride to the land of Never, to fetch the wedding-dress of the Princess Vasilissa from the bottom of the deep blue sea. Besides, the dress is wanted for the Tzar's wedding, and I love the Princess myself."

"What did I tell you?" says the horse of power. "I told you that there would be trouble if you picked up the golden feather from the fire-bird's burning breast. Well, do not be afraid. The trouble is not yet; the trouble is to come. Up! Into the saddle with you, and away for the wedding-dress of the Princess Vasilissa!"

The young archer leapt into the saddle, and the horse of power, with his thundering hoofs, carried him swiftly through the green forests and over the bare plains, till they came to the edge of the world, to the land of Never, where the red sun rises in flame from behind the deep blue sea. There they rested, at the very edge of the sea.

The young archer looked sadly over the wide waters, but the horse of power tossed its mane and did not look at the sea, but on the shore. This way and that it looked, and saw at last a huge lobster moving slowly, sideways, along the golden sand.

Nearer and nearer came the lobster, and it was a giant among lobsters, the tzar of all the lobsters; and it moved slowly along the shore, while the horse of power moved carefully and as if by accident, until it stood between the lobster and the sea. Then when the lobster came close by, the horse of power lifted an iron hoof and set it firmly on the lobster's tail.

"You will be the death of me!" screamed the lobster—as well he might, with the heavy foot of the horse of power pressing his tail into the sand. "Let me live, and I will do whatever you ask of me."

"Very well," says the horse of power, "we will let you live," and he slowly lifted his foot. "But this is what you shall do for us. In the middle of the blue sea lies a great stone, and under that stone is hidden the wedding-dress of the Princess Vasilissa. Bring it here."

The lobster groaned with the pain in his tail. Then he cried out in a voice that could be heard all over the deep blue sea. And the sea was disturbed, and from all sides lobsters in thousands made their way towards the bank. And the huge lobster that was the oldest of them all, and the tzar of all the lobsters that live between the rising and the setting of the sun, gave them the order and sent them back into the sea. And the young archer sat on the horse of power and waited.

After a little time the sea was disturbed again, and the lobsters in their thousands came to the shore, and with them they brought a golden casket in which was the wedding-dress of the Princess Vasilissa. They had taken it from under the great stone that lay in the middle of the sea.

The tzar of all the lobsters raised himself painfully on his bruised tail and gave the casket into the hands of the young archer, and instantly the horse of power turned himself about and galloped back to the palace of the Tzar, far, far away, at the other side of the green forests and beyond the treeless plains.

The young archer went into the palace and gave the casket into the hands of the Princess, and looked at her with sadness in his eyes, and she looked at him with love. Then she went away into an inner chamber, and came back in her wedding-dress, fairer than the spring itself. Great was the joy of the Tzar. The wedding feast was made ready, and the bells rang, and flags waved above the palace.

The Tzar held out his hand to the Princess, and looked at her with his old eyes. But she would not take his hand.

"No," says she, "I will marry nobody until the man who brought me here has done penance in boiling water."

Instantly the Tzar turned to his servants and ordered them to make a great fire, and to fill a great cauldron with water and set it on the fire, and, when the water should be at its hottest, to take the young archer and throw him into it, to do penance for having taken the Princess Vasilissa away from the land of Never.

There was no gratitude in the mind of that Tzar.

Swiftly the servants brought wood and made a mighty fire, and on it they laid a huge cauldron of water, and built the fire round the walls of the cauldron. The fire burned hot and the water steamed. The fire burned hotter, and the water bubbled and seethed. They made ready to take the young archer, to throw him into the cauldron.

"Oh, misery!" thought the young archer. "Why did I ever take the golden feather that had fallen from the fire-bird's burning breast? Why did I not listen to the wise words of the horse of power?" And he remembered the horse of power, and he begged the Tzar:

"O lord Tzar, I do not complain. I shall presently die in the heat of the water on the fire. Suffer me, before I die, once more to see my horse."

"Let him see his horse," says the Princess.

"Very well," says the Tzar. "Say goodbye to your horse, for you will not ride him again. But let your farewells be short, for we are waiting."

The young archer crossed the courtyard and came to the horse of power, who was scraping the ground with his iron hoofs.

"Farewell, my horse of power," says the young archer. "I should have listened to your words of wisdom, for now the end is come, and we shall never more see the green trees pass above us and the ground disappear beneath us, as we race the wind between the earth and the sky."

"Why so?" says the horse of power.

"The Tzar has ordered that I am to be boiled to death—thrown into that cauldron that is seething on the great fire."

"Fear not," says the horse of power, "for the Princess Vasilissa has made him do this, and the end of these things is better than I thought. Go back, and when they are ready to throw you in the cauldron, do you run boldly and leap yourself into the boiling water."

The young archer went back across the courtyard, and the servants made ready to throw him into the cauldron.

"Are you sure that the water is boiling?" says the Princess Vasilissa.

"It bubbles and seethes," said the servants.

"Let me see for myself," says the Princess, and she went to the fire and waved her hand above the cauldron. And some say there was something in her hand, and some say there was not.

"It is boiling," says she, and the servants laid hands on the young archer; but he threw them from him, and ran and leapt boldly before them all into the very middle of the cauldron.

Twice he sank below the surface, borne round with the bubbles and foam of the boiling water. Then he leapt from the cauldron and stood before the Tzar and the Princess. He had become so beautiful a youth that all who saw cried aloud in wonder.

"This is a miracle," says the Tzar. And the Tzar looked at the beautiful young archer, and thought of himself—of his age, of his bent back, and his gray beard, and his toothless gums. "I too will become beautiful," thinks he, and he rose from his throne and clambered into the cauldron, and was boiled to death in a moment.

And the end of the story? They buried the Tzar, and made the young archer Tzar in his place. He married the Princess Vasilissa, and lived many years with her in love and good fellowship. And he built a golden stable for the horse of power, and never forgot what he owed to him.

YOUNG BLACK BEAUTY

When Black Beauty *was first published, over a hundred years ago, it carried a subtitle—*The Autobiography of a Horse. *The book was written by Anna Sewell as a protest against what she saw as Victorian England's cruelty to horses, but* Black Beauty *is really a moving and timeless story. In the first three chapters, which are printed below,* Black Beauty *introduces himself.*

My Early Home

THE FIRST PLACE that I can well remember was a large pleasant meadow with a pond of clear water in it. Some shady trees leaned over it, and rushes and water lilies grew at the deep end. Over the hedge on one side we looked into a plowed field, and on the other we looked over a gate at our master's house, which stood by the roadside. At the top of the meadow was a plantation of fir trees, and at the bottom there was a swiftly running brook overhung by a steep bank.

While I was young I lived upon my mother's milk, as I could not eat grass. In the daytime I ran by her side, and at night I lay down close by her. When it was hot, we used to stand by the pond in the shade of the trees, and when it was cold, we had a nice warm shed near the plantation.

As soon as I was old enough to eat grass, my mother went out to work in the daytime and came back in the evening.

There were six young colts in the meadow besides me. They were older than I was; some were nearly as large as grown-up horses. I ran with them and had great fun. We used to gallop all together round and round the field, as hard as we could go. Sometimes we had rather rough play, for the older colts would frequently bite and kick as well as gallop.

One day when there was a good deal of kicking, my mother whinnied to me to come to her, and then she said, "I wish you to pay attention to what I am going to say to you. The colts who live here are very good colts, but they are cart-horse colts, and, of course, they have not learned manners. You have been well bred and well born. Your father has a great name in these parts, and your grandfather won the cup two years at the Newmarket races; your grandmother had the sweetest temper of any horse I ever knew, and I think you have never seen me kick or bite. I hope you will grow up gentle and good, and never learn bad ways. Do your work with a will, lift your feet up well when you trot, and never bite or kick even in play."

I have never forgotten my mother's advice. I knew she was a wise old horse, and our master thought a great deal of her. Her name was Duchess, but many is the time he called her Pet.

Our master was a good, kind man. He gave us good food, good lodging, and kind words. He spoke as kindly to us as he did to his little children. We were all fond of him, and my mother loved him very much. When she saw him at the gate, she would neigh with joy and trot up to him. He would pat and stroke her and say, "Well, old Pet, and how is your little Darkie?" I was a dull black, so he called me Darkie. Then he would give me a piece of bread, which was very good, and sometimes he brought a carrot for my mother. All the horses would come to him, but I think we were his favorites. My mother always took him to town on a market day in a light gig.

There was a plowboy, Dick, who sometimes came into our field to pluck blackberries from the hedge. When he had eaten all he wanted, he would have what he called fun with the colts, throwing stones and sticks at them to make them gallop. We did not much mind him, for we could gallop off. But sometimes a stone would hit and hurt us.

One day he was at this game and did not know that the master was in the next field. But he was there, watching what was going on. Over the hedge he jumped in a snap, and, catching Dick by the arm, he gave him such a box on the ears as made him roar with pain and surprise. As soon as we saw the master, we trotted up nearer so that we could see what went on.

"Bad boy!" he said. "Bad boy to chase the colts. This is not the first time nor the second, but it shall be the last! There! Take your money and go home. I shall not want you on my farm again."

So we never saw Dick any more. Old Daniel, the man who looked after the horses, was just as gentle as our master, so we were well off.

The Hunt

I was two years old when a circumstance happened which I have not forgotten. It was early in the spring. There had been a little frost in the night, and a light mist still hung over the plantations and meadows. The other colts and I were feeding at the lower part of the field when we heard, in the distance, what sounded like the cry of dogs. The oldest of the colts raised his head, pricked his ears, and said, "There are the hounds!" He immediately cantered off, followed by the rest of us, to the upper part of the field where we could look over the hedge and see several fields beyond. My mother and an old riding horse of our master's were also standing near and seemed to know all about it.

"They have found a hare," said my mother. "If they come this way, we shall see the hunt."

And soon the dogs were all tearing down the field of young wheat next to ours. I never heard such a noise as they made. They did not bark, nor howl, nor whine, but kept up a "Yo! Yo-o-o! Yo! Yo-o-o!" at the top of their voices. After them came a number of men on horseback, some of them in green coats, all galloping as fast as they could. The old horse snorted and looked eagerly after them, and we young colts wanted to be galloping after them, but they were soon away into the fields lower down. Here it seemed as if they had come to a stand. The dogs left off barking, and ran about every way with their noses to the ground.

"They have lost the scent," said the old horse. "Perhaps the hare will get off."

"What hare?" I said.

"Oh! I don't know *what* hare. Likely enough it may be one of our own hares out of the plantation. Any hare they can find will do for the dogs and men to run after."

Before long the dogs began their "Yo! Yo-o-o!" again. And back they came all together at full speed, making straight for our meadow at the part where the high bank and hedge overhang the brook.

"Now we shall see the hare," said my mother. And just then a hare, wild with fright, rushed by.

On came the dogs! They burst over the bank, leaped the stream, and came dashing across the field, followed by the huntsmen. Six or eight men leaped their horses over, close upon the dogs. The hare tried to get through the fence. It was too thick, and she turned sharp round to make for the road. But it was too late. The dogs were upon her with their wild cries. We heard one shriek, and that was the end of the hare.

One of the huntsmen rode up and whipped off the dogs, who would soon have torn her to pieces. He held her up by the leg, torn and bleeding, and all the gentlemen seemed well pleased.

As for me, I was so astonished that I did not at first see what was going on by the brook. But when I did look, there was a sad sight. Two fine horses were down; one was struggling in the stream, and the other was groaning on the grass. One of the riders was getting out of the water covered with mud. The other lay quite still.

"His neck is broken," said my mother.

"And serves him right, too," said one of the colts.

I thought the same, but my mother did not join with us.

"Well, no," she said. "You must not say that. But though I am an old horse, and have seen and heard a great deal, I never yet could make out why men are so fond of this sport. They often hurt themselves, often spoil good horses and tear up the fields, and all for a hare or a fox or a stag that they could get more easily some other way. But we are only horses and don't know."

While my mother was saying this, we stood and looked on. Many of the riders had gone to the young man. But my master, who had been watching what was going on, was the first to raise him. His head fell back and his arms hung down, and everyone looked very serious. There was no noise now. Even the dogs were quiet and seemed to know that something was wrong. They carried him to our master's house. I heard afterward that it was young George Gordon, the squire's only son, a fine, tall young man, and the pride of his family.

There was now riding off in all directions to the doctor's, to the farrier's, and no doubt to Squire Gordon's, to let him know about his son. When Mr. Bond, the farrier, came to look at the black horse that lay groaning on the grass, he felt him all over and shook his head; one of his legs was broken. Then someone ran to our master's house and came back with a gun. Presently there was a loud bang and a dreadful shriek, and then all was still. The black horse moved no more.

My mother seemed much troubled. She said she had known that horse for years, and that his name was Rob Roy. He was a good, bold horse, and there was no vice in him. She never would go to that part of the field afterward.

Not many days after, we heard the church bell tolling for a long time. Looking over the gate, we saw a long, strange black coach that was covered with black cloth and was drawn by black horses. After that came another and another and another, and all were black, while the bell kept tolling, tolling. They were carrying young Gordon to the churchyard to bury him. He would never ride again.

What they did with Rob Roy I never knew. But 'twas all for one little hare.

My Breaking In

I was now beginning to grow handsome; my coat had grown fine and soft, and was bright black. I had one white foot and a pretty white star on my forehead. I was thought very handsome.

My master would not sell me till I was four years old. He said lads ought not to work like men, and colts ought not to work like horses till they were quite grown up.

When I was four years old, Squire Gordon came to look at me. He examined my eyes, my mouth, and my legs. He felt them all down, and then I had to walk and trot and gallop before him. He seemed to like me and said, "When he has been well broken in, he will do very well."

My master said he would break me in himself, as he should not like me to be frightened or hurt.

He lost no time about it, for the next day he began.

Everyone may not know what breaking in is; therefore I will describe it. It means to teach a horse to wear a saddle and bridle and to carry on his back a man, woman, or child; to go just the way his rider wishes, and to go quietly. Besides this, he has to learn to wear a collar, a crupper, and a breeching, and to stand still while they are put on; then to have a cart or a chaise fixed behind him, so that he cannot walk or trot without dragging it after him. And he must go fast or slow, as his driver wishes. He must never start at what he sees, nor speak to other horses, nor bite, nor kick, nor have any will of his own; but always do his master's will, even though he may be very tired or hungry. But the worst of all is, when his harness is once on, he may neither jump for joy nor lie down for weariness. So you see this breaking in is a great thing.

I had, of course, long been used to a halter and a headstall, and to being led about in the field and lanes quietly. But now I was to have a bit and a bridle. My master gave me some oats as usual, and after a good deal of coaxing he got the bit into my mouth and the bridle fixed.

But it was a nasty thing! Those who have never had a bit in their mouths cannot think how bad it feels. A great piece of cold hard steel as thick as a man's finger is pushed into one's mouth, between one's teeth, and over one's tongue! Its ends come out at the corner of your mouth and are held fast there by straps over your head, under your throat, round your nose, and under your chin, so that in no way in the world can you get rid of the nasty hard thing. It is very bad! Yes, very bad!

At least I thought so; but I knew my mother always wore one when she went out, and all horses did when they were grown up. So, what with the nice oats, and what with my master's pats, kind words, and gentle ways, I learned to wear my bit and bridle.

Next came the saddle, but that was not half so bad. My master put it on my back very gently, while old Daniel held my head. He then

made the girths fast under my body, patting and talking to me all the time. Then I had a few oats, then a little leading about. This he did every day, till I began to look for the oats and the saddle.

At length, one morning my master got on my back and rode me round the meadow on the soft grass. It certainly did feel queer. But I must say I felt rather proud to carry my master, and as he continued to ride me a little every day, I soon became accustomed to it.

The next unpleasant business was putting on the iron shoes; that, too, was very hard at first. My master went with me to the smith's forge, to see that I was not hurt or got any fright. The blacksmith took my feet in his hand, one after the other, and cut away some of the hoof. It did not pain me, so I stood still on three legs till he had done them all. Then he took a piece of iron the shape of my foot, and clapped it on, and drove some nails through the shoe quite into my hoof, so that the shoe was firmly on. My feet felt very stiff and heavy, but in time I got used to it.

And now, having got so far, my master went on to break me to harness; there were more new things to wear. First, a stiff, heavy collar just on my neck, and a bridle with great sidepieces against my eyes, called blinkers. And blinkers they were, for I could not see on either side, but only straight in front of me. Next there was a small saddle with a nasty stiff strap that went right under my tail. That was the crupper. I hated the crupper—to have my long tail doubled up and poked through a strap was almost as bad as the bit. I never felt more like kicking, but of course I could not kick such a good master.

So in time I got used to everything and could do my work as well as my mother.

I must not forget to mention one part of my training, which I have always considered a very great advantage. My master sent me for a fortnight to a neighboring farmer's, who had a meadow which was skirted on one side by the railway. Here were some sheep and cows, and I was turned in among them.

I shall never forget the first train that ran by. I was feeding quietly near the pales which separated the meadow from the railway, when I heard a strange sound at a distance. Before I knew whence it came—with a rush and a clatter and a puffing out of smoke—a long black train of something flew up and was gone, almost before I could draw my breath. I turned and galloped to the farther side of the meadow as fast as I could go, and there I stood snorting with astonishment and fear. In the course of the day many other trains went by, some more slowly. These drew up at the station close by and sometimes made an awful shriek and groan before they stopped. I thought it very dreadful, but the cows went on eating very quietly and hardly raised their heads as the black frightful thing came puffing and grinding past.

For the first few days I could not feed in peace; but as I found that this terrible creature never came into the field or did me any harm, I began to disregard it. Very soon I cared as little about a train passing as the cows and sheep did.

Since then I have seen many horses much alarmed and restive at the sight or sound of a steam engine. But thanks to my good master's care, I am as fearless at railway stations as in my own stable.

Now, if anyone wants to break in a young horse well, that is the way.

My master often drove me in double harness with my mother, because she was steady and could teach me how to go better than a strange horse. She told me the better I behaved, the better I should be treated, and that it was wisest to do my best to please my master.

"But," said she, "there are a great many kinds of men. There are good, thoughtful men like our master, that any horse may be proud to serve; but there are bad, cruel men, who never ought to have a horse or dog to call their own. Besides, there are a great many foolish men, vain, ignorant, and careless, who never trouble themselves to think. These spoil more horses than all, just for want of sense. They don't mean it, but they do it for all that. I hope you will fall into good hands; but a horse never knows who may buy him or who may drive him. It is all chance for us.

"But still I say, do your best wherever it is and keep up your good name."

THE CAT
WHO BECAME
HEAD-FORESTER

A Russian Fairytale

IF YOU DROP Vladimir by mistake, you know he always falls on his feet. And if Vladimir tumbles off the roof of the hut, he always falls on his feet. Cats always fall on their feet, on their four paws, and never hurt themselves. And as in tumbling, so it is in life. No cat is ever unfortunate for very long. The worse things look for a cat, the better they are going to be.

Well, once upon a time, not so very long ago, an old peasant had a cat and did not like him. He was a tom-cat, always fighting; and he had lost one ear, and was not very pretty to look at. The peasant thought he would get rid of his old cat, and buy a new one from a neighbor. He did not care what became of the old tom-cat with one ear, so long as he never saw him again. It was no use thinking of killing him, for it is a life's work to kill a cat, and it's likely enough that the cat would come alive at the end.

So the old peasant he took a sack, and he bundled the tom-cat into the sack, and he sewed up the sack and slung it over his back, and walked off into the forest. Off he went, trudging along in the summer sunshine, deep into the forest. And when he had gone very many versts into the forest, he took the sack with the cat in it and threw it away among the trees.

"You stay there," says he, "and if you do get out in this desolate place, much good may it do you, old quarrelsome bundle of bones and fur!"

And with that he turned round and trudged home again, and bought a nice-looking, quiet cat from a neighbor in exchange for a little tobacco, and settled down comfortably at home with the new cat in front of the stove; and there he may be to this day, so far as I know. My story does not bother with him, but only with the old tom-cat tied up in the sack away there out in the forest.

The bag flew through the air, and plumped down through a bush to the ground. And the old tom-cat landed on his feet inside it, very much frightened but not hurt. Thinks he, this bag, this flight through the air, this bump, mean that my life is going to change. Very well; there is nothing like something new now and again.

And presently he began tearing at the bag with his sharp claws. Soon there was a hole he could put a paw through. He went on, tearing and scratching, and there was a hole he could put two paws through. He went on with his work, and soon he could put his head through, all the easier because he had only one ear. A minute or two after that he had wriggled out of the bag, and stood up on his four paws and stretched himself in the forest.

"The world seems to be larger than the village," he said. "I will walk on and see what there is in it."

He washed himself all over, curled his tail proudly up in the air, cocked the only ear he had left, and set off walking under the forest trees.

"I was the head-cat in the village," says he to himself. "If all goes well, I shall be head here too." And he walked along as if he were the Tzar himself.

Well, he walked on and on, and he came to an old hut that had belonged to a forester. There was nobody there, nor had been for many years, and the old tom-cat made himself quite at home. He climbed up into the loft under the roof, and found a little rotten hay.

"A very good bed," says he, and curls up and falls asleep.

When he woke he felt hungry, so he climbed down and went off in the forest to catch little birds and mice. There were plenty of them in the forest, and when he had eaten enough he came back to the hut, climbed into the loft, and spent the night there very comfortably.

You would have thought he would be content. Not he. He was a cat. He said, "This is a good enough lodging. But I have to catch all my own food. In the village they fed me every day, and I only caught mice for fun. I ought to be able to live like that here. A person of my dignity ought not to have to do all the work for himself."

Next day he went walking in the forest. And as he was walking he met a fox, a vixen, a very pretty young thing, gay and giddy like all girls. And the fox saw the cat, and was very much astonished.

"All these years," she said—for though she was young she thought she had lived a long time—"all these years," she said, "I've lived in the forest, but I've never seen a wild beast like that before. What a strange-looking animal! And with only one ear. How handsome!"

And she came up and made her bows to the cat, and said:

"Tell me, great lord, who you are. What fortunate chance has brought you to this forest? And by what name am I to call your Excellency?"

Oh! the fox was very polite. It is not every day that you meet a handsome stranger walking in the forest.

The cat arched his back, and set all his fur on end, and said, very slowly and quietly:

"I have been sent from the far forests of Siberia to be Head-forester over you. And my name is Cat Ivanovitch."

"O Cat Ivanovitch!" says the pretty young fox, and she makes more bows. "I did not know. I beg your Excellency's pardon. Will your Excellency honor my humble house by visiting it as a guest?"

"I will," says the cat. "And what do they call you?"

"My name, your Excellency, is Lisabeta Ivanova."

"I will come with you, Lisabeta," says the cat.

And they went together to the fox's earth. Very snug, very neat it was inside; and the cat curled himself up in the best place, while Lisabeta Ivanova, the pretty young fox, made ready a tasty dish of game. And while she was making the meal ready, and dusting the furniture with her tail, she looked at the cat. At last she said, shyly:

"Tell me, Cat Ivanovitch, are you married or single?"

"Single," says the cat.

"And I too am unmarried," says the pretty young fox, and goes busily on with her dusting and cooking.

Presently she looks at the cat again.

"What if we were to marry, Cat Ivanovitch? I would try to be a good wife to you."

"Very well, Lisabeta," says the cat; "I will marry you."

The fox went to her store and took out all the dainties that she had, and made a wedding feast to celebrate her marriage to the great Cat Ivanovitch, who had only one ear, and had come from the far Siberian forests to be Head-forester.

They ate up everything there was in the place.

Next morning the pretty young fox went off busily into the forest to get food for her grand husband. But the old tom-cat stayed at home, and cleaned his whiskers and slept. He was a lazy one, was that cat, and proud.

The fox was running through the forest, looking for game, when she met an old friend, the handsome young wolf, and he began making polite speeches to her.

"What had become of you, gossip?" says he. "I've been to all the best earths and not found you at all."

"Let be, fool," says the fox very shortly. "Don't talk to me like that. What are you jesting about? Formerly I was a young, unmarried fox; now I am a wedded wife."

"Whom have you married, Lisabeta Ivanova?"

"What!" says the fox, "you have not heard that the great Cat Ivanovitch, who has only one ear, has been sent from the far Siberian forests to be Head-forester over all of us? Well, I am now the Head-forester's wife."

"No, I had not heard, Lisabeta Ivanova. And when can I pay my respects to his Excellency?"

"Not now, not now," says the fox. "Cat Ivanovitch will be raging angry with me if I let anyone come near him. Presently he will be taking his food. Look you. Get a sheep, and make it ready, and bring it as a greeting to him, to show him that he is welcome and that you know how to treat him with respect. Leave the sheep nearby, and hide yourself so that he shall not see you; for, if he did, things might be awkward."

"Thank you, thank you, Lisabeta Ivanova," says the wolf, and off he goes to look for a sheep.

The pretty young fox went idly on, taking the air, for she knew that the wolf would save her the trouble of looking for food.

Presently she met the bear.

"Good day to you, Lisabeta Ivanova," says the bear; "as pretty as ever, I see you are."

"Bandy-legged one," says the fox; "fool, don't come worrying me. Formerly I was a young, unmarried fox; now I am a wedded wife."

"I beg your pardon," says the bear, "whom have you married, Lisabeta Ivanova?"

"The great Cat Ivanovitch has been sent from the far Siberian forests to be Head-forester over us all. And Cat Ivanovitch is now my husband," says the fox.

"Is it forbidden to have a look at his Excellency?"

"It is forbidden," says the fox. "Cat Ivanovitch will be raging angry with me if I let anyone come near him. Presently he will be taking his food. Get along with you quickly; make ready an ox, and bring it by way of welcome to him. The wolf is bringing a sheep. And look you. Leave the ox nearby, and hide yourself so that the great Cat Ivanovitch shall not see you; or else, brother, things may be awkward."

The bear shambled off as fast as he could go to get an ox.

The pretty young fox, enjoying the fresh air of the forests, went slowly home to her earth, and crept in very quietly, so as not to awake the great Head-forester, Cat Ivanovitch, who had only one ear and was sleeping in the best place.

Presently the wolf came through the forest, dragging a sheep he had killed. He did not dare to go too near the fox's earth, because of

Cat Ivanovitch, the new Head-forester. So he stopped, well out of sight, and stripped off the skin of the sheep, and arranged the sheep so as to seem a nice tasty morsel. Then he stood still, thinking what to do next. He heard a noise, and looked up. There was the bear, struggling along with a dead ox.

"Good day, brother Michael Ivanovitch," says the wolf.

"Good day, brother Levon Ivanovitch," says the bear. "Have you seen the fox, Lisabeta Ivanova, with her husband, the Head-forester?"

"No, brother," says the wolf. "For a long time I have been waiting to see them."

"Go on and call out to them," says the bear.

"No, Michael Ivanovitch," says the wolf, "I will not go. Do you go; you are bigger and bolder than I."

"No, no, Levon Ivanovitch, I will not go. There is no use in risking one's life without need."

Suddenly, as they were talking, a little hare came running by. The bear saw him first, and roared out:

"Hi, Squinteye! trot along here."

The hare came up, slowly, two steps at a time, trembling with fright.

"Now then, you squinting rascal," says the bear, "do you know where the fox lives, over there?"

"I know, Michael Ivanovitch."

"Get along there quickly, and tell her that Michael Ivanovitch the bear and his brother Levon Ivanovitch the wolf have been ready for a long time, and have brought presents of a sheep and an ox, as greetings to his Excellency. . . ."

"His Excellency, mind," says the wolf, "don't forget."

The hare ran off as hard as he could go, glad to have escaped so easily. Meanwhile the wolf and the bear looked about for good places in which to hide.

"It will be best to climb trees," says the bear. "I shall go up to the top of this fir."

"But what am I to do?" says the wolf. "I can't climb a tree for the life of me. Brother Michael, Brother Michael, hide me somewhere or other before you climb up. I beg you, hide me, or I shall certainly be killed."

"Crouch down under these bushes," says the bear, "and I will cover you with the dead leaves."

"May you be rewarded," says the wolf, and he crouched down under the bushes, and the bear covered him up with dead leaves, so that only the tip of his nose could be seen.

Then the bear climbed slowly up into the fir tree, into the very top, and looked out to see if the fox and Cat Ivanovitch were coming.

They were coming; oh yes, they were coming! The hare ran up and knocked on the door, and said to the fox:

"Michael Ivanovitch the bear and his brother Levon Ivanovitch the wolf have been ready for a long time, and have brought presents of a sheep and an ox as greetings to his Excellency."

"Get along, Squinteye," says the fox; "we are just coming."

And so the fox and the cat set out together.

The bear, up in the top of the tree, saw them, and called down to the wolf:

"They are coming, Brother Levon; they are coming, the fox and her husband. But what a little one he is, to be sure!"

"Quiet, quiet," whispers the wolf. "He'll hear you, and then we are done for."

The cat came up, and arched his back and set all his furs on end, and threw himself on the ox, and began tearing the meat with his teeth and claws. And as he tore he purred. And the bear listened, and heard the purring of the cat, and it seemed to him that the cat was angrily muttering, "Small, small, small . . ."

And the bear whispers: "He's no giant, but what a glutton! Why, we couldn't get through a quarter of that, and he finds it not enough. Heaven help us if he comes after us!"

The wolf tried to see, but could not, because his head, all but his nose, was covered with the dry leaves. Little by little he moved his head, so as to clear the leaves away from in front of his eyes. Try as he would to be quiet, the leaves rustled, so little, ever so little, but enough to be heard by the one ear of the cat.

The cat stopped tearing the meat and listened.

"I haven't caught a mouse today," he thought.

Once more the leaves rustled.

The cat leapt through the air and dropped with all four paws, and his claws out, on the nose of the wolf. How the wolf yelped! The leaves flew like dust, and the wolf leapt up and ran off as fast as his legs could carry him.

Well, the wolf was frightened, I can tell you, but he was not so frightened as the cat.

When the great wolf leapt up out of the leaves, the cat screamed and ran up the nearest tree, and that was the tree where Michael Ivanovitch the bear was hiding in the topmost branches.

"Oh, he has seen me. Cat Ivanovitch has seen me," thought the bear. He had no time to climb down, and the cat was coming up in long leaps.

The bear trusted to Providence, and jumped from the top of the tree. Many were the branches he broke as he fell; many were the bones he broke when he crashed to the ground. He picked himself up and stumbled off, groaning.

The pretty young fox sat still, and cried out, "Run, run, Brother Levon! . . . Quicker on your pins, Brother Michael! His Excellency is behind you; his Excellency is close behind!"

Ever since then all the wild beasts have been afraid of the cat, and the cat and the fox live merrily together, and eat fresh meat all the year round, which the other animals kill for them and leave a little way off.

And that is what happened to the old tom-cat with one ear, who was sewn up in a bag and thrown away in the forest.

"Just think what would happen to our handsome Vladimir if we were to throw him away!" said Vanya.

THE DOG AND HIS SHADOW

A DOG, CARRYING A piece of meat in his mouth, was crossing a stream on a narrow footbridge. He happened to look into the water and there he saw his shadow, but he thought it another dog with a piece of meat larger than his. He made a grab for the other dog's meat; but in doing so, of course, he dropped his own, and therefore was without any.

Greediness may cause one to lose everything.

THE GOOSE WITH THE GOLDEN EGGS

ONCE UPON A time a man had a goose that laid a golden egg every day. Although he was gradually becoming rich, he grew impatient. He wanted to get all his treasure at once; therefore he killed the Goose. Cutting her open, he found her—just like any other goose. He learned to his sorrow:

It takes time to win success.

CHARLES G. D. ROBERTS

IN THE DEEP
OF THE GRASS

MISTY GRAY GREEN, washed with tints of the palest violet, spotted with red clover-blooms, white oxeyes, and hot orange Canada lilies, the deep-grassed levels basked under the July sun. A drowsy hum of bees and flies seemed to distill, with warm aromatic scents, from the sun-steeped blooms and grass-tops. The broad, blooming, tranquil expanse, shimmering and softly radiant in the heat, seemed the very epitome of summer. Now and again a small cloud-shadow sailed across it. Now and again a little wind, swooping down upon it gently, bent the grass-tops all one way, and spread a sudden silvery pallor. Save for the droning bees and flies there seemed to be but one live creature astir between the grass and the

blue. A solitary marsh-hawk, far over by the rail fence, was winnowing slowly, slowly, hither and thither, lazily hunting.

All this was in the world above the grass-tops. But below the grass-tops was a very different world—a dense, tangled world of dim green shade, shot with piercing shafts of sun, and populous with small, furtive life. Here, among the brown and white roots, the crowded green stems, and the mottled stalks, the little earth kindreds went busily about their affairs and their desires, giving scant thought to the aerial world above them. All that made life significant to them was here in the warm green gloom; and when anything chanced to part the grass to its depths they would scurry away in unanimous indignation.

On a small stone, over which the green closed so thickly that, when he chanced to look upward, he caught but the scantiest shreds of sky, sat a half-grown fieldmouse, washing his whiskers with his dainty claws. His tiny, bead-like eyes kept ceaseless watch, peering through the shadowy tangle for whatever might come near in the shape of foe or prey. Presently two or three stems above his head were beaten down, and a big green grasshopper, alighting clumsily from one of his blind leaps, fell sprawling on the stone. Before he could struggle to his long legs and climb back to the safer region of the grass-tops, the little mouse was upon him. Sharp, white teeth pierced his green mail, his legs kicked convulsively twice or thrice, and the faint iridescence faded out of his big, blank, foolish eyes. The mouse made his meal with relish, daintily discarding the dry legs and wing-cases. Then amid the green debris scattered upon the stone, he sat up, and once more went through his fastidious toilet.

But life for the little mouse in his grass-world was not quite all watching and hunting. When his toilet was complete, and he had amiably let a large black cricket crawl by unmolested, he suddenly began to whirl round on the stone, chasing his own tail. As he was amusing himself with this foolish play, another mouse, about the same size as himself, and probably of the same litter, jumped upon the stone, and knocked him off. He promptly retorted in kind; and for several minutes, as if the game were a well-understood one, the two kept it up, squeaking soft merriment, and apparently forgetful of all peril. The grass-tops above this play rocked and rustled in a way that would certainly have attracted attention had there been any eyes to see. But the marsh-hawk was still hunting lazily at the other side of the field, and no tragedy followed the childishness.

Both seemed to tire of the sport at the same instant; for suddenly they stopped, and hurried away through the grass on opposite sides of the stone, as if remembered business had just called to them. Whatever the business was, the first mouse seemed to forget it very speedily, for in half a minute he was back upon the stone again, combing his fine whiskers and scratching his ears. This done to his satisfaction, he dropped like a flash from his seat, and disappeared into a small hollow beneath it. As he did so, a hairy black spider darted out, and ran away among the roots.

A minute or two after the disappearance of the mouse, a creature came along which appeared gigantic in the diminutive world of the grass folk. It was nearly three feet long, and of the thickness of a man's finger. Of a steely gray-black, striped and reticulated in a mysterious pattern with a clear whitish yellow, it was an ominous shape indeed, as it glided smoothly and swiftly, in graceful curves, through the close green tangle. The cool shadows and thin lights touched it flickeringly as it went, and never a grass-top stirred to mark its sinister approach. Without a sound of warning it came straight up to the stone, and darted its narrow, cruel head into the hole.

There was a sharp squeak, and instantly the narrow head came out again, ejected by the force of the mouse's agonized spring. But the snake's teeth were fastened in the little animal's neck. The doom of the green world had come upon him while he slept.

But doomed though he was, the mouse was game. He knew there was no poison in those fangs that gripped him, and he struggled desperately to break free. His powerful hind legs kicked the ground with a force which the snake, hampered at first by the fact of its length being partly trailed out through the tangle, was unable to quite control. With unerring instinct—though this was the first snake he had ever encountered—the mouse strove to reach its enemy's back and sever the bone with the fine chisels of his teeth. But it was just this that the snake was watchful to prevent. Three times in his convulsive leaps the mouse succeeded in touching the snake's body—but with his feet only, never once with those destructive little teeth. The snake held him inexorably, with a steady, elastic pressure which yielded just so far, and never quite far enough. And in a minute or two the mouse's brave struggles grew more feeble.

All this, however—the lashing and the wriggling and the jumping—had not gone on without much disturbance to the grass-tops. Timothy head and clover-bloom, oxeye, and feathery plume-grass, they had bowed and swayed and shivered till the commotion, very conspicuous to one looking down upon the tranquil, flowery sea of green, caught the attention of the marsh-hawk, which at that moment chanced to be perching on a high fence stake. The lean-headed, fierce-eyed, trim-feathered bird shot from his perch, and sailed on long wings over the grass to see what was happening. As the swift shadow hovered over the grass-tops, the snake looked up. Well he understood the significance of that sudden shade. Jerking back his fangs with difficulty from the mouse's neck, he started to glide off under the thickest matting of the roots. But lightning quick though he was, he was not quite quick enough. Just as his narrow head darted under the roots, the hawk, with wings held straight up, and talons reaching down, dropped upon him, and clutched the middle of his back in a grip of steel. The next moment he was jerked into the air, writhing and coiling, and striking in vain frenzy at his captor's mail of hard feathers. The hawk flew off with him over the sea of green to the top of the fence stake, there to devour him at leisure. The mouse, sore wounded but not past recovery, dragged himself back to the hollow under the stone. And over the stone the grass-tops, once more still, hummed with flies, and breathed warm perfumes in the distilling heat.

THE RELUCTANT DRAGON

The Boy has made the acquaintance of a most unusual dragon who would rather quote poetry than fight. When the great dragon-hunter St. George comes to town, the Boy must find a way to keep St. George from hurting his dragon friend.

ONE DAY THE Boy, on walking into the village, found everything wearing a festal appearance which was not to be accounted for in the calendar. Carpets and gay-colored stuffs were hung out of the windows, the church bells clamored noisily, the little street was flower-strewn, and the whole population jostled each other along either side of it, chattering, shoving and ordering each other to stand back. The Boy saw a friend of his own age in the crowd and hailed him.

"What's up!" he cried. "Is it the players, or bears, or a circus, or what?"

"It's all right," his friend hailed back. "He's a-coming."

"*Who's* a-coming?" demanded the Boy, thrusting into the throng.

"Why, St. George, of course," replied his friend. "He heard tell of our dragon, and he's comin' on purpose to slay the deadly beast, and free us from his horrid yoke. O my! won't there be a jolly fight!"

Here was news indeed! The Boy felt that he ought to make quite sure for himself, and he wriggled himself in between the legs of his good-natured elders, abusing them all the time for their unmannerly habit of shoving. Once in the front rank, he breathlessly awaited the arrival.

216

Presently from the faraway end of the line came the sound of cheering. Next, the measured tramp of a great war-horse made his heart beat quicker, and then he found himself cheering with the rest, as, amidst welcoming shouts, shrill cries of women, uplifting of babies and waving of handkerchiefs, St. George paced slowly up the street. The Boy's heart stood still and he breathed with sobs, the beauty and the grace of the hero were so far beyond anything he had yet seen. His fluted armor was inlaid with gold, his plumed helmet hung at his saddlebow, and his thick fair hair framed a face gracious and gentle beyond expression till you caught the sternness in his eyes. He drew rein in front of the little inn, and the villagers crowded round with greetings and thanks and voluble statements of their wrongs and grievances and oppressions. The Boy heard the grave gentle voice of the Saint, assuring them that all would be well now, and that he would stand by them and see them righted and free them from their foe; then he dismounted and passed through the doorway and the crowd poured in after him. But the Boy made off up the hill as fast as he could lay his legs to the ground.

"It's all up, dragon!" he shouted as soon as he was within sight of the beast. "He's coming! He's here now! You'll have to pull yourself together and *do* something at last!"

The dragon was licking his scales and rubbing them with a bit of house-flannel the Boy's mother had lent him, till he shone like a great turquoise.

"Don't be *violent*, Boy," he said without looking round. "Sit down and get your breath, and try and remember that the noun governs the verb, and then perhaps you'll be good enough to tell me *who's* coming?"

"That's right, take it coolly," said the Boy. "Hope you'll be half as cool when I've got through with my news. It's only St. George who's coming, that's all; he rode into the village half an hour ago. Of course you can lick him—a great big fellow like you! But I thought I'd warn you, 'cos he's sure to be round early, and he's got the longest, wickedest-looking spear you ever did see!" And the Boy got up and began to jump round in sheer delight at the prospect of the battle.

"O deary, deary me," moaned the dragon. "This is too awful. I won't see him, and that's flat. I don't want to know the fellow at all. I'm sure he's not nice. You must tell him to go away at once, please. Say he can write if he likes, but I can't give him an interview. I'm not seeing anybody at present."

"Now dragon, dragon," said the Boy imploringly, "don't be perverse and wrongheaded. You've *got* to fight him sometime or other, you know, 'cos he's St. George and you're the dragon. Better get it over, and then we can go on with the sonnets. And you ought to consider other people a little, too. If it's been dull up here for you, think how dull it's been for me!"

"My dear little man," said the dragon solemnly, "just understand, once for all, that I can't fight and I won't fight. I've never fought in my life, and I'm not going to begin now, just to give you a Roman holiday. In old days I always let the other fellows—the *earnest* fellows—do all the fighting, and no doubt that's why I have the pleasure of being here now."

"But if you don't fight he'll cut your head off!" gasped the Boy, miserable at the prospect of losing both his fight and his friend.

"Oh, I think not," said the dragon in his lazy way. "You'll be able to arrange something. I've every confidence in you, you're such a *manager*. Just run down, there's a dear chap, and make it all right. I leave it entirely to you."

The Boy pursued his way to the inn, and passed into the principal chamber, where St. George now sat alone, musing over the chances of the fight, and the sad stories of rapine and of wrong that had so lately been poured into his sympathetic ears.

"May I come in, St. George?" said the Boy politely, as he paused at the door. "I want to talk to you about this little matter of the dragon, if you're not tired of it by this time."

"Yes, come in, Boy," said the Saint kindly. "Another tale of misery and wrong, I fear me. Is it a kind parent, then, of whom the tyrant has bereft you? Or some tender sister or brother? Well, it shall soon be avenged."

"Nothing of the sort," said the Boy. "There's a misunderstanding somewhere, and I want to put it right. The fact is, this is a *good* dragon."

"Exactly," said St. George, smiling pleasantly, "I quite understand. A good *dragon*. Believe me, I do not in the least regret that he is an adversary worthy of my steel, and no feeble specimen of his noxious tribe."

"But he's *not* a noxious tribe," cried the Boy distressedly. "Oh dear, oh dear, how *stupid* men are when they get an idea into their heads! I tell you he's a *good* dragon, and a friend of mine, and tells me the most beautiful stories you ever heard, all about old times and when he was little. And he's been so kind to mother, and mother'd do anything for him. And father likes him too, though father doesn't hold with art and poetry much, and always falls asleep when the dragon starts talking about *style*. But the fact is, nobody can help liking him when once they know him. He's so engaging and so trustful, and as simple as a child!"

"Sit down, and draw your chair up," said St. George. "I like a fellow who sticks up for his friends, and I'm sure the dragon has his good points, if he's got a friend like you. But that's not the question. All this evening I've been listening, with grief and anguish unspeakable, to tales of murder, theft, and wrong; rather too highly colored, perhaps, not always quite convincing, but forming in the main a most serious roll of crime. History teaches us that the greatest rascals often possess all the domestic virtues; and I fear that your cultivated friend, in spite of the qualities which have won (and rightly) your regard, has got to be speedily exterminated."

"Oh, you've been taking in all the yarns those fellows have been telling you," said the Boy impatiently. "Why, our villagers are the biggest storytellers in all the country round. It's a known fact. You're a stranger in these parts, or else you'd have heard it already. All they want is a *fight*. They're the most awful beggars for getting up fights—it's meat and drink to them. Dogs, bulls, dragons—anything so long as it's a fight. Why, they've got a poor innocent badger in the stable behind here, at this moment. They were going to have some fun with him today, but they're saving him up now till *your* little affair's over. And I've no doubt they've been telling you what a hero you were, and how you were bound to win, in the cause of right and justice, and so on; but let me tell you, I came down the street just now, and they were betting six to four on the dragon freely!"

"Six to four on the dragon!" murmured St. George sadly, resting his cheek on his hand. "This is an evil world, and sometimes I begin to think that all the wickedness in it is not entirely bottled up inside the dragons. And yet—may not this wily beast have misled you as to his real character, in order that your good report of him may serve as a cloak for his evil deeds? Nay, may there not be, at this very moment, some hapless Princess immured within yonder gloomy cavern?"

The moment he had spoken, St. George was sorry for what he had said, the Boy looked so genuinely distressed.

"I assure you, St. George," he said earnestly, "there's nothing of the sort in the cave at all. The dragon's a real gentleman, every inch of him, and I may say that no one would be more shocked and grieved than he would, at hearing you talk in that—that *loose* way about matters on which he has very strong views!"

"Well, perhaps I've been over-credulous," said St. George. "Perhaps I've misjudged the animal. But what are we to do? Here are the dragon and I, almost face to face, each supposed to be thirsting for each other's blood. I don't see any way out of it, exactly. What do you suggest? Can't you arrange things, somehow?"

"That's just what the dragon said," replied the Boy, rather nettled. "Really, the way you two seem to leave everything to me—I suppose you couldn't be persuaded to go away quietly, could you?"

"Impossible, I fear," said the Saint. "Quite against the rules. *You* know that as well as I do."

"Well, then, look here," said the Boy, "it's early yet—would you mind strolling up with me and seeing the dragon and talking it over? It's not far, and any friend of mine will be most welcome."

"Well, it's *irregular*," said St. George, rising, "but really it seems about the most sensible thing to do. You're taking a lot of trouble on your friend's account," he added, good-naturedly, as they passed out through the door together. "But cheer up! Perhaps there won't have to be any fight after all."

"Oh, but I hope there will, though!" replied the little fellow, wistfully.

"I've brought a friend to see you, dragon," said the Boy, rather loud.

The dragon woke up with a start. "I was just—er—thinking about things," he said in his simple way. "Very pleased to make your acquaintance, sir. Charming weather we're having!"

"This is St. George," said the Boy, shortly. "St. George, let me introduce you to the dragon. We've come up to talk things over quietly, dragon, and now for goodness' sake do let us have a little straight common sense, and come to some practical businesslike arrangement, for I'm sick of views and theories of life and personal tendencies, and all that sort of thing. I may perhaps add that my mother's sitting up."

"So glad to meet you, St. George," began the dragon rather nervously, "because you've been a great traveler, I hear, and I've always been rather a stay-at-home. But I can show you many antiquities, many interesting features of our countryside, if you're stopping here any time—"

"I think," said St. George, in his frank, pleasant way, "that we'd really better take the advice of our young friend here, and try to come to some understanding, on a business footing, about this little affair of ours. Now don't you think that after all the simplest plan would be just to fight it out, according to the rules, and let the best man win? They're betting on you, I may tell you, down in the village, but I don't mind that!"

"Oh, yes, *do*, dragon," said the Boy, delightedly. "It'll save such a lot of bother!"

"My young friend, you shut up," said the dragon severely. "Believe me, St. George," he went on, "there's nobody in the world I'd rather oblige than you and this young gentleman here. But the whole thing's nonsense, and conventionality, and popular thick-headedness. There's absolutely nothing to fight about, from beginning to end. And anyhow I'm not going to, so that settles it!"

"But supposing I make you?" said St. George, rather nettled.

"You can't," said the dragon, triumphantly. "I should only go into my cave and retire for a time down the hole I came up. You'd soon get heartily sick of sitting outside and waiting for me to come out and fight you. And as soon as you'd really gone away, why, I'd come up again gaily, for I tell you frankly, I like this place, and I'm going to stay here!"

St. George gazed for a while on the fair landscape around them.

"But this would be a beautiful place for a fight," he began again persuasively. "These great bare rolling Downs for the arena—and me in my golden armor showing up against your big blue scaly coils! Think what a picture it would make!"

"Now you're trying to get at me through my artistic sensibilities," said the dragon. "But it won't work. Not but what it would make a very pretty picture, as you say," he added, wavering a little.

"We seem to be getting rather nearer to *business*," put in the Boy. "You must see, dragon, that there's got to be a fight of some sort, 'cos you can't want to have to go down that dirty old hole again and stop there till goodness knows when."

"It might be arranged," said St. George, thoughtfully. "I *must* spear you somewhere, of course, but I'm not bound to hurt you very much. There's such a lot of you that there must be a few *spare* places somewhere. Here, for instance, just behind your foreleg. It couldn't hurt you much, just here!"

"Now you're tickling, George," said the dragon, coyly. "No, that place won't do at all. Even if it didn't hurt—and I'm sure it would, awfully—it would make me laugh, and that would spoil everything."

"Let's try somewhere else, then," said St. George, patiently. "Under your neck, for instance—all these folds of thick skin—if I speared you here you'd never even know I'd done it!"

"Yes, but are you sure you can hit off the right place?" asked the dragon, anxiously.

"Of course I am," said St. George, with confidence. "You leave that to me!"

"It's just because I've *got* to leave it to you that I'm asking," replied the dragon, rather testily. "No doubt you would deeply regret any error you might make in the hurry of the moment; but you wouldn't regret it half as much as I should! However, I suppose we've got to trust somebody, as we go through life, and your plan seems, on the whole, as good a one as any."

"Look here, dragon," interrupted the Boy, a little jealous on behalf of his friend, who seemed to be getting all the worst of the bargain. "I don't quite see where *you* come in! There's to be a fight, apparently, and you're to be licked; and what I want to know is, what are *you* going to get out of it?"

"St. George," said the dragon, "just tell him, please, what will happen after I'm vanquished in the deadly combat?"

"Well, according to the rules I suppose I shall lead you in triumph down to the marketplace or whatever answers to it," said St. George.

"Precisely," said the dragon. "And then—"

"And then there'll be shootings and speeches and things," continued St. George. "And I shall explain that you're converted, and see the error of your ways, and so on."

"Quite so," said the dragon. "And then—?"

"Oh, and then—" said St. George, "why, and then there will be the usual banquet, I suppose."

"Exactly," said the dragon; "and that's where *I* come in. Look here," he continued, addressing the Boy, "I'm bored to death up here, and no one really appreciates me. I'm going into Society, I am, through the kindly aid of our friend here, who's taking such a lot of trouble on my account; and you'll find I've got all the qualities to endear me to people who entertain! So now that's all settled, and if you don't mind—I'm an old-fashioned fellow—don't want to turn you out, but—"

"Remember, you'll have to do your proper share of the fighting, dragon!" said St. George, as he took the hint and rose to go. "I mean ramping, and breathing fire, and so on!"

"I can *ramp* all right," replied the dragon, confidently. "As to breathing fire, it's surprising how easily one gets out of practice; but I'll do the best I can. Good night!"

They had descended the hill and were almost back in the village again, when St. George stopped short. "*Knew* I had forgotten something," he said. "There ought to be a Princess. Terror-stricken and chained to a rock, and all that sort of thing. Boy, can't you arrange a Princess?"

The Boy was in the middle of a tremendous yawn. "I'm tired to death," he wailed, "and I *can't* arrange a Princess, or anything more, at this time of night. And my mother's sitting up, and *do* stop asking me to arrange more things till tomorrow!"

ROBERT FROST

THE RUNAWAY

ONCE WHEN THE snow of the year was beginning to fall,
We stopped by a mountain pasture to say, "Whose colt?"
A little Morgan had one forefoot on the wall,
The other curled at his breast. He dipped his head
And snorted at us. And then he had to bolt.
We heard the miniature thunder where he fled,
And we saw him, or thought we saw him, dim and gray,
Like a shadow against the curtain of falling flakes.
"I think the little fellow's afraid of the snow.
He isn't winter-broken. It isn't play
With the little fellow at all. He's running away.
I doubt if even his mother could tell him, 'Sakes,
It's only weather.' He'd think she didn't know!
Where is his mother? He can't be out alone."
And now he comes again with clatter of stone,
And mounts the wall again with whited eyes
And all his tail that isn't hair up straight.
He shudders his coat as if to throw off flies.
"Whoever it is that leaves him out so late,
When other creatures have gone to stall and bin,
Ought to be told to come and take him in."

ANDREW LANG

THE TWO FROGS

A Japanese Fairytale

ONCE UPON A time in the country of Japan there lived two frogs, one of whom made his home in a ditch near the town of Osaka, on the sea coast, while the other dwelt in a clear little stream which ran through the city of Kioto. At such a great distance apart, they had never even heard of each other; but, funnily enough, the idea came into both their heads at once that they should like to see a little of the world, and the frog who lived at Kioto wanted to visit Osaka, and the frog who lived at Osaka wished to go to Kioto, where the great Mikado had his palace.

So one fine morning in the spring they both set out along the road that led from Kioto to Osaka, one from one end and the other from the other. The journey was more tiring than they expected, for they did not know much about traveling, and halfway between the two towns there arose a mountain which had to be climbed. It took them a long time and a great many hops to reach the top, but there they were at last, and what was the surprise of each to see another frog before him! They looked at each other for a moment without speaking, and then fell into conversation, explaining the cause of their meeting so far from their homes. It was delightful to find that they both felt the same wish—to learn a little more of their native country—and as there was no sort of hurry they stretched themselves out in a cool, damp place, and agreed that they would have a good rest before they parted to go their ways.

"What a pity we are not bigger," said the Osaka frog; "for then we could see both towns from here, and tell if it is worth our while going on."

"Oh, that is easily managed," returned the Kioto frog. "We have only got to stand up on our hind legs, and hold onto each other, and then we can each look at the town he is traveling to."

This idea pleased the Osaka frog so much that he at once jumped up and put his front paws on the shoulders of his friend, who had risen also. There they both stood, stretching themselves as high as they could, and holding each other tightly, so that they might not fall down. The Kioto frog turned his nose towards Osaka, and the Osaka frog turned his nose towards Kioto; but the foolish things forgot that when they stood up their great eyes lay in the backs of their heads, and that though their noses might point to the places to which they wanted to go their eyes beheld the places from which they had come.

"Dear me!" cried the Osaka frog, "Kioto is exactly like Osaka. It is certainly not worth such a long journey. I shall go home!"

"If I had had any idea that Osaka was only a copy of Kioto I should never have traveled all this way," exclaimed the frog from Kioto, and as he spoke he took his hands from his friend's shoulders, and they both fell down on the grass. Then they took a polite farewell of each other, and set off for home again, and to the end of their lives they believed that Osaka and Kioto, which are as different to look at as two towns can be, were as like as two peas.

THE UGLY DUCKLING

IT WAS GLORIOUS out in the country. It was summer, and the cornfields were yellow, and the oats were green; the hay had been put up in stacks in the green meadows, and the stork went about on his long red legs, and chattered Egyptian, for this was the language he had learned from his good mother. All around the fields and meadows were great forests, and in the midst of these forests lay deep lakes. Yes, it was really glorious out in the country. In the midst of the sunshine there lay an old farm, surrounded by deep canals, and from the wall down to the water grew great burdocks, so high that little children could stand upright under the loftiest of them. It was just as wild there as in the deepest wood. Here sat a Duck upon her nest, for she had to hatch her young ones; but she was almost tired out before the little ones came; and then she so seldom had visitors. The other ducks liked better to swim about in the canals than to run up to sit down under a burdock, and cackle with her.

At last one egg shell after another burst open. "Piep! piep!"

it cried, and in all the eggs there were little creatures that stuck out their heads.

"Rap! rap!" they said; and they all came rapping out as fast as they could, looking all round them under the green leaves; and the mother let them look as much as they chose, for green is good for the eyes.

"How wide the world is!" said the young ones, for they certainly had much more room now than when they were in the eggs.

"Do you think this is all the world?" asked the mother. "That extends far across the other side of the garden, quite into the parson's field, but I have never been there yet. I hope you are all together," she continued, and stood up. "No, I have not all. The largest egg still lies

there. How long is that to last? I am really tired of it." And she sat down again.

"Well, how goes it?" asked an old Duck who had come to pay her a visit.

"It lasts a long time with that one egg," said the Duck who sat there. "It will not burst. Now, only look at the others; are they not the prettiest ducks one could possibly see? They are all like their father: the bad fellow never comes to see me."

"Let me see the egg which will not burst," said the old visitor. "Believe me, it is a turkey's egg. I was once cheated in that way, and had much anxiety and trouble with the young ones, for they are afraid of the water. I could not get them to venture in. I quacked and clucked, but it was no use. Let me see the egg. Yes, that's a turkey's egg! Let it lie there, and teach the other children to swim."

"I think I will sit on it a little longer," said the Duck. "I've sat so long now that I can sit a few days more."

"Just as you please," said the old Duck; and she went away.

At last the great egg burst. "Piep! piep!" said the little one, and crept forth. It was very large and very ugly. The Duck looked at it.

"It's a very large duckling," said she; "none of the others look like that: can it really be a turkey chick? Now we shall soon find it out. It must go into the water, even if I have to thrust it in myself."

The next day the weather was splendidly bright, and the sun shone on all the green trees. The Mother Duck went down to the water with all her little ones. Splash she jumped into the water. "Quack! quack!" she said, and one duckling after another plunged in. The water closed over their heads, but they came up in an instant, and swam capitally; their legs went of themselves, and there they were all in the water. The ugly gray Duckling swam with them.

"No, it's not a turkey," said she; "look how well it can use its legs, and how upright it holds itself. It is my own child! On the whole it's quite pretty, if one looks at it rightly. Quack! quack! come with me, and I'll lead you out into the great world, and present you in the poultry yard; but keep close to me, so that no one may tread on you, and take care of the cats!"

And so they came into the poultry yard. There was a terrible riot going on in there, for two families were quarreling about an eel's head, and the cat got it after all.

"See, that's how it goes in the world!" said the Mother Duck; and she whetted her beak, for she, too, wanted the eel's head. "Only use your legs," she said. "See that you can bustle about, and bow your heads before the old Duck yonder. She's the grandest of all here; she's of Spanish blood—that's why she's so fat; and do you see, she has a red rag around her leg; that's something particularly fine, and the greatest distinction a duck can enjoy: it signifies that one does not want to lose her, and that she's to be recognized by man and beast. Shake yourselves—don't turn in your toes; a well brought up duck turns its toes quite out, just like father and mother, so! Now bend your necks and say 'Rap!'"

And they did so; but the other ducks round about looked at them, and said quite boldly:

"Look there! Now we're to have these hanging on as if there were not enough of us already! And—fie!—how that Duckling yonder looks; we won't stand that!" And one duck flew up immediately, and bit it in the neck.

"Let it alone," said the mother; "it does no harm to anyone."

"Yes, but it's too large and peculiar," said the Duck who had bitten it; "and therefore it must be buffeted."

"Those are pretty children that the mother has there," said the old Duck with the rag round her leg. "They're all pretty but that one; that was a failure. I wish she could alter it."

"That cannot be done, my lady," replied the Mother Duck. "It is not pretty, but it has a really good disposition, and swims as well as any other; I may even say it swims better. I think it will grow up pretty, and become smaller in time; it has lain too long in the egg, and therefore is not properly shaped." And then she pinched it in the neck, and smoothed its feathers. "Moreover, it is a drake," she said, "and therefore it is not of so much consequence. I think he will be very strong: he makes his way already."

"The other ducklings are graceful enough," said the old Duck. "Make yourself at home; and if you find an eel's head, you may bring it to me."

And now they were at home. But the poor Duckling which had crept last out of the egg, and looked so ugly, was bitten and pushed and jeered at, as much by the ducks as by the chickens.

"It is too big!" they all said. And the turkey cock, who had been born with spurs, and therefore thought himself an emperor, blew himself up like a ship in full sail, and bore straight down upon it; then he gobbled, and grew quite red in the face. The poor Duckling did not know where it should stand or walk; it was quite melancholy because it looked ugly, and was scoffed at by the whole yard.

So it went on the first day; and afterward it became worse and worse. The poor Duckling was hunted about by everyone; even its brothers and sisters were quite angry with it, and said, "If the cat would only catch you, you ugly creature!" And the mother said, "If you were only far away!" And the ducks bit it, and the chickens beat it, and the girl who had to feed the poultry kicked at it with her foot.

Then it ran and flew over the fence, and the little birds in the bushes flew up in fear.

"That is because I am so ugly!" thought the Duckling; and it shut its eyes, but flew on farther; thus it came out into the great moor, where the wild ducks lived. Here it lay the whole night long; and it was weary and downcast.

Toward morning the wild ducks flew up, and looked at their new companion.

"What sort of a one are you?" they asked; and the Duckling turned in every direction, and bowed as well as it could. "You are remarkably ugly!" said the wild ducks. "But that is very indifferent to us, so long as you do not marry into our family."

Poor thing! It certainly did not think of marrying, and only hoped to obtain leave to lie among the reeds and drink some of the swamp water.

Thus it lay two whole days; then came thither two wild geese, or, properly speaking, two wild ganders. It was not long since each had crept out of an egg, and that's why they were so saucy.

"Listen, comrade," said one of them. "You're so ugly that I like you. Will you go with us, and become a bird of passage? Near here, in another moor, there are a few sweet lovely wild geese, all unmarried, and all able to say 'Rap!' You've a chance of making your fortune, ugly as you are!"

"Piff! paff!" resounded through the air; and the two ganders fell down dead in the swamp, and the water became blood-red. "Piff! paff!" it sounded again, and whole flocks of wild geese rose up from the reeds. And then there was another report. A great hunt was going on. The hunters were lying in wait all round the moor, and some were even sitting up in the branches of the trees, which spread far over the reeds. The blue smoke rose up like clouds among the dark trees, and was wafted far away across the water; and the hunting dogs came— splash, splash!—into the swamp, and the rushes and the reeds bent down on every side. That was a fright for the poor Duckling! It turned its head, and put it under its wing; but at that moment a frightful great dog stood close by the Duckling. His tongue hung far out of his mouth and his eyes gleamed horrible and ugly; he thrust out his nose close against the Duckling, showed his sharp teeth, and—splash, splash!—on he went, without seizing it.

"Oh, Heaven be thanked!" sighed the Duckling. "I am so ugly that even the dog does not like to bite me!"

And so it lay quiet, while the shots rattled through the reeds and gun after gun was fired. At last, late in the day, silence was restored; but the poor Duckling did not dare to rise up; it waited several hours before it looked round, and then hastened away out of the moor as fast as it could. It ran on over field and meadow; there was such a storm raging that it was difficult to get from one place to another.

Toward evening the Duckling came to a little miserable peasant's hut. This hut was so dilapidated that it did not know on which side it should fall; and that's why it remained standing. The storm whistled round the Duckling in such a way that the poor creature was obliged to sit down, to stand against it; and the tempest grew worse and worse. Then the Duckling noticed that one of the hinges of the door had given way, and the door hung so slanting that the Duckling could slip through the crack into the room.

Here lived a woman, with her Tom Cat and her Hen. And the Tom Cat, whom she called Sonnie, could arch his back and purr, he could even give out sparks; but for that one had to stroke his fur the wrong way. The Hen had quite little short legs, and therefore she was called Chickabiddy-shortshanks; she laid good eggs, and the woman loved her as her own child.

In the morning the strange Duckling was at once noticed, and the Tom Cat began to purr, and the Hen to cluck.

"What's this?" said the woman, and looked all round; but she could not see well, and therefore she thought the Duckling was a fat duck that had strayed. "This is a rare prize!" she said. "Now I shall have duck's eggs. I hope it is not a drake. We must try that."

And so the Duckling was admitted on trial for three weeks; but no eggs came. And the Tom Cat was master of the house, and the Hen was the lady, and always said, "We and the world!" for she thought they were half the world, and by far the better half. The Duckling thought one might have a different opinion, but the Hen would not allow it.

"Can you lay eggs?" she asked.

"No."

"Then you'll have the goodness to hold your tongue."

And the Tom Cat said, "Can you curve your back, and purr, and give out sparks?"

"No."

"Then you cannot have any opinion of your own when sensible people are speaking."

And the Duckling sat in a corner and was melancholy; then the fresh air and the sunshine streamed in; and it was seized with such a strange longing to swim on the water, that it could not help telling the Hen of it.

"What are you thinking of?" cried the Hen. "You have nothing to do, that's why you have these fancies. Purr or lay eggs, and they will pass over."

"But it is so charming to swim on the water!" said the Duckling, "so refreshing to let it close above one's head, and to dive down to the bottom."

"Yes, that must be a mighty pleasure truly," quoth the Hen. "I fancy you must have gone crazy. Ask the Cat about it—he's the cleverest animal I know—ask him if he likes to swim on the water, or to dive down: I won't speak about myself. Ask our mistress, the old woman; no one in the world is cleverer than she. Do you think she has any desire to swim, and to let the water close above her head?"

"You don't understand me," said the Duckling.

"We don't understand you? Then pray who is to understand you? You surely don't pretend to be cleverer than the Tom Cat and the woman—I won't say anything of myself. Don't be conceited, child, and be grateful for all the kindness you have received. Did you not get into a warm room, and have you not fallen into company from which you may learn something? But you are a chatterer, and it is not pleasant to associate with you. You may believe me, I speak for your good. I tell you disagreeable things, and by that one may always know one's true friends! Only take care that you learn to lay eggs, or to purr and give out sparks!"

"I think I will go out into the wide world," said the Duckling.

"Yes, do go," replied the Hen.

And the Duckling went away. It swam on the water, and dived, but it was slighted by every creature because of its ugliness.

Now came the autumn. The leaves in the forest turned yellow and brown; the wind caught them so that they danced about, and up in the air it was very cold. The clouds hung low, heavy with hail and snowflakes, and on the fence stood the raven, crying, "Croak! croak!" for mere cold; yes, it was enough to make one feel cold to think of this. The poor little Duckling certainly had not a good time. One evening—the sun was just setting in his beauty—there came a whole flock of great handsome birds out of the bushes; they were dazzlingly white, with long flexible necks; they were swans. They uttered a very peculiar cry, spread forth their glorious great wings, and flew

away from that cold region to warmer lands, to fair, open lakes. They mounted so high, so high! and the ugly little Duckling felt quite strangely as it watched them. It turned round and round in the water like a wheel, stretched out its neck toward them, and uttered such a strange loud cry as frightened itself. Oh! it could not forget those beautiful, happy birds; and so soon as it could see them no longer, it dived down to the very bottom, and when it came up again, it was quite beside itself. It knew not the name of those birds, and knew not whither they were flying; but it loved them more than it had ever loved anyone. It was not at all envious of them. How could it think of wishing to possess such loveliness as they had? It would have been glad if only the ducks would have endured its company—the poor, ugly creature!

And the winter grew cold, very cold! The Duckling was forced to swim about in the water, to prevent the surface from freezing entirely; but every night the hole in which it swam about became smaller and smaller. It froze so hard that the icy covering crackled again; and the Duckling was obliged to use its legs continually to prevent the hole from freezing up. At last it became exhausted, and lay quite still, and thus froze fast into the ice.

Early in the morning a peasant came by, and when he saw what had happened, he took his wooden shoe, broke the ice crust to pieces, and carried the Duckling home to his wife. Then it came to itself again. The children wanted to play with it; but the Duckling thought they would do it an injury, and in its terror fluttered up into the milk pan, so that the milk spurted down into the room. The woman clapped her hands, at which the Duckling flew down into the butter tub, and then into the meal barrel and out again. How it looked then! The woman screamed, and struck at it with the fire tongs; the children tumbled over one another in their efforts to catch the Duckling; and they laughed and screamed finely! Happily the door stood open, and the poor creature was able to slip out between the shrubs into the newly fallen snow; and there it lay quite exhausted.

But it would be too melancholy if I were to tell all the misery and care which the Duckling had to endure in the hard winter. It lay out on the moor among the reeds when the sun began to shine again and the larks to sing: it was a beautiful spring.

Then all at once the Duckling could flap its wings: they beat the air more strongly than before, and bore it strongly away; and before it well knew how all this happened, it found itself in a great garden, where the elder-trees smelt sweet, and bent their long green branches down to the canal that wound through the region. Oh, here it was so beautiful, such a gladness of spring! and from the thicket came three glorious white swans; they rustled their wings, and swam lightly on the water. The Duckling knew the splendid creatures, and felt oppressed by a peculiar sadness.

"I will fly away to them, to the royal birds! and they will kill me, because I, that am so ugly, dare to approach them. But it is of no consequence! Better to be killed by them than to be pursued by ducks, and beaten by fowls, and pushed about by the girl who takes care of the poultry yard, and to suffer hunger in winter!" And it flew out into the water, and swam toward the beautiful swans: these looked at it, and came sailing down upon it with outspread wings. "Kill me!" said the poor creature, and bent its head down upon the water, expecting nothing but death. But what was this that it saw in the clear water? It beheld its own image; and, lo! it was no longer a clumsy dark gray bird, ugly and hateful to look at, but—a swan!

It matters nothing if one is born in a duck-yard, if one has only lain in a swan's egg.

It felt quite glad at all the need and misfortune it had suffered; now

it realized its happiness in all the splendor that surrounded it. And the great swans swam round it, and stroked it with their beaks.

Into the garden came little children, who threw bread and corn into the water; and the youngest cried, "There is a new one!" and the other children shouted joyously, "Yes, a new one has arrived!" And they clapped their hands and danced about, and ran to their father and mother; and bread and cake were thrown into the water; and they all said, "The new one is the most beautiful of all! so young and handsome!" and the old swans bowed their heads before him.

Then he felt quite ashamed, and hid his head under his wing, for he did not know what to do; he was so happy, and yet not at all proud. He thought how he had been persecuted and despised; and now he heard them saying that he was the most beautiful of all birds. Even the elder-tree bent its branches straight down into the water before him, and the sun shone warm and mild. Then his wings rustled, he lifted his slender neck, and cried rejoicingly from the depths of his heart:

"I never dreamed of so much happiness when I was still the ugly Duckling!"

THE MONKEY AND THE JELLY-FISH

A Japanese Fairytale

CHILDREN MUST OFTEN have wondered why jelly-fishes have no shells, like so many of the creatures that are washed up every day on the beach. In old times this was not so; the jelly-fish had as hard a shell as any of them, but he lost it through his own fault, as may be seen in this story.

The sea-queen Otohime grew suddenly very ill. The swiftest messengers were sent hurrying to fetch the best doctors from every country under the sea, but it was all of no use; the queen grew rapidly worse instead of better. Everyone had almost given up hope, when one day a doctor arrived who was cleverer than the rest, and said that the only thing that would cure her was the liver of an ape. Now apes do not dwell under the sea, so a council of the wisest heads in the nation was called to consider the question how a liver could be obtained. At length it was decided that the turtle, whose prudence was well known, should swim to land and contrive to catch a living ape and bring him safely to the ocean kingdom.

It was easy enough for the council to entrust this mission to the turtle, but not at all so easy for him to fulfill it. However, he swam to a part of the coast that was covered with tall trees, where he thought the apes were likely to be; for he was old, and had seen many things. It was some time before he caught sight of any monkeys, and he often grew tired with watching for them, so that one hot day he fell fast asleep, in spite of all his efforts to keep awake. By-and-by some apes, who had been peeping at him from the tops of the trees, where they had been carefully hidden from the turtle's eyes, stole noiselessly down, and stood round staring at him, for they had never seen a turtle before, and did not know what to make of it. At last one young monkey, bolder than the rest, stooped down and stroked the shining shell that the strange new creature wore on its back. The movement, gentle though it was, woke the turtle. With one sweep he seized the monkey's hand in his mouth, and held it tight, in spite of every effort to pull it away. The other apes, seeing that the turtle was not to be trifled with, ran off, leaving their young brother to his fate.

Then the turtle said to the monkey, "If you will be quiet, and do what I tell you, I won't hurt you. But you must get on my back and come with me."

The monkey, seeing there was no help for it, did as he was bid; indeed he could not have resisted, as his hand was still in the turtle's mouth.

Delighted at having secured his prize, the turtle hastened back to the shore and plunged quickly into the water. He swam faster than he had ever done before, and soon reached the royal palace. Shouts of joy broke forth from the attendants when he was seen approaching, and some of them ran to tell the queen that the monkey was there, and that before long she would be as well as ever she was. In fact, so great was their relief that they gave the monkey such a kind welcome, and were so anxious to make him happy and comfortable, that he soon forgot all the fears that had beset him as to his fate, and was generally quite at his ease, though every now and then a fit of homesickness would come over him, and he would hide himself in some dark corner till it had passed away.

It was during one of these attacks of sadness that a jelly-fish happened to swim by. At that time jelly-fishes had shells. At the sight of the gay and lively monkey crouching under a tall rock, with his eyes closed and his head bent, the jelly-fish was filled with pity, and stopped, saying, "Ah, poor fellow, no wonder you weep; a few days more, and they will come and kill you and give your liver to the queen to eat."

The monkey shrank back horrified at these words and asked the jelly-fish what crime he had committed that deserved death.

"Oh, none at all," replied the jelly-fish, "but your liver is the only thing that will cure our queen, and how can we get at it without killing you? You had better submit to your fate, and make no noise about it, for though I pity you from my heart there is no way of helping you." Then he went away, leaving the ape cold with horror.

At first he felt as if his liver was already being taken from his body, but soon he began to wonder if there was no means of escaping this terrible death, and at length he invented a plan which he thought would do. For a few days he pretended to be gay and happy as before, but when the sun went in, and rain fell in torrents, he wept and howled from dawn to dark, till the turtle, who was his head keeper, heard him,

and came to see what was the matter. Then the monkey told him that before he left home he had hung his liver out on a bush to dry, and if it was always going to rain like this it would become quite useless. And the rogue made such a fuss and moaning that he would have melted a heart of stone, and nothing would content him but that somebody should carry him back to land and let him fetch his liver again.

The queen's councillors were not the wisest of people, and they decided between them that the turtle should take the monkey back to his native land and allow him to get his liver off the bush, but desired the turtle not to lose sight of his charge for a single moment. The monkey knew this, but trusted to his power of beguiling the turtle when the time came, and mounted on his back with feelings of joy, which he was, however, careful to conceal. They set out, and in a few hours were wandering about the forest where the ape had first been caught, and when the monkey saw his family peering out from the treetops, he swung himself up by the nearest branch, just managing to save his hind leg from being seized by the turtle. He told them all the dreadful things that had happened to him, and gave a war cry which brought the rest of the tribe from the neighboring hills. At a word from him they rushed in a body to the unfortunate turtle, threw him on his back, and tore off the shield that covered his body. Then with mocking words they hunted him to the shore, and into the sea, which he was only too thankful to reach alive. Faint and exhausted he entered the queen's palace, for the cold of the water struck upon his naked body, and made him feel ill and miserable. But wretched though he was, he had to appear before the queen's advisers and tell them all that had befallen him, and how he had suffered the monkey to escape. But, as sometimes happens, the turtle was allowed to go scot-free, and had his shell given back to him, and all the punishment fell on the poor jelly-fish, who was condemned by the queen to go shieldless for ever after.

A MAD TEA-PARTY

One hot afternoon, a girl named Alice followed a smartly dressed white rabbit down a rabbit hole and found Wonderland. You will learn all of what happened to her there if you read Alice's Adventures in Wonderland *by Lewis Carroll. "A Mad Tea-Party" (which Alice finds by following directions from a Cheshire Cat) will give you a good introduction to Wonderland, a place of the impossible.*

THERE WAS A table set out under a tree in front of the house, and the March Hare and the Hatter were having tea at it: a Dormouse was sitting between them, fast asleep, and the other two were using it as a cushion, resting their elbows on it, and talking over its head. "Very uncomfortable for the Dormouse," thought Alice; "only as it's asleep, I suppose it doesn't mind."

The table was a large one, but the three were all crowded together at one corner of it. "No room! No room!" they cried out when they saw Alice coming. "There's *plenty* of room!" said Alice indignantly, and she sat down in a large armchair at one end of the table.

"Have some wine," the March Hare said in an encouraging tone.

Alice looked all round the table, but there was nothing on it but tea. "I don't see any wine," she remarked.

"There isn't any," said the March Hare.

"Then it wasn't very civil of you to offer it," said Alice angrily.

"It wasn't very civil of you to sit down without being invited," said the March Hare.

"I didn't know it was *your* table," said Alice: "it's laid for a great many more than three."

"Your hair wants cutting," said the Hatter. He had been looking at Alice for some time with great curiosity, and this was his first speech.

"You should learn not to make personal remarks," Alice said with some severity: "It's very rude."

The Hatter opened his eyes very wide on hearing this; but all he *said* was, "Why is a raven like a writing desk?"

"Come, we shall have some fun now!" thought Alice. "I'm glad they've begun asking riddles—I believe I can guess that," she added aloud.

"Do you mean that you think you can find out the answer to it?" said the March Hare.

"Exactly so," said Alice.

"Then you should say what you mean," the March Hare went on.

"I do," Alice hastily replied; "at least—I mean what I say—that's the same thing, you know."

"Not the same thing a bit!" said the Hatter. "Why, you might just as well say that 'I see what I eat' is the same thing as 'I eat what I see'!"

"You might just as well say," added the March Hare, "that 'I like what I get' is the same thing as 'I get what I like'!"

"You might just as well say," added the Dormouse, which seemed to be talking in its sleep, "that 'I breathe when I sleep' is the same thing as 'I sleep when I breathe'!"

"It *is* the same thing with you," said the Hatter, and here the conversation dropped, and the party sat silent for a minute, while Alice thought over all she could remember about ravens and writing desks, which wasn't much.

The Hatter was the first to break the silence. "What day of the month is it?" he said, turning to Alice: he had taken his watch out of his pocket, and was looking at it uneasily, shaking it every now and then, and holding it to his ear.

Alice considered a little, and then said, "The fourth."

"Two days wrong!" sighed the Hatter. "I told you butter wouldn't suit the works!" he added, looking angrily at the March Hare.

"It was the *best* butter," the March Hare meekly replied.

"Yes, but some crumbs must have got in as well," the Hatter grumbled: "you shouldn't have put it in with the bread knife."

The March Hare took the watch and looked at it gloomily: then he dipped it into his cup of tea, and looked at it again: but he could think of nothing better to say than his first remark, "It was the *best* butter, you know."

Alice had been looking over his shoulder with some curiosity. "What a funny watch!" she remarked. "It tells the day of the month, and doesn't tell what o'clock it is!"

"Why should it?" muttered the Hatter. "Does *your* watch tell you what year it is?"

"Of course not," Alice replied very readily: "but that's because it stays the same year for such a long time together."

"Which is just the case with *mine*," said the Hatter.

Alice felt dreadfully puzzled. The Hatter's remark seemed to her to have no sort of meaning in it, and yet it was certainly English. "I don't quite understand you," she said, as politely as she could.

"The Dormouse is asleep again," said the Hatter, and he poured a little hot tea upon its nose.

The Dormouse shook its head impatiently, and said, without opening its eyes, "Of course, of course: just what I was going to remark myself."

"Have you guessed the riddle yet?" the Hatter said, turning to Alice again.

"No, I give it up," Alice replied. "What's the answer?"

"I haven't the slightest idea," said the Hatter.

"Nor I," said the March Hare.

Alice sighed wearily. "I think you might do something better with the time," she said, "than wasting it in asking riddles that have no answers."

"If you knew Time as well as I do," said the Hatter, "you wouldn't talk about wasting *it*. It's *him*."

"I don't know what you mean," said Alice.

"Of course you don't!" the Hatter said, tossing his head contemptuously. "I daresay you never even spoke to Time!"

"Perhaps not," Alice cautiously replied; "but I know I have to beat time when I learn music."

"Ah! That accounts for it," said the Hatter. "He won't stand beating. Now, if you only kept on good terms with him, he'd do almost anything you liked with the clock. For instance, suppose it were nine o'clock in the morning, just time to begin lessons: you'd only have to whisper a hint to Time, and round goes the clock in a twinkling! Half-past one, time for dinner!"

("I only wish it was," the March Hare said to itself in a whisper.)

"That would be grand, certainly," said Alice thoughtfully; "but then—I shouldn't be hungry for it, you know."

"Not at first, perhaps," said the Hatter: "but you could keep it to half-past one as long as you liked."

"Is that the way *you* manage?" Alice asked.

The Hatter shook his head mournfully. "Not I!" he replied. "We quarreled last March—just before *he* went mad, you know—" (pointing with his teaspoon at the March Hare) "—it was at the great concert given by the Queen of Hearts, and I had to sing

> *'Twinkle, twinkle, little bat!*
> *How I wonder what you're at!'*

You know the song, perhaps?"

"I've heard something like it," said Alice.

"It goes on, you know," the Hatter continued, "in this way:

> *'Up above the world you fly,*
> *Like a tea-tray in the sky.*
> *Twinkle, twinkle—'"*

Here the Dormouse shook itself, and began singing in its sleep, "*Twinkle, twinkle, twinkle, twinkle—*" and went on so long that they had to pinch it to make it stop.

"Well, I'd hardly finished the first verse," said the Hatter, "when the Queen bawled out, 'He's murdering the time! Off with his head!'"

"How dreadfully savage!" exclaimed Alice.

"And ever since that," the Hatter went on in a mournful tone, "he won't do a thing I ask! It's always six o'clock now."

A bright idea came into Alice's head. "Is that the reason so many tea things are put out here?" she asked.

"Yes, that's it," said the Hatter with a sigh: "it's always teatime, and we've no time to wash the things between whiles."

"Then you keep moving round, I suppose?" said Alice.

"Exactly so," said the Hatter: "as the things get used up."

"But what happens when you come to the beginning again?" Alice ventured to ask.

"Suppose we change the subject," the March Hare interrupted, yawning. "I'm getting tired of this. I vote the young lady tells us a story."

"I'm afraid I don't know one," said Alice, rather alarmed at the proposal.

"Then the Dormouse shall!" they both cried. "Wake up, Dormouse!" And they pinched it on both sides at once.

The Dormouse slowly opened its eyes. "I wasn't asleep," it said in a hoarse, feeble voice, "I heard every word you fellows were saying."

"Tell us a story!" said the March Hare.

"Yes, please do!" pleaded Alice.

"And be quick about it," added the Hatter, "or you'll be asleep again before it's done."

"Once upon a time there were three little sisters," the Dormouse began in a great hurry; "and their names were Elsie, Lacie, and Tillie; and they lived at the bottom of a well—"

"What did they live on?" said Alice, who always took a great interest in questions of eating and drinking.

"They lived on treacle," said the Dormouse, after thinking a minute or two.

"They couldn't have done that, you know," Alice gently remarked. "They'd have been ill."

"So they were," said the Dormouse; "*very* ill."

Alice tried a little to fancy to herself what such an extraordinary way of living would be like, but it puzzled her too much: so she went on: "But why did they live at the bottom of a well?"

"Take some more tea," the March Hare said to Alice, very earnestly.

"I've had nothing yet," Alice replied in an offended tone: "so I can't take more."

"You mean you can't take *less*," said the Hatter: "It's very easy to take *more* than nothing."

"Nobody asked *your* opinion," said Alice.

"Who's making personal remarks now?" the Hatter asked triumphantly.

Alice did not quite know what to say to this: so she helped herself to some tea and bread-and-butter, and then turned to the Dormouse, and repeated her question. "Why did they live at the bottom of a well?"

The Dormouse again took a minute or two to think about it, and then said, "It was a treacle well."

"There's no such thing!" Alice was beginning very angrily, but the Hatter and the March Hare went "Sh! Sh!" and the Dormouse sulkily remarked, "If you can't be civil, you'd better finish the story for yourself."

"No, please go on!" Alice said very humbly. "I won't interrupt you again. I daresay there may be *one*."

"One, indeed!" said the Dormouse indignantly. However, he consented to go on. "And so these three little sisters—they were learning to draw, you know—"

"What did they draw?" said Alice, quite forgetting her promise.

"Treacle," said the Dormouse, without considering at all, this time.

"I want a clean cup," interrupted the Hatter: "let's all move one place on."

He moved on as he spoke, and the Dormouse followed him: the March Hare moved into the Dormouse's place, and Alice rather unwillingly took the place of the March Hare. The Hatter was the only one who got any advantage from the change; and Alice was a good deal worse off than before, as the March Hare had just upset the milk jug into his plate.

Alice did not wish to offend the Dormouse again, so she

began very cautiously: "But I don't understand. Where did they draw the treacle from?"

"You can draw water out of a water well," said the Hatter; "so I should think you could draw treacle out of a treacle well—eh, stupid?"

"But they were *in* the well," Alice said to the Dormouse, not choosing to notice this last remark.

"Of course they were," said the Dormouse: "well in."

This answer so confused poor Alice that she let the Dormouse go on for some time without interrupting it.

"They were learning to draw," the Dormouse went on, yawning and rubbing its eyes, for it was getting very sleepy; "and they drew all manner of things—everything that begins with an M—"

"Why with an M?" said Alice.

"Why not?" said the March Hare.

Alice was silent.

The Dormouse had closed its eyes by this time, and was going off into a doze; but, on being pinched by the Hatter, it woke up again with a little shriek, and went on: "—that begins with an M, such as mouse-traps, and the moon, and memory, and muchness—you know you say things are 'much of a muchness'—did you ever see such a thing as a drawing of a muchness!"

"Really, now you ask me," said Alice, very much confused, "I don't think—"

"Then you shouldn't talk," said the Hatter.

This piece of rudeness was more than Alice could bear: she got up in great disgust, and walked off: the Dormouse fell asleep instantly, and neither of the others took the least notice of her going, though she looked back once or twice, half hoping that they would call after her: the last time she saw them, they were trying to put the Dormouse into the teapot.

"At any rate I'll never go *there* again!" said Alice, as she picked her way through the wood. "It's the stupidest tea-party I ever was at in all my life!"

THE AUTHORS

Hans Christian Andersen *(1805–1875)*

The son of a poor shoemaker, Hans Christian Andersen grew up in the small town of Odense in Denmark. After his father's death he worked in a factory. He soon displayed a talent for poetry and the arts, and went to Copenhagen in the hopes of working in the theater but was rejected for his lack of education. He next tried to become a singer but found he was unsuited for the stage. Finally, with the help of some generous friends, he went to school. He wrote many works in his lifetime but it was his fairy tales, such as *The Ugly Duckling*, *The Emperor's New Clothes*, and *The Snow Queen*, that earned him an international reputation as one of the greatest storytellers of all time.

L. Frank Baum *(1856–1919)*

Lyman Frank Baum was born in Chittenango, New York. He was privately tutored at home and then attended Peekskill Military Academy. Baum is best known for his fantasies for children, particularly *The Wonderful Wizard of Oz* (1900). The thirteen sequels to *The Wonderful Wizard of Oz* include *The Marvelous Land of Oz* (1904), *Ozma of Oz* (1907), *The Road to Oz* (1909), *The Emerald City of Oz* (1910), and *The Lost Princess of Oz* (1917).

Lewis Carroll (1832–1898)

Lewis Carroll was the pen name of Charles Lutwidge Dodgson, an English mathematician and children's book writer. Born in Daresbury, near Warrington, the third of eleven children, he was educated at Rugby and Christ Church College, Oxford. He is best known for writing the children's classic *Alice's Adventures in Wonderland* (1865) and its sequel, *Through the Looking Glass* (1872). He also published mathematics books under his own name.

Robert Frost (1874–1963)

Born in San Francisco, Robert Lee Frost moved to New England with his family at the age of ten. After attending Dartmouth College and Harvard University, he worked a variety of jobs—making shoes, working in a mill, editing a country newspaper, teaching school, and farming. He moved to England in 1912, where he published his first book of poetry. Upon returning to the United States in 1915, he became professor of English at Amherst College. Frost's poetry collections include *Twilight* (1894), *North of Boston* (1914), *Mountain Interval* (1916), *West-Running Brook* (1928), *You Came Too: Favorite Poems for Young Readers* (1959), and *In the Clearing* (1962).

Kenneth Grahame (1859–1932)

Kenneth Grahame, the son of an advocate, was born in Edinburgh, Scotland. He was educated at St. Edward's School, Oxford, and in 1876 became a gentleman clerk at the Bank of England. His early work consisted of collected essays and country tales. In 1908 he published his masterpiece, *The Wind in the Willows*, an animal fantasy created for his young son. It has become a children's classic and was dramatized by A. A. Milne as *Toad of Toad Hall*.

E. Pauline Johnson *(1861–1913)*

Pauline Johnson, daughter of a Mohawk father and an English mother, was born on the Six Nations Reserve near Brantford, Ontario. She was, for the most part, educated informally, but was exposed at an early age to the great Victorian poets. Her reputation as a poet owed a great deal to her popularity as a performer. She emphasized her Indian heritage—often wearing Indian dress during her recitals—but her work was clearly derived from a European tradition. Pauline Johnson's books include *The White Wampum* (1895), *Legends of Vancouver* (1911), and *Flint and Feather* (1912).

Rudyard Kipling *(1865–1936)*

Rudyard Kipling was an English writer, born in Bombay, India. He was educated in England, at the United Services College, Westward Ho!, but returned to India in 1880, where he worked as a journalist. In 1889 he went back to London. The people and animals of India are a predominant theme in the many novels and short stories he wrote for adults and children. The two *Jungle Books* (1894–1895) and the *Just So Stories* (1902) have won a place among the classic animal stories. In 1907 he was awarded the Nobel prize for literature.

Andrew Lang *(1844–1912)*

Born in Scotland, Andrew Lang was a well-known historian and folklore scholar. He attended Edinburgh Academy, St. Andrews, Glasgow, and Balliol College, Oxford. In 1875 he moved to London to take up journalism and became one of the most versatile and famous writers of his day. His writings include historical works, anthropological essays, novels, and a series of children's books, beginning with *The Blue Fairy Tale Book* (1889).

R. D. Lawrence *(1921–)*

R. D. Lawrence was born at sea on board a British passenger ship. He received his education in Spain. Just shy of his fifteenth birthday, at the outbreak of the Spanish Civil War, Lawrence enlisted in the Republican army. He was wounded in 1937, interned, and finally released and sent to England in 1938. He served with British forces in the Second World War. After the war, he studied biology and worked as a journalist, emigrating to Canada in 1954. Lawrence has alternately homesteaded in northern Ontario and worked as a journalist. He now lives on 100 acres in Ontario's Haliburton Highlands with his wife, two timber wolves, and a variety of other fauna. Lawrence's books include *Wildlife in Canada* (1966), *Cry Wild* (1970), *The North Runner* (1979), *The Ghost Walker* (1983), *The Shark* (1985), and *Trail of the Wolf* (1993).

Edward Lear *(1812–1888)*

Edward Lear, born in London, was an artist, traveler, and humorist. He first attracted attention for his paintings of birds, and later turned to landscapes. He traveled in Italy, Greece, Egypt, and India, publishing books on his travels with his own illustrations. He popularized the limerick in his *A Book of Nonsense*, which he published anonymously in 1846. Later he published *Nonsense Songs, Stories, Botany, and Alphabets* (1870), *More Nonsense Rhymes* (1871), and *Laughable Lyrics* (1876). He spent most of his latter years in Italy.

Cyrus Macmillan *(1882–1953)*

Cyrus Macmillan was born in Wood Islands, Prince Edward Island. He taught for some years in Charlottetown before joining the English department at McGill University, where he remained for the rest of his career. He was Dean of Arts and Sciences from 1940 to 1947, and also served as a Member of Parliament, representing a Prince Edward Island constituency during the Second World War. Macmillan wrote *Canadian Wonder Tales* (1918) and *Canadian Fairy Tales* (1922), as well as a history of McGill. A number of the stories from the two anthologies were reprinted after his death in *Glooskap's Country* (1955).

Farley Mowat *(1921–)*

Farley Mowat was born in Belleville, Ontario, and raised in Saskatoon, Saskatchewan. He attended the University of Toronto, then served with the Canadian forces (Hastings and Prince Edward Regiment) during the Second World War. After the war, he resumed his academic studies, spending two years in Canada's far north before completing his degree. Mowat has written many books about animals, the North, and native peoples, including *People of the Deer* (1952), *The Desperate People* (1959), *Never Cry Wolf* (1963), and *Sea of Slaughter* (1984). Specifically for children he has written *The Dog Who Wouldn't Be* (1957) and *Owls in the Family* (1961).

E. Nesbit *(1858–1924)*

Edith Nesbit was born in London, the daughter of an agricultural chemist who died when she was three. She was educated in a French convent, and began her literary career writing poetry. She married a journalist in 1880, and began writing popular fiction and children's stories to help with the family's finances. A number of her books have become well-loved children's classics, including *The Story of the Treasure Seekers* (1899), *The Railway Children* (1906), and *The Enchanted Castle* (1907).

Arthur Ransome *(1884–1967)*

Born in Leeds, Arthur Mitchell Ransome was a writer and journalist, who served as the correspondent in Russia for the *Daily News* during the First World War and the Russian Revolution. He had been a published author for a quarter of a century before the appearance of *Swallows and Amazons* (1930), the first of twelve perennially popular novels featuring two families of adventurous but responsible children who spend their school holidays reveling in the open air, free from adult restrictions.

Knud Rasmussen *(1879–1933)*

Knud Johan Victor Rasmussen, a Danish explorer and ethnologist, was born in Greenland of a Danish Eskimo mother. He directed several expeditions to Greenland and, in 1921–1924, he crossed from Greenland to the Bering Strait by dog sled to visit all the Eskimo groups along the route.

Charles G. D. Roberts *(1860–1943)*

Sir Charles George Douglas Roberts was born in Douglas, near Fredericton, New Brunswick, and educated at the University of New Brunswick. He taught in Chatham and Fredericton before accepting a position as professor of English at King's College, Nova Scotia. By 1897 he was earning a living as a freelance journalist, novelist, and poet. He lived for a while in New York, then went to England, where he spent 17 years. He fought with the Canadian forces overseas during the First World War. He was knighted in 1935. Roberts' books include *Orion, and Other Poems* (1880), *The Canadian Guide-Book* (1891), *The Raid from Beauséjour* (1894), *The Land of Evangeline* (1895), *A History of Canada* (1897), and *Canada in Flanders* (1918).

Ernest Thompson Seton (d. *1946*)

Ernest Thompson (he adopted the name "Seton" as an adult) was born in South Shields, Durham, England. The family moved to Canada in 1866. Seton was educated in Toronto public schools, then studied art at the Ontario College of Art in Toronto, and in schools overseas. He was appointed naturalist to the Manitoba government in 1890. In 1896 he moved to the United States. He founded a youth movement devoted to outdoor activities and was subsequently involved in the Boy Scouts of America organization. In 1930 he founded the New Mexico Institute of Wildlife and Woodcraft which remained, with his writing, the focus of his attention until his death in 1946. Seton wrote and illustrated about 40 books. They include *Wild Animals I Have Known* (1898), *Lives of the Hunted* (1901), *Two Little Savages* (1903), *Life Histories of Northern Animals* (1909), and *Lives of Game Animals* (four volumes, 1925–1928).

Anna Sewell (1820–1878)

Anna Sewell was born in Yarmouth, England, and was an invalid for most of her life. Her only published work, *Black Beauty, The Autobiography of a Horse* (1877), is perhaps the most famous fictional work about horses. Although now read as a children's book, it originally was written as a plea for more humane treatment of horses by adults.

Wallace Wadsworth (b. *1894*)

Born in Indiana, Wallace Wadsworth lived most of his life in Indianapolis. He was educated at Butler University and later became a publisher's representative for several publishing houses. His books include *Paul Bunyan and His Great Blue Ox* (1926) and *The Modern Story Book* (1931).

THE ILLUSTRATORS

VictoR GAD
The Owl and the Pussy Cat; A Mad Tea-Party

Colin Gillies
Young Black Beauty

Richard Hook
Brer Rabbit

Robert Johannsen
The Bremen Town Musicians; Then There Were Three; "If You Talk to the Animals . . ."; The Ugly Duckling

Peter Kovalic
The Grasshopper and the Ants; The Hare and the Tortoise; A Lion and a Mouse; A Wolf in Sheep's Clothing; Belling the Cat; The Town Mouse and the Country Mouse; The Dog and His Shadow; The Goose with the Golden Egg

John Lupton
All Gone; Coyote and Water Serpent; The Last of the Dragons; The Mock Turtle's Story; The Runaway

Renée Mansfield

The Springfield Fox

Sharon Matthews

The Elephant's Child

Paul McCusker

Mutt Makes His Mark; The Riverbank; The Train Dogs

Michelle Nidenoff

In the Deep of the Grass

Brian Price Thomas

The Wonderful Ox

ACKNOWLEDGMENTS

ARE HAS BEEN TAKEN to trace ownership of copyright material contained in this book. The publishers will gladly receive any information that will enable them to rectify any reference or credit line in subsequent editions.

"All Gone" by Walter de la Mare. From *Animal Stories* by Walter de la Mare, published by Faber and Faber, © 1939.

"The Beginning of the Armadillos" and "The Elephant's Child" by Rudyard Kipling. From *Just So Stories* by Rudyard Kipling, © 1902.

"The Cat Who Became Head-Forester" and "The Fire-Bird, the Horse of Power, and the Princess Vasilissa" by Arthur Ransome. From *Old Peter's Russian Tales* by Arthur Ransome, published by Nelson, © 1916.

"The Cowardly Lion" by L. Frank Baum. From *The Wonderful Wizard of Oz* by L. Frank Baum, © 1899.

"The Dance of the Royal Ants" by Alice Gall and Fleming Crew. From *The Little Black Ant* by Alice Gall and Fleming Crew, published by Walck, © 1936.

"The Great Sea Serpent" and "The Ugly Duckling" by Hans Christian Andersen. From *The Complete Fairy Tales and Stories of Hans Christian Andersen* by Hans Christian Andersen.

"How Some Wild Animals Became Tame Ones" by Andrew Lang. From *The Orange Fairy Book* by Andrew Lang, published by Dover publications, © 1933.

"How the Rabbit Lost His Tail" by Cyrus Macmillan. From *Canadian Wonder Tales* by Cyrus Macmillan, © 1918.

"If You Talk to Animals . . ." by Chief Dan George. From *My Heart Soars* by Chief Dan George, published by Hancock House Publishers, © 1974. Reprinted by permission of Hancock House Publishers Ltd.

"In the Deep of the Grass" by Charles G. D. Roberts. From *Watchers of the Trails* by Charles G. D. Roberts.

"The Last of the Dragons" by E. Nesbit. From *The Complete Book of Dragons*.

"A Mad Tea-Party" and "The Mock Turtle's Story" by Lewis Carroll. From *Alice's Adventures in Wonderland* by Lewis Carroll, first published by Macmillan & Co. Ltd., © 1865.

"The Monkey and the Jelly-Fish" and "The Two Frogs" by Andrew Lang. From *The Violet Fairy Book* by Andrew Lang, published by Dover Publications, © 1901.

"Mutt Makes His Mark" by Farley Mowat. From *The Dog Who Wouldn't Be* by Farley Mowat, © 1957. Reprinted by permission of the author.

"The Owl and the Pussy Cat" by Edward Lear. Reprinted from *A Treasury of the World's Best-Loved Poems*, published by Crown Publishers, Inc., © 1961. Reprinted by permission of Crown Publishers, Inc.

"The Raven and the Goose" by Knud Rasmussen, translated by W. Worster. From *Eskimo Folk-Tales* by Knud Rasmussen, translated by W. Worster, © 1921.

"The Reluctant Dragon" by Kenneth Grahame. From *Dream Days* by Kenneth Grahame, © 1898.

"The Riverbank" by Kenneth Grahame. From *The Wind in the Willows* by Kenneth Grahame, © 1908.

"The Runaway" by Robert Frost. From *You Come Too: Favorite Poems for Young Readers* by Robert Frost, published by Holt, Rinehart and Winston, Inc., © 1959. Copyright © renewed 1964 by Lesley Frost Ballantine.